SCION'S SACRIFICE

THE GUARDIANS OF LIGHT: BOOK 3

R. MICHAEL CARD

Gryphon's Gate Publishing

Scion's Sacrifice

Copyright © 2017 R. Michael Card

Gryphon's Gate Publishing

550 King St. N.

PO Box 42088 Conestoga

Waterloo, ON.

N2L 6K5

ebook ISBN978-1-988115-43-6

Print ISBN978-1-988115-42-9

*M*aster Elia rushed to the High Abbot's chambers. She wasn't pleased at having been summoned, not when she was needed out on the walls.

Outside and all around St. Antin Abbey the Blacklord's army pressed their offensive, attacking yet again, throwing ever more of their seemingly innumerable men against the fifty-foot walls and battle-ready monks of Embreth. The monks were far better trained and for every monk that fell in battle, twenty to fifty of the enemy fell. Still, Elia feared it wouldn't be enough. There were far more of the enemy than her monks.

Two factors helped to level the playing field. The first were the sisters of Ehlani, healers who could bring a monk back from the brink of death. The second and far more influential in this fight, were the two scions who battled to defend St. Antin.

Senia and Wyllea were a blessing. Two Guardians of Aehryn in an age when all were thought to be lost. Long ago

The Greatest of the Gods, Aehryn of All Things, had given of herself, dying in order to bless certain people with powerful magic weapons. These special few and their descendants, or scions, became the Guardians of Aehryn. One scion was worth a hundred monks, if not more. The two women were both fierce warriors and an inspiration to her monks. She thanked Embreth for those scions every night. More recently, the armies of the west had also arrived to help. But since they were unable to fit within the confines of the abbey. They were camped in the mountains to the west. As of yet they had only sent out a few parties to skirmish with the enemy — as it was difficult to find any good battleground in the forested hills. These armies could be a great boon if they could somehow manage to coordinate their efforts.

Elia stopped before the High Abbot's door and pounded on the door.

Impatient and frustrated that she'd been taken away from helping those she'd trained and raised — her monks, her people — she tried to put on a pleasant face. She could be civil, if she wanted to be. She should be fighting, but when the High Abbot called, she obeyed. Besides, the high abbot was never disturbed or distressed, always serene. So she knew her agitation would serve her little in this meeting.

A quiet attendant ushered her into the sitting room of the High Abbot's modest suite. The room was large for private quarters, but when compared to many other rooms in the massive abbey it was still quite small. To Elia's left stood a long table with several simple wooden chairs around it. The tabletop was set with maps and papers, the defense of St. Antin. Beyond the table was a wall with a single door, which led to the sleeping chambers of the High Abbot. On the wall to her right and continuing around to the wall behind her were floor to ceiling bookshelves, filled with the High Abbot's private collection of tomes and scrolls. Before her was a large sitting area defined by a large, thick rug in front of the great hearth, which roared with a new fire. Four comfortable, well-cushioned high back chairs had been set out. Two of those chairs were occupied, one by the High Abbot herself, the other by High Sister Olinda, the ranking member of the Daughters of Ehlani in the Abbey. This made Master Elia even more curious.

She took a seat and glanced at the fourth chair, a further curiosity. Was someone else expected?

"High Abbot, if I may ask, are we waiting on another?" Elia asked, all formal courtesy despite the urgency within her to be back out on the walls in the fight.

The High Abbot of Embreth was a woman only slightly older than Elia herself, but of a much more *pleasant* look and demeanor. Where Elia knew she was short and harsh — all sharp angles and steel-gray hair with a steely attitude to match — Ullanine, the high abbot, nearly always wore a smile, which was amplified by an inner light in her sky blue eyes. She was tall and regal, and her blond hair was fading to a stark, pure, white. If Elia had cared about such things, she might have been just the tiniest bit jealous. Luckily, she didn't care. Ullanine was wise and knowledgeable and the right choice for the High Abbot.

Ullanine's smile broadened for just a moment. "Yes. I could say it's a surprise and keep you in suspense, Embreth is the keepers of secrets after all, but I won't. We await a young woman. Her name is Ragnalla of Scandia. I'm told, in their tongue, the name means 'wise counsel.' I'm hoping she will prove her name to be accurate tonight."

Elia didn't ask why three of the wisest and strongest

women in their fields would need some young thing to counsel them, but she was curious. She was also curious why the scions weren't present for this meeting. The two women, even though Wyllea was still fairly new, were the center of everything done here in the Abbey.

She stayed her questions with effort, trying to remain somewhat composed. As much as she respected Ullanine's leadership, the woman's perpetual calm grated on Elia, especially now. They were at war. People were dying on the walls and still Ullanine seemed unaffected, serene. Elia was a woman formed in harsh times, in a harsh place, a woman of war and action. She'd asked the High Abbot once why she was always so peaceful and soft-spoken. Ullanine's answer had been simple: as the High Abbot, it was her job to show her faith in Embreth, to display the tranquility which comes with knowing the deeper secrets of the world, the peace of knowing all would work out, given time.

Elia wasn't so sure she believed things would work out. So she tried to contain her aggravation and concern and relax but found it impossible. She needed to be moving, fighting, not sitting.

She glanced over at High Sister Olinda of the Sisters of Ehlani. She was younger than Elia or Ullanine, but not by much. Her hair, once soft brown waves, was now a cascade of salt and pepper framing an oval face with dark brown eyes. The woman had a sort of hawkish look with a prominent, curved nose and intense gaze. She caught Elia's look and nodded solemnly. Elia nodded back and looked away into the fire, wondering how long they would have to wait.

It wasn't long.

A knock on the door heralded the arrival of young

Ragnalla, ushered in by an attendant who then promptly left, closing the door behind her.

When the young woman stepped tentatively into the light shed by the fire, Elia wondered even more at her presence. She was very young, perhaps fifteen, looking rather abashed and uncertain. She was a waif of a girl, too thin — as some girls of that age were — with long red-blond hair reaching to her thighs. The hair was pulled back from her face and braided in the Scandian style. Her face was plain, eyes brown, mouth small, nose straight. She wore a long simple dress that brushed the floor, hiding legs and feet. Not practical for fighting, but Elia suspected the girl did little of that.

She gave a fleeting smile and curtseyed. Once her hands had dropped from holding her skirt she reached for her long braid and began playing with it. It seemed a habitual action, unconscious, comforting.

"Thank you for coming, my dear," Ullanine said, her voice soft and calm. "Please have a seat." She motioned to the empty chair.

The girl sat in the chair, which seemed oversized for her. She even tucked her legs up beside her as some children did in chairs too large for them. She continued to fiddle with her braid.

Ullanine spoke, "Ragnalla has a gift. When we sought aid from the Kingdoms of the West, the Scandians were one of the first to pledge their support. When their armies marched, they brought Ragnalla with them. She does not fight, does not cook, but she has a place of honor in their ranks. She is seen as a good omen, partly because she has visions which help the army plan and prepare for the future."

Now Elia was intrigued. The True Sight was a rare and powerful gift.

Ullanine's gaze met Elia's, stern and yet hopeful. It was clear the girls gift was no trifle. "When I learned of this, I went to see the girl myself. I was skeptical of her abilities. She told me our scion would be captured. I did not think this possible given Senia's abilities and yet that came to pass. She told me we would hold within our walls at once a darkness and a great hope. I did not know what this meant, but with the arrival of Wyllea and the Blacklord's son I can see how Wyllea could be seen as a great hope for our future and the man as a great darkness. So I came to trust her abilities."

Ullanine reached across to grasp one of Ragnalla's small hands. "And now she's had another vision, but this one is different than any before. I brought her here tonight to share with you what she has seen." She turned to the girl, "Please tell us."

Ragnalla's voice was soft and hard to hear when she spoke, but with each word she gained a little confidence, enough that Elia could hear her at least. Her Scandian accent was also thick, making it harder to understand her, but Elia listened keenly so as not to miss anything. "There is a dark tide which washes against a great rock. A great light shines from the rock and will overwhelm the dark tide. Yet the ocean from which the tide came is vast and deep and at its core is a pure darkness." The girl gave an involuntary shiver before continuing. "The tide will be defeated, that is known, but after that, there are two possible futures."

Ullanine interrupted. "And that's why this vision is unlike any other. Usually, there's one clear path, but here there are two, both clear, and which will come to pass is unknown." The High Abbot's gaze was intense as it came to Elia, then passed to Olinda. Elia could sense the gravity which hung heavy over this moment. "Go on, youngling."

Ragnalla nodded. "The first of these futures is dark. The ocean is vast and deep and black and in time will swell to flood all the lands. There will be no second "dark tide," just a steady rising of water which will quench all light, covering all lands."

Well Elia certainly didn't like the sound of that. Would their fighting be for naught? Would their scions fail under the sheer power of the Blacklord? It wasn't something she wished to ponder.

"The other future is a path into the light. There are six bright fish." Ragnalla grimaced. "No, that is not right. There are five bright fish and one dark fish with only speckles of light." She stopped, shaking her head. "I am sorry, it is very hard to find the words in your language for the things I see."

"It is well, Ragnalla, we understand," Ullanine said, patting Ragnalla's hand. "Take your time."

Ragnalla nodded, taking a moment to steady herself. "There are six who must go into the heart of the ocean," she said with confidence. "Perhaps given time I can give you more details, but I know this: one who must go is of blue-fire, one is of green winds, and one is of gold and contains all the base elements. The darker one is also of all the base elements." She pressed her lips together in concentration for a moment, then shook her head. "That is all I have for now. These few and only these few must go to the depths of the black ocean, to the core. Some may not survive, but they are the only ones who have any chance to dispel the heart of the darkness. If they can do this, the dark ocean will recede from all lands and light shall prevail once more." Ragnalla's eyes gazed upon some distant sight none of the rest of them could see. Her hands had, for that brief moment, stopped playing with her braid. Then she blinked and was returned to them.

The only sound in the room was the crackle and hiss of the fire.

So there was hope. Despite the death and strife that plagued them continuously these days, perhaps there would be an end to the Blacklord within her lifetime. Elia grimaced. Did Ullanine already know such things? Was that how she managed to remain calm through it all? Yet even this sense of hope was clouded by knowing there was another equally as possible future which was far worse.

Ullanine spoke breaking the short silence. "Thank you Ragnalla, we appreciate your strength in helping us see your visions as you do. You may go now, youngling."

Ragnalla unfolded herself from the chair and with a quick bow of her head to the three older women, scurried from the room.

Elia shook her head. "Amazing." The single word seemed to hang in the air.

Ullanine looked into the fire, her hands folded in her lap, her gaze intense. "Truly," the High Abbot said, taking another long moment to ponder the flames before turning back to Elia and Olinda. "Now to our task. We must ensure that this second future comes to pass." For the first time, Elia heard an urgency in the High Abbot's voice, a break in the ever-present serenity. If she hadn't been looking for it she might not have noticed the way one hand in the High Abbott's lap grasped the other intently.

"It would seem a daunting task. How are we to know who to send?" Elia asked, starting to get curious at High Sister Olinda's silence. Unlike the other two, Elia had to move. She rose and strode toward the fire. Once there she turned to face the other two again.

Ullanine said with assurance, "I think we all know who the 'blue-fire' is."

"Senia, yes. And the 'green wind' must be Wyllea, but who is the one of all elements. I haven't heard of such a multi-talent in generations." Elia shrugged.

"That is why I am here," Olinda said finally. The High Sister was a little too still in her chair, arms folded in her lap. It was a tranquility that came from effort, keeping oneself still.

"Oh?" Elia asked, seeing a look pass between Ullanine and Olinda. They knew something she didn't.

"One of my daughters is such a talent."

Elia knew that to be a healer of any great effect one needed the earth talent which was connected to the body. As such, most Daughters of Ehlani were earth talents to some degree. Even minor earth talents could heal most wounds. Yet someone with all elements, able to heal body, mind, soul, and spirit would be a very rare talent indeed. Elia could understand why the High Sister might want to keep this a secret.

"Her name is Cassine," Olinda said, voice measured. "And her eyes, in the right light might be said to shine like gold. The High Abbot believes Cassine is the third member of this party."

"Very well then," Elia said, "but that still leaves three members unknown, one being a 'dark one' whatever that means. How shall we know these people?" She began to pace, a short stretch back and forth in front of the fire, the heat from the hearth stimulating her into action.

Ullanine drew in a long breath. "I have been thinking about this. It is only a guess, though it feels right. But if Senia were going on any journey, who do you think would be next to her no matter what we said to him?"

Elia grimaced. "Ahrn." She nodded. Ahrn was Senia's lover and bonded mate. He was named for the Vanished God, Aehryn of All Things, who once ruled the heavens. "You're right. Most likely he will be one of those going. He would never let Senia go alone, even if it meant his death."

"Which it may," Olinda said with a sigh. "You heard what the girl said, not all of them may survive." She shook her head. "I've already brought that boy back from death's door once."

"For which he and I, and Senia are eternally grateful, High Sister," Elia said.

"Also," Ullanine went on, "if we follow that formula, then it would seem that Wyllea's man might also be another of those to go."

Elia arched a brow. "I don't see him being much help. He's only just starting his training. He has a long way to go before he'd be ready for such a quest."

"Yet from what I hear, he and Wyllea would die for each other as well and are not likely to go anywhere without the other."

Elia had to agree. "True."

"This leaves only the dark one," Olinda said.

"Yes, he or she is the mystery." Ullanine's gaze turned to the fire.

Elia had a thought. "Though if we follow the pattern, then it would be the man who loves your multi-talent," Elia said to Olinda.

"Cassine?" Olinda seemed surprised. "She has no man in her life. She is a devoted and dedicated Daughter of Ehlani and as far as I know she's never even known the touch of a man."

Elia grimaced. That hope had died quickly.

"And so," Ullanine said, "the question remains, who is this dark one?"

Elia stopped her pacing. "Who indeed?"

CHAPTER 1

*C*assine's hope of escape vanished. She yelled for help, but her voice was drowned out amidst the din of combat and the screams of the dying all around her. The Blacklord's armies swelled around the keep in yet another night raid. She couldn't be heard and she wouldn't be seen. A magical darkness shrouded her and her captor, the Blacklord's son, as he made his way across the bailey of St. Antin Abbey toward the outer wall.

He'd captured her only moments before as she'd tended to him in the dungeons of the Abbey. He'd snapped the chains attaching him to the wall as if they'd been strings. He still wore the magical manacles that kept him from accessing his Scion-Weapon and its magic, but he was a strong multi-talent on top of his scion abilities. No one had suspected this. Only she knew. Being a multi-talent herself, she was one of the few who could see the magic within him.

He held her close in front of him. He only needed one arm, great muscles pressing against her like a vice, wrapped around her ribcage just below her breasts. His other hand, kept close by the manacles, rested on her hip. Her feet didn't even touch the ground. Her arms were pinned, yet she could kick and thrash her head, but this seemed to affect him little.

Her heart thundered in her chest, blood boiling with an intense desire to be free of this man. But she wasn't scared, not yet. If she could find a way to escape while still within the confines of St. Antin she doubted he'd come back for her. She wasn't that important a person.

Physically she wasn't strong, but her talent with earth magic was significant and that affected the body. She stopped moving for a moment as she pumped everything she had into strengthening herself. Then she pushed away from him with all her earth-talent enhanced strength. With any normal man she would have easily pried her way out of his grip, but this was no normal man. His arm around her flexed as she tried to escape and she succeeded only in freeing one arm before he yanked her back, tight to him. His earth talent was amazing! A moment later he'd caught her free arm and was pinning it to her side once again.

"You are a feisty one aren't you?" A deep baritone rumbled from within him.

Her stomach clenched in panic, blood pounding in her ears. She was losing time, but she had so much more at her disposal than just her earth-talent.

Unable to see through the darkness around her, Cassine sent out her life-sense. There were many others around, dashing through the bailey or lying too still as their life-essence faded. Yet she found it hard to sense those nearby as her life-sense was half-blinded by her captor's brilliant bloom of life energy. No wonder he'd been able to overpower her earth-talent enhanced strength. He was a potent individual, powerful in many respects, physically for sure, but the pure power of spirit within him was like a beacon in the night. This shook her to her core and nearly overwhelmed her. She doubted any of her magic would affect him. He was simply far too powerful.

Her strongest talent was with water and soul magic, but there was little that could do to him, except dishearten him perhaps. She tried to push at his soul, making him doubt himself, uncertain. Yet she found his soul to be an inky, oily place which disgusted her.

He hesitated for just a moment, her effects on him clear, but his determination to escape was too strong and he was moving again a moment later.

Her thoughts danced, frantic. Her heart raced, trapped in her chest like she was trapped in this man's arms. His pure life energy would give him away in an instant to any who were looking for it, but no one else here, even either of the scions, could see life as she could. Cassine's life-sense was an ability of water and soul. It was enhanced by her link to fire and spirit as well as to earth and the physical body, but she doubted anyone else could see things the same way. If Senia was nearby she might become aware of this man's spirit, which was incredibly strong, but Senia was likely out beyond the walls fighting, and it might be too late by the time she caught up with them.

Cassine's terror bloomed into a black cloud of doubt and fear. She now felt what she'd been trying to make him feel. How could she ever hope to escape this man?

"Please," she tried one last time. "Don't do this. I know there's good in you." She had seen it. His soul might have been a twisted, dark thing, but mixed into the warped wounds was more than one strand of empathy, of kindness. They might not be large, nor many, but they were there.

"There is no good in me," he growled, his voice a low, deep and husky.

"Perhaps you can't see it, but I can."

He tightened his grip on her, his free hand moving up to grasp her throat, choking her. "Speak of this again and you'll know how evil I am."

Despite his words, he released her neck. He could have killed her, yet he hadn't.

He crouched and leapt. They were close to the walls. The life-essences of those in the bailey stopped abruptly. She felt the rush of warm wind on her face, tousling her long hair.

His leap took them well above the fifty-foot walls, the life essences of those on the wall sinking farther and farther below them.

She'd hoped he wouldn't take her this far, that he'd discard her before this, but he hadn't. She had to do something quickly or she'd be neck deep in the Blacklord's armies. He alone was bad enough, but there were other mages serving the Blacklord as well and she'd have little hope once she was in amidst all of that magic. She trembled, yet still some core of strength within her sought for a way out, something to save her.

She couldn't affect him, so she needed to do something else, but what?

There was one thing.

She'd only ever done it once before and that had been by accident nearly twenty years ago as a child.

Yet she knew it was possible and she remembered how it had felt, the memory ingrained into her being. It took all elements and a great deal of power. She had no idea if it would work, but it was her only hope, the only magic she could think of to free herself. Desperation pushed her. She had to try, even if she had no clue what would happen. She knew only if she stayed with this man she couldn't imagine a worse fate.

She tried to calm herself as he began his descent, gathering her energies. First, she drew upon water, her most significant talent. She felt her own blood, the liquid life within her as well as the aura that was her soul. These were like her hands or face, so well known to her as to be taken for granted. Then she gathered her strength in earth, her second strongest talent, the ability to heal, which had gotten her into the Daughters of Ehlani. She used the knowledge of the body to strengthen her muscles and harden herself for what was to come. Next was fire and spirit, closer to soul than mind, but still not a strong element for her. She reached out with her spirit to a distant place, sensing the world around her, knowing the feel of all things, as spirit was the element that created and connected all things. Finally air, her weakest element and connected to the mind. She calmed her thoughts, ready now for the extreme effort she needed to push herself out of her own being, taking mind, body, soul and spirit with her to another place in an instant.

The only problem was, she couldn't control where she went.

She felt the tearing of the fabric of reality as she pushed herself to some other, distant place. Her body would have been torn apart if not for the earth magic she'd pushed into it. There was disorientation and pain. It was incredibly intense, but only for an instant. There was a cry, from whom, she didn't know, she was a being of magic at the moment and the needs and sensations of her body were distant. She floated free, detached, in all places at once and none. The sensation lasted a mere heartbeat and yet stretched for an eternity, one breath drawn out for what seemed like hours.

She landed, feeling solid earth under her feet. She'd done it. Her soul elated, celebrated. She was free!

Snapping out of the trance she'd needed to teleport herself, she came to her senses despite her entire being: body, soul, mind, and spirit, feeling drained and weak.

Instantly she realized something had gone wrong.

When she'd done this as a child, she'd been alone. This time, she hadn't been, and somehow she'd taken her captor with her.

By all the Gods, no!

Yet even as her heart sank, his grip loosened and released. He fell to the ground behind her with a heavy thud. She wanted to run away, to cry out with joy, but with her own weakness she couldn't do anything but collapse to her knees. She sat there for a moment, still trying desperately to get up, away from this place and that man.

There was no strength in her however. She doubled over onto her hands.

Perhaps she could crawl.

Instead, she found herself taking several long, deep breaths to keep from blacking out. It wasn't enough. She sank to the ground as everything slowly went dark.

For a moment, her mind still functioned before unconsciousness took her. One thought circled in her mind: she lay in some unknown place with her captor still close by. The Gods must hate her.

CHAPTER 2

*D*avar woke in a rush.

He sat up, knowing something was wrong and trying to bring himself to alertness, but his entire body hurt and his head spun with the effort. A thousand soldiers marched in time in his skull, pounding his thoughts to mist. He opened his eyes only to have light stab into them, burning. He brought his hands, still bound by the manacles that cut him off from his Scion-Blade, to his forehead and shut his eyes.

What in all the blazes of the Void had happened?

He'd been in the middle of jumping over the walls of St. Antin when...

Well, he had no idea what had happened.

He tried tentatively opening his eyes again. This time he blinked away the stabbing pain forcing himself to look at what was around him and it was clear he was nowhere near St. Antin Abbey.

It was dawn. He was high up on the side of a mountain,

able to see the sun far to the east cresting the curve of the world. But everything was wrong. The sun was too far north for Hallania and the land around these mountains was thick forest, nothing like the lands around Maalkin's Rise. He had no clue where he was or how he'd gotten here. He recalled a sensation like a giant hand trying to rend him in all directions at once. He'd pushed his earth magic to its limits, barely quick enough to resist being torn apart, but it had drained him and sent him reeling.

He stood, or at least tried to, but his legs wouldn't support him, weak as a kitten. So he continued to massage his forehead as he took in his surroundings. To the east high hills and deep gorges, mostly covered in thick forest, rolled away from the mountain plateau on which he sat. The north held a steep mountainside jutting up to a high, snow-capped peak. This definitely wasn't Maalkin's Rise. There was no snow on those mountains except in winter. Also, Maalkin's Rise had much more rounded tops than the jagged, pointed spikes of this stretch of mountains. To the west, the plateau rose slowly and narrowed into a crevice between two steep slopes. To the south was a low, sparsely forested hill with higher mountains beyond it.

The woman he'd captured lay nearby so whatever had happened to him had happened to her as well. His gaze lingered on her: the way the sun caught her hair and turned it to gold, the lush curves of her body, the exposed slender ankle in a delicate stocking, the peaceful face. It reminded him of...

Someone...

Who...?

It was a very faint memory — or was it a memory at all? It

was some image of a woman captured in his mind. His mother? He'd never known his mother. He'd been told he had no mother, that he'd been created by his father's magic alone. He wasn't sure if he believed that. The Blacklord rarely told the truth, even to his own son, preferring to bend all things to reflect his dark view of the world.

Thinking of his father reminded him he was outside the enchantment of the abbey walls. He should be able to hear and feel his father in his mind, and yet...

There was something, but it was so faint as to be hardly there at all. It was like a whisper that was just too far away to hear. He knew someone was trying to speak to him, but knew not what they said. He must be far to the west, farther from his father than he'd ever been. This gave him a suspicion of where he was, probably the Silver Mountains. He couldn't be sure, but it was a reasonable guess.

He tried to remember the maps he'd studied of the world. How far away were the Silver Mountains? How long would it take him, moving as fast as he could, to get back east? He estimated at least a week, probably closer to two.

Knowing this did little to improve his mood. The resounding silence he'd felt in the dungeons of St. Antin consumed him once more. A profound loss and emptiness echoed through his soul. He didn't know what to do with such a feeling. A great anger swelled and bellowed within him.

It gave him the strength to stand.

A part of him knew his anger would be of little use in figuring a way out of this mess. Yet each breath he drew in to quell it only fanned the flames of his distemper to a bonfire. He clenched his jaw, feeling his muscles tense and bunch.

Why was this happening to him?

Looking at the prone figure on the ground, he knew she had to be involved somehow. He took out his anger on her, kicking her backside. His strength was such that he sent her rolling several feet away. "Wake up!"

As angry as he was the kick still sent him off balance and he staggered to one side nearly falling. He was still drained from resisting... whatever it was that had brought them here.

The woman stirred, but didn't wake. Whatever had put them here had hit her harder. That didn't surprise him. His abilities were exceptional, far beyond mere mortals, even scions. It had taken two scions to bring him in after all.

He stalked over to her, each step stronger, then kicked her again harder. This time she lifted off the ground before landing with a thump and a groan.

Her eyes fluttered open, but only for a moment before closing again. She muttered something intelligible and rolled over.

He was tempted to just leave her, but something compelled him to wake her. She needed to know how angry he was. The more he thought about it the more he was sure this was her fault. She might look like some woman of his dreams, but right now he was simply too frustrated to leave her be.

He got down on one knee next to her. He raised his hands, balled together to bash her across the face, but paused. Her face was nothing short of angelic. It would be a shame to break and bruise such beauty.

Had he really just thought that? His mind must be addled. What did it matter what she looked like? She was infuriating even in her sleep and needed to be punished!

He screamed and brought his fists down hard. They sunk

deep into the ground above her head. He raised them again, this time sure he would hit her, but they froze, trembling with frustration and rage. It probably wouldn't wake her anyway. He'd probably hit her too hard and knock her out again or kill her.

So he grabbed her by the shoulders and shook her, yelling at her. "Wake up, wench!"

She let out a long low groan, followed by another one. He stopped his assault and sat back with a grim smile. Now she'd know his wrath!

Her eyes opened slowly, long lashes fluttering like butterfly wings revealing her soft brown eyes which shone like pools of gold in the newly risen sun.

By all the Gods! Those eyes pulled at him, drew him in, held him.

He shook that off, his anger resuming. "What did you do?"

She seemed to come fully awake, actually seeing him. Her eyes flashed with defiance and she rolled away from him, coming smoothly to her feet. She was quick, lithe and grace-ful, like a dancer. Yet once standing she had to steady herself, waving and wobbling a bit, arms out to balance herself. She seemed just as weak as he was.

Once steady, she winced and rubbed her rump. "Did you kick me?"

"No."

She glared at him.

He gave her a cruel smile.

"You did kick me."

"Tell me what you did. Where are we?"

She glared at him, lips tight. Her breast rose and fell with quick breaths, showing off the lush curves hidden by her dress. Now that she was standing, he noticed she was tall for a woman. Her figure was well rounded and full, not like some of the waifs he'd bedded in brothels. Her face was round with well-defined cheeks, a slender nose, and full lips. Her eyes shone like the sun, full of fire at the moment. Then there was her hair, long and straight, golden and flowing like a field of ripe wheat swaying in the wind. She would make an excellent match for him. His anger began to fade as arousal built within him.

He shook his head. Why couldn't he remain mad at her? Why did her mere presence keep distracting him? He was starting to question why he'd even bothered to bring her out of the dungeons. It seemed more and more like that had been a mistake.

He let out a roar of frustration, pleased to see her shrink back. Then he turned from her and began walking. He couldn't stand to look at her, that unearthly beauty. He needed to be far from this place. Yet despite the intensity of his need to be away from here, away from her, he stopped after only a few paces.

He was gulping air now, seething. The sun before him became flashes of her soft hair and golden eyes. She'd enchanted him. That had to be it. She'd done something when she'd brought him here, and he'd find out what, then kill her.

He put all the threat he could into his voice as he turned back to her weaving all the dark passion and danger of who he was behind every word. "What did you do to me?"

She flinched, but mostly looked confused. That was not the reaction he'd been expecting. Scared, defiant, those were emotions that would have made sense, but confusion?

When she spoke, her voice was calm, even. That annoyed him even more. "All I did was try to get away from you."

"You did a horrible job."

"I'm aware of that, thank you."

"Where are we?"

She looked around and seemed just as baffled as he'd been. "I don't know."

He couldn't take it anymore. He leapt and landed next to her, catching her off guard. He grabbed her head, a hand cupping each cheek.

Whatever he'd meant to do was lost the instant his flesh touched hers. An overwhelming sensation filled him as the full force of her entire being was shunted into him. Her mind, soul, and spirit fused with his. Her feelings merged and mingled with the dark emotions in his soul. Everything she was, such beauty and purity, filled him and intermingled with his twisted malevolence.

He couldn't move, though his hands did release her reflexively as if touching hot coals. She staggered back with a long, "Oh," of exhaled air. He guessed the look of utter shock and overwhelm on her face matched his. Whatever had happened to him, had happened to her.

Yet still he couldn't fathom the joining which had just occurred. He could feel her. He knew her on such an intimate level that he lost his own being. He *was* her in every way but the physical. Even that wasn't far removed for he could feel the way the fabric of her dress moved over her skin, feel the wind in her hair.

It was far too much to take in so quickly. He knew everything about her, memories of her parents, her feelings about him and the war, the confusion over where they were — so apparently she really didn't know — the bright buoyancy of her spirit, always open and hopeful.

Yet, far worse than knowing and feeling her was the incongruence of how that countered his own thoughts and feelings and spirit. There was a great internal conflict as these two forces collided and tried to be at home in one body but couldn't come to any agreeable terms.

He finally managed to stammer out some words. "What was that?" But even as he spoke he knew the answer. He had no idea how or why it had happened, but the result was clear enough, echoing within him. Somehow he and Cassine, he knew her name now like it was his own, had completely merged mind, soul, and spirit.

She fell to her knees still breathing hard. "We..." She couldn't get the words out, but he heard everything she intended to say: *we are one, we merged, but how? Is this because of the teleportation?*

What teleportation? Had he said those words out loud? No, he hadn't. And he already knew the answer. He knew her thoughts, what she'd done, how they'd come to be here. Despite his knowing she still responded to him.

I tried to teleport myself away from you, but I'd never done it with someone holding me before. I took us both.

He already knew all of that. He could feel her power and knew she was a multi-talent of no small ability but he still had to ask: *What are you?* There was far more at work here than a simple spell. Well, teleportation wasn't a *simple* spell at all, but it alone only explained how they'd arrived here, it didn't explain what had happened just a moment ago. He hadn't done it, which meant it had to come from her. Yet he knew everything about her and knew that she'd never done or experienced anything like this before either. Which meant if it wasn't him and wasn't her, then...

"It's something about the connection between us. Two multi-talents touching..." she said having followed his train of thoughts.

It made no sense to him, yet it also seemed the most likely explanation. He'd touched her skin to skin before now, just not since...

"The teleportation," she said, finishing his thoughts once again. "Somehow, using a spell which combines all the elements while we were together has joined us. It just required a physical touch to activate it?" She was uncertain of what she was saying, as was he. Yet it was currently the only explanation that made sense.

Another thought came to him.

"You're a multi-talent," he said, his thoughts already spinning ahead and she knew where they were going.

"No!" she said vehemently.

"You can remove these bindings!"

"Why would I want to free you?"

It was an excellent question. His gut reaction was 'because I'll kill you if you don't' but even as that thought flashed through his head — and hers — he knew he wouldn't.

"See," she said slowly, her thoughts already known to him, far ahead of her words, "I told you there was good in you."

"No!" He needed to get away from her, from anyone knowing him so deeply. Only his father was allowed in, not this woman. He stalked away, first with long strides, then running, soon bounding in a long leap from this plateau to the lower peak to the south. He landed in a large clearing with evergreen trees loosely placed all around. He turned, looking back at the plateau far away and the speck of a woman.

He could still feel her, but thankfully, distance had diminished the connection. He could still hear her thoughts, but they were quieter. Her feelings weren't as raw and intense in his soul, her spirit not blinding him with its purity. He shuddered and fell to his knees, so tired from everything that had happened since they'd arrived here. He needed a break. He needed to think without her in his head, but that would be impossible. He'd need to be a lot farther away for that to happen and he didn't have the strength to run at the moment. He sat back, elbows on his knees, head in his hands. He needed to get her out and get back to being himself.

Yet of all the things she'd said, there was one that stuck like a thorn in his mind and soul. He was not a good man. He'd done and seen and ordered far too many evil things to be good. How could she say he was good?

Especially now that he knew her. She was everything that was pure and virtuous. She was like a sun within him dispelling the night of his own being, stuck in a permanent conflict of dawn or dusk, depending on how you saw it. He was black, like his father, evil through and through... and yet... he knew what she'd seen in him, those select few fibers of light in an otherwise twisted and sinister soul. Sure they were there, he could admit that, but that meant nothing against the sheer volume of hatred and vileness that was the rest of him. It was insignificant... wasn't it? He didn't even know where those strands came from and didn't care. He'd banish them if he could, but they formed some deep core of who he was. Yet that didn't mean he was a good man.

I just said you had good in you. Not that you were a good man. Her voice echoed through his mind.

He tried to push her out. He needed to think.

So he stayed there, brooding, chaffing, sorting through his thoughts and feelings, and hating every minute of it. He was a man of action, not introspection. He'd never questioned himself before, so why now? Because he needed proof that he was who he thought he was. Proof enough to dissuade this woman who could see his soul. Proof enough to overcome his fledgling doubts and permanently squash the very faint light within him.

Why not just kill her? The questioned echoed through his thoughts. *She's a threat. She knows too much.*

He could. Despite her powers, he could still rip her in two if he wanted, but... something was stopping him. At first, he thought it was her benevolent thoughts and feelings polluting him, but after a moment, he knew that wasn't the case. He could have killed her back at the abbey, but hadn't. Why?

Again, the image of that other woman flashed into his mind. Whoever she was she was behind this. He couldn't kill Cassine because some faint memory of another woman was stopping him. But who was she? How did that brief memory have the power to stop him from killing, which came naturally to him?

Thoughts warred within him, feelings battling alongside, twisted and confused.

His stomach rumbled.

He quelled the hunger with a thought. Being strong in the element of earth meant he was well connected to his body and able to go for days without eating if needed.

If you're hungry you should eat, she said into his mind.

What do you care? The really sickening part was: she did care. By all that was dark and evil! They were enemies, yet she cared for him. She seemed to think of it as something called 'common decency.' She treated her enemies with kindness and a certain respect. She was good to people who were mean to her. She didn't like him at all, but she'd be nice to him? What sort of person lived like that?

Her thoughts and emotions grew stronger. Cassine was coming. He'd known for some time. She'd taken a rather long circuitous route to get to him. She'd been hunting. He looked up as she entered the clearing carrying several small dead animals.

He knew from their connection that her father was a woodsman and a hunter. She'd helped him as a child and learned some of his craft.

"Dinner?" She laid her catch on the ground and crouched across from him. She wasn't happy about any of this. She felt a vile revulsion toward him and yet here she was offering him food.

"Why?" He didn't need to ask the rest of the questions. She knew them. Why help me? Why come back to me? Why are you here? What do you want?

"You know why," she said, and he did. This was what 'good' people did. They did for others as they hoped others would do for them. It made no sense to him, but apparently it was the only thing that made sense to her.

She smiled. It was forced, but still pleasant looking. "I'll go get some firewood."

I'll do it. He rose in a flash, reaching out to stop her but his hand halted itself inches from her wrist. He wouldn't touch her, skin to skin, again. He wasn't afraid...

Yes you are.

Ok, maybe he was. He didn't want to renew the connection. Even now, though she was there with him he could feel it slipping away, not as crisp or clear as it had been at first. He turned away, stalking into the woods to find dry wood. He needed to walk, get away.

This woman was going to drive him insane, perhaps she already had. Maybe that was why he questioned everything he was.

CHAPTER 3

*C*assine listened to the fire crackle and snap as fat from the spitted squirrel dripped onto the leaping flames. It was late afternoon and the sun had already disappeared behind the high peaks to the west. The air was cooling quickly. Also slipping away was the deep connection she'd shared with Davar earlier that day.

Cassine sat and waited to eat as Davar finished sucking the meat from the bones of the first squirrel she'd cooked. He'd demanded to be fed first, stroking his ego and hiding his uncertainty. It was infuriating and yet, it was who he was. The fact that they were 'sharing' a meal at all was incredible... for both of them. She'd let him have his way, taking just a little joy from how much her generosity had infuriated him.

He was an intimidating man, as large as they came. She was tall, built sturdy and strong, so there were few men who loomed over her. He was one of them. A head taller than she and built like a bear, thick through chest and shoulders with great muscular arms and long, massive legs. His face was angular with a heavy brow, thick nose, and sharp strong jawline. His eyes were dark brown, almost black to match his hair, which was a tousled mane around his face, falling to his shoulders.

Yet despite his great size and savage look, it was his magic that intimidated her the most. With any larger than her she might still be able to overpower them with her earth magic, but with Davar...

She shivered, remembering how easily he'd overpowered her back at the abbey, how futile her magically enhanced strength had been against him.

She was in no way upset as the connection with him faded. It had been horrid being connected to one so dark and broken, feeling the slimy filth of his soul fouling and staining hers. She'd had to keep from being physically sick at the feel of such vile and corrupt thoughts and feelings mingling with hers.

It had taken all her will to do... anything for a long time after they'd bonded. He was as dark and depraved a man as she'd ever met and she didn't want any part of him anywhere near her.

And yet she felt compelled to help him, to heal him.

She was more than just a healer by trade but had always felt a certain drive to help those in need. He didn't want her help, but to her all that darkness was like a wound. Only this wound was in his soul; a great gaping sore, which could be healed... given a lot of time and effort. Once she'd recovered from feeling sick, she knew she had to help him.

You can't fix me.

Cassine sighed, wondering how much of what she was thinking he was hearing at the moment. She decided she didn't care and continued with her train of thought.

It was true he was 'the enemy.' Yet what she'd seen when

she'd been intimately connected to him was more like a lost and troubled boy. He might be the Blacklord's son, but she wondered idly who'd been his mother? According to his thoughts earlier, he believed he had no mother, that he was created by magic. But Cassine found that difficult to believe.

She knew much of magic, specifically the sub-element of creation, which lay between the elements of water and earth, her two prime talents. She was quite knowledgeable about creation, conception, and birth. She'd been the best midwife of all of the Daughters of Ehlani. It was true that with strong enough magic nearly anything was possible, but she didn't think even the Blacklord with all his powers would be able to generate that level of pure creation. Perhaps he could. She suspected a more likely explanation was that a woman had carried Davar while much dark magic had been used to conceive and develop the boy. She also suspected that the woman had probably not been allowed to live much past Davar's birth.

Yet his creation was not as much a concern to her as the one thought she kept circling back to: could he be healed?

He didn't want to be. He'd made that clear. But that hadn't stopped her in the past. She'd seen soldiers praying for death, a release, and been able to bring them back from the brink to a full and healthy life. High Sister Olinda had once told her she was the most skilled healer of all the Daughters of Ehlani, perhaps even better than the High Sister herself. She had faith that she could heal this man's twisted soul.

Davar took the spitted squirrel from the fire and removed the spit. He glanced at her, then tossed her the spit. She set about skewering the last of the three she'd caught, already cleaned and waiting. She placed the spit back over the fire without a word and waited.

He glared at her.

Then with a sneer, he broke the cooked squirrel he was holding in half then tossed her part. She caught it.

"Thank you," she said simply.

His eyes narrowed, then he looked away confused. Finally, he shook his head and began devouring his half of the carcass.

Yes, she decided, he could be healed.

He need not have given her any food. He was stronger than she was, and she wouldn't have been able to take it from him by force. Had he felt something for her? Had he let some of that light seep through, then regretted it immediately?

"I know what you're thinking, remember," he said, his voice the deep, gruff baritone she'd come to know. "You can't change me."

Could she? Was his next immediate thought.

She nibbled on her food to hide her growing smile. There were doubts enough there for her to work with. She knew part of his uncertainty came from the empty space within him where the voice of the Blacklord had once been. Davar was too far away now to hear his 'father's' commands. He didn't have someone controlling him, telling him what to do, which meant he had to figure out who he was on his own. If she had any say in it, he'd start to see the light within him.

"It's up to you," she said softly. "If you want those bindings off then perhaps you'll let me try." It was a gamble. She knew the bindings kept him from summoning his Scion-Sword. With them gone, he'd have access to a great weapon. What he'd do with that she really didn't know, despite their connection.

He glared at her again. "I could just race back to my armies and have them do it."

"You haven't yet."

"I like the night. I was waiting for full dark and a good meal before starting."

"As you say." She shrugged. "It's up to you."

His thoughts might have been mostly hidden from her now, but his soul wasn't. She could feel the turmoil within him at the thought of leaving her. She wasn't quite sure why except that he seemed to have some desire, some infatuation with her. He'd thought of her as 'angelic' earlier. She wasn't sure where that had come from, but she'd apparently made a deep impression on him. Whether it was that, the light of her soul mixed with his, or something else beyond either of their understandings that made him stay, it didn't matter. As long as he stayed, she had a chance to help him.

It was a long shot, but perhaps she could try another approach. "Don't you want to know about your mother?"

His head snapped up, eyes burning with suspicion and anger. "I had no mother."

"I can tell you for sure, one way or the other, if you'd like."

"My father has no reason to lie to me." Even as he said the words, his emotions clenched with uncertainty and a deeper, frustration-driven, anger. It was strong enough that she felt it clearly. His father lied to him all the time. It was the man's nature.

"We both know that's not true. Aren't you curious?" She was, certainly. If she could help him see his mother, perhaps that would begin the process of healing. Yet her curiousness went deeper still. What if the Blacklord was powerful enough to simply create this man from nothing, what did that say? Would there be any way to stop a man who could mimic the power of the Gods and create life? She wanted to know if Davar had a mother perhaps more than he did.

He was curious too. She'd sensed it, yet he was still keeping Cassine at bay. He wasn't going to give in easily. He didn't want her inside his head any more than she already was. Searching through his soul for the connection to his mother was no easy task and would involve a deep scan through the fiber of his being. She already knew he didn't like the fact that they'd been so closely connected earlier. She didn't relish the thought of them 'reconnecting' either, but she couldn't help but want to try, even if it meant sifting through that slimy soul once again.

Why?

His question rang through her with its usual endings *why are you doing this? Why are you staying?* And so many others.

"You know why," she said softly. If he could still feel as much from her as she could from him, he'd know she wanted to help him.

"But why do you want to help me?" he asked, gruff. He was actually confused on that point. He didn't know. Then it occurred to Cassine that she didn't necessarily have a clear answer to that question either. She wanted to help everyone in need, but that wasn't really a straight answer. Sure she was compelled to help, it was in her nature, but why him specifically and why now?

She considered for a moment before she answered. "Because I think you've been dealt a great injustice."

He gave a harrumph with a dismissive grimace.

She went on unperturbed, "You've never had any chance to explore who you really are. You were raised by a man of evil and he's been in your head controlling you since you were a boy. You can't deny I'm right. I know. I saw all of your thoughts earlier. You don't really know who you are without him. Perhaps you're the man you think you are... but you aren't certain. So let me help you figure that out. If you find you are the terrible man you believe yourself to be, then I'll go. I won't want to be near you anyway. But you'll never be certain unless you know everything about yourself and that includes knowing your mother."

He sniffed, chewing silently, glaring at her. She could sense his turmoil, the conflict within him to know more about who he was, and yet also not allow her to be right or get too close.

"How?" He was still skeptical. *I know of no way to do what you're proposing and I'm a stronger multi-talent than you.*

"Water and soul are your weakest talents," she said bluntly. They both knew it was true. "Soul is my strongest ability. I can search back through the line of your soul to the moment of your birth. Using some spirit, I can go even further back, to when she carried you and your soul would have been connected to hers. If indeed you had a mother, then I can link to her soul and reveal that to you. I've done it before." It had been long ago when she'd only just been starting as a healer in her village. She'd helped orphans find out more about their parents.

He grunted. It wasn't an affirmation or a negation. She still felt the roil of emotions within him: hate, anger, curiosity, desire, traces of hope and even joy at the prospect of knowing his mother and starting to decipher who he was. There was also fear. He didn't want her sifting around in his soul. He didn't want to risk them touching and renewing the connection they'd had. Yet despite his fear, she knew it was still a tantalizing prospect for him.

"And if I let you do this, you'll free me from these?" He held up his manacled wrists.

She nodded.

Here again, she felt a surge of emotion, mostly his longing to be rejoined with his weapon. Though dark and twisted like him, it held a special place in his soul. The Blacklord had been the only father figure Davar had ever known and his sword, in many ways, was like a sibling.

"Then do it."

She smiled. She'd gotten through to him. This could be the start of a great healing for him if he ever let it happen. "I should rest, it will take a lot and—"

"Do it now!"

She flinched at the intensity of his voice and the wave of jumbled emotions thrown her way.

She drew a breath, giving herself a moment to recover, and said, "Fine, but I'll need a moment to regain some strength, and I'll need that last squirrel." She pointed to the spit on the fire.

He grunted with a nod. "Be quick about it."

The squirrel wasn't quite ready yet, so she stood. "There's a stream not far off into those woods." She pointed. She'd passed it earlier when she'd been hunting. "I'm going to get some water and clean myself up a little. When I return, I'll have that squirrel and we can begin."

He nodded again, and she left. She found the stream easily despite that evening shadows and darkness were growing deeper. She used her water talent to assess the water. It was clean and drinkable. She drank heavily knowing she was depleted. Then she stripped off her dress and waded into the stream. It only came to her knee at its deepest, but she crouched and quickly bathed herself. The stream was frigid, made of cold mountain waters. She used her fire talent and warmed herself a little. She scrubbed as best she could with her hands, even laid back to douse her hair and scrub it out as well.

It didn't take too long and when finished she waded out. She used her water talent to force the remaining drops off her until she was dry. She dressed, then had another long drink from a spot just upstream from where she'd bathed before returning to Davar.

She'd needed that break. Being away from him dimmed their connection, which was tenuous now and only revealed the strongest thoughts or emotions when they were close to one another. She knew she was about to delve into the nearly unfathomable darkness of his soul and had wanted desperately to simply be alone and clean and fresh for a moment before she tried it.

As she walked back, she grew more and more conflicted. She was afraid of what he might do once freed from those restraints. There were multiple fears actually. He was strong enough to rip her apart if he didn't like what she was doing. So yes, she feared for her life, but she also feared for his. What if he rejected the light within and returned to the overwhelming darkness?

Questions whirled in her mind: what would she find? What would he do once he had his Scion-Weapon back? Would she get the chance to fully heal him? Could she do it? Would he give her that much time and effort? It certainly didn't seem likely, but she had to try. It was that last bit of determination that pushed her up the hill to return to him. Even though it might mean her life, she would do this.

She returned and took the last squirrel from the spit, noticing a leg had been removed. It would do no good to glare at him; one look at his satisfied smile told her he'd done it just to spite her. A disapproving glance would only give him what he wanted. So she ate quietly, it would be enough.

Once finished she readied herself, moved around the fire, and knelt next to him.

It was full dark now, only the light of their fire and the stars above illuminated them.

Being this close their connection was revived and she could feel his fear and uncertainty... or was that hers projected onto him? Apparently, neither of them was certain of what would happen next.

"Lay back and relax. This may be very uncomfortable, but I'm sure you can cope with that."

He laughed as he laid back. "Do your worst." Despite the nonchalant words, she could feel his resistance grow. Strong thoughts pushed into her mind. He didn't like being in any sort of a submissive position. He'd never trusted anyone before in his life, so he couldn't help but think this was some sort of trick or trap. Images flashed of all the ways he could hurt or incapacitate her if he needed to. He wasn't worried that he could best her.

"I don't expect you to trust me," she said softly as she positioned herself next to his upper torso. "But our connection will probably renew when I touch you in a moment. Go ahead and read all my intentions. I think you already know I have no trick up my sleeve. I just want to help you because... it's who I am."

He glared at her.

She began to unlace his shirt and her fingers brushed his skin reviving the connection. It was not as strong this time. Their minds, souls, and spirits merged, but it wasn't nearly as jarring or as intense as it had been. Nor was it as deep. There were hidden corners, distant thoughts and feelings of his she couldn't access. It was still uncomfortable and near to overwhelming, but not as shocking as the first time.

Once again, she was forced to deal with the slick and slippery, inky nature of his essence. Just as she knew that he was gritting his teeth at the brightness of her soul and thoughts. But also he'd know she had no ill intentions, her motives were pure.

She slid her hand under his shirt along the bulging muscle of his chest to a place over his heart. The heart was the source of blood and the part of the body most connected to the soul.

His thoughts, as her hand pressed to the mountain that was his pectoral muscle, were far from pure. In a rather short time, he'd gone from images of how to hurt or subdue her to images of ripping away her dress and a whole barrage of thoughts that followed which made her blush and grow rather uncomfortably warm. His desire for her was intense. The fact that he knew she'd never been with a man seemed to stoke his lust even more. Something about being the one to deflower her excited him.

These thoughts were not helping her do what she needed to do. She closed her eyes, all of his thoughts and hers warring within her. Slowly, carefully, she cleared her mind of his doubts and lust and fears as well as her own fears and curiosity at his raging emotions, focusing on her own soul. Then she made the connection with his.

The initial connection was easy since they were linked. She focused still, digging deep into his soul. It was a slow process, grueling for them both as she sifted through the tangled jumble of his feelings and his very life essence. It helped that she was connected to spirit as well and could retrace his spirit-line back through his soul, back through so much torment and torture and vileness.

Gods! His life had been one horror after another, forced to kill and do much worse. The atrocities his father had made him commit as a boy weren't meant for any child to endure. She wept, though the sensation of the streams of tears on her cheeks was distant.

She forced herself to go on, back even farther to the agonizing and terrifying moment of his birth.

This is where things got that much harder. She delved further, before the moment of birth, to a place of physical, spiritual, and emotional darkness; made one-thousand fold darker for the brew of evil magic which had surrounded him. A person's soul was not instilled at birth, but some time while they were still in the womb. So she was able to trace his soul into this place, though it was disorienting and difficult. As much as the soul exists, it isn't fully formed. Emotions are only buds of the flowers they will eventually become in life. Things were murky here, like swimming through a muddy pond.

Yet it was here, before he was born, that his spirit and soul would have been connected inseparable with his mother's.

Trying to find that connection however, was incredibly hard. Her ability with spirit wasn't as strong as with soul. She groped and probed, trying to extend her essence out to that other person if indeed there had been anyone there. If there wasn't, she could flounder in this dark and disorienting place for an eternity, searching for a spirit and soul that didn't exist. This process was never easy, but usually if she just concentrated on the spirit-link, she could trace it to the mother. She grasped onto Davar's spirit, or rather that remembered spirit of him as he'd been before he was even born and used that.

She climbed that line of spirit like a rope up an unfathomable mountainside...

And she found Davar's mother.

It was only for an instant, a flickered image of a woman, a heartbeat, one tortured moment as the face and pain of Davar's mother became known to both of them. Despite the mere fraction of a moment they were connected to her, it was one of the most horrible things Cassine had ever felt. They couldn't tell what was being done to the woman — and she thanked all the Gods for that — but they felt every inch of the woman's agony. She was screaming. Not the yelling of someone cursing in pain, but the wordless, unending shriek of one far gone into torment. It clawed at their ears and tore at their souls.

The scream was just the tip of the iceberg of horrific emotions and sensations. Her body and soul were being torn apart, shredded, twisted, and corrupted. This was how the Blacklord had gestated his son, with torment beyond reason.

All of this was experienced in one terrible instant.

Then the raw intensity of the woman's soul-scream pushed Cassine's essence right out of Davar.

Cassine sat back, dazed, head aching, the scream of a long-dead woman still echoing in her mind. When she'd offered to help Davar find his mother, she'd never expected anything like that.

"Gods," she whispered and began to weep, too overwhelmed with pain and grief to do anything else.

CHAPTER 4

*D*avar stared at nothing but the remembrance of his mother's torment. He hadn't moved since Cassine had been thrust out of his soul by that same memory. He lay on the grass in the dark, the fire snapping and hissing not far away. His breathing came quick and shallow.

He didn't weep like Cassine, but he felt hot tears leave his eyes, running down into his ears. It was annoying, but he didn't move to wipe the wetness away.

He knew his father was cruel and evil. The Blacklord was literally heartless, having sacrificed his heart long ago in a ritual to gain immortality. Davar had had a vicious childhood, raised brutally to be the hard, dark man he was. His father cared for no one, not even him. He was a tool to his father, not family. He knew this and still couldn't fathom the horrors that his mother had been subjected to.

Despite having only experienced a single instant of her suffering, he knew enough of his father to surmise what the Blacklord had put that woman through: dark rituals and vile torture designed to inflict the maximum possible pain without killing her. The entire pregnancy she'd probably lived on the fine line where pain met death, until the day she birthed him and finally died.

His father had been partly right. It had been dark magic that had, in part, shaped him into what he was today. Yet to see, to know what had happened to his mother was overwhelming. Davar didn't shock easily, and yet he felt bile rise in his throat. He was horrified and angry. He hated his father for what he'd done and hated Cassine for having revealed it to him.

She'd been a scion, his mother. He knew that now, though he didn't know where this understanding had come from. He also suddenly understood why his father had so desperately wanted him to catch Senia alive. He'd wanted another scion woman to spawn a child for him.

Davar should have been fine with that thought, but right now it disgusted him. Perhaps it was his connection with Cassine... or maybe even his brief vision of his mother, but he felt a purity within him which reviled what his father had planned for the scions.

There was something about the sparkling stars and brilliant moon above him, the soft forest sounds, even Cassine's weeping, which soothed him. It spoke of a peace and innocence which contrasted all the darkness within him. It resonated with a place deep within him, long buried.

This once, he didn't fight it.

Instead, he questioned everything else in his life.

He'd never liked his father. He'd feared and respected the man's power yes, but nothing ever close to a familial love. He'd always hated his father, but he'd hated the world more and saw no other way to live than to follow the most powerful man in existence and bring the world to heel. But had that been his own thought? He'd always had his father inside his head, always present, always watching, always commanding him. Did he hate the world, or was that an extension of his father's seething ire at everything?

It occurred to him that he'd been without his father's presence for nearly a week now between the days in the dungeon of St. Antin and then here in the west. He'd hated the silence, but now...

Yet it wasn't silent now.

Cassine lingered in his thoughts, in his soul.

There was something about that light and purity that ate at him.

He suddenly needed to move. He stood and strode away. If she were as connected to him as he to her, she'd know he needed time to think, to work out everything that had been turned upside down in his life in such a short period of time.

He was quickly in the forest which covered most of the hillside. A light wind stirred the branches above him in a soft wash and murmur of leaves. Twigs snapped as he stepped on them, the debris of the forest floor crunching lightly with every step.

He was tired, so incredibly tired. The past day had been exhausting and he just wanted to sleep, but his mind wouldn't let him rest. Cassine had said he needed to figure out who he was, but suddenly that didn't seem like a quick or easy process. He'd never had a chance, until now, to be anything other than what his father commanded him to be.

Perhaps he'd start there.

Is that the life he wanted? Did he want to go back? It had been his single desire for most of the past week, but now... he wasn't sure. It would be easier that was certain. He wouldn't have to think for himself, just do as commanded. He'd have some free thought, acting in the moment to carry out the Blacklord's commands, but still his father would be there, close, watching. If he went back, he wouldn't have to figure any of this out. He wouldn't need to know who he was. His father would tell him. Everything would be clear... but would it be right?

He stopped suddenly as he walked through the darkness of the new night. Where had that thought come from?

From Cassine, of course.

Except it hadn't.

It might have been some side effect of her connection to him, but that thought had been his. Did he suddenly care about what was right?

The fact that he didn't immediately answer himself with a 'no' was telling and shook the foundation of his entire existence.

Right and wrong had never been a consideration. It had always been: follow commands and otherwise do what pleased you.

An owl called somewhere in the distant darkness of the forest. An eerie and haunting sound amidst the relative silence of the night.

He began walking again, more briskly this time. He put that troubling thought aside and went back to his first dilemma, would he return to his father?

Do you want to be free? That was her thought.

He didn't answer her. He didn't want her to know how he felt about that question, which was idiotic because she already knew.

Did he want to be free? Well, of course he did... didn't he? But if he went back to his father he wouldn't be.

Well, actually that wasn't true. If he went back, he'd be

free from having to decide, having to make a choice, having to think for himself and do all this work to figure out who he was. That was the 'freedom' his father offered. But he knew from her thoughts that wasn't freedom at all. Freedom was the ability to make a choice without interference, to truly do as one felt. So which was it? Did he want freedom or the simplicity of his father's control?

Gods! Why did this have to be so frustrating and complicated?

He punched a tree as he passed it. It had a sturdy trunk, thick and heavy, but it shook with the impact of his fist. Leaves fluttered down on him for a moment afterward. He left a two-inch indentation in the wood, his knuckles coming away bleeding, yet already healing from his earth talent.

He was a man of action. He wanted to fight this problem, but he couldn't. This wasn't something he could hit.

So he gritted his teeth and attacked the problem head on, logically.

Did he like his father's control? Well no, not really.

Sure, he was perfectly fine with the acts and atrocities he was committing, but having someone else in charge wasn't what he wanted. He was a strong and powerful man in his own right, perhaps the second most powerful person in the world next to his father. Why let the one man more powerful than him control him? Which meant he didn't want his father. He wanted freedom. Just because he was free didn't mean he had to be a pure-hearted do-gooder like Cassine. He could do whatever he wanted. Yes, he wanted that, wanted to be free.

Are you certain? Her voice again.

Yes, he replied. *I don't have to be like you.*

True, but if you really want to be free of your father than you'll need to do more than simply not return to him. His influence is stamped on your soul. If you really want to be free, you'll need to know who you are without that influence. You'll need to get rid of your father's stain then *see who you want to be.*

He halted once again. He didn't want to admit it, but the blasted woman was right. That would be true freedom. Even now, without his father's voice directly in his head, he knew that it would be the shadow of his father that directed his actions. He would commit atrocities and evil without a second thought. That was what his father would do, but what would the real Davar do? He didn't know.

He swore a long string of curses and another tree was left with an indentation of his fist.

"Why do you have to make everything so difficult?" he shouted into the night and into her mind.

It's not me making it difficult. It's what the Blacklord has done to you.

He could see the truth in that as much as he didn't want to admit it. That didn't do anything to improve his mood, though. He picked up a rock and threw it into the night. He heard it crash through the forest for a moment.

The owl hooted again.

He sighed, suddenly exhausted. Thinking or walking any farther seemed like far too much work.

He returned to their small fire.

Cassine was sitting staring into the flames her breathing still ragged from crying.

He stood next to her and thrust out his still manacled arms. "Remove these."

She looked up at him, her eyes red and raw. "I'm exhausted. Can it wait until morning?"

He was about to say no and command her to do it. Then

he realized that that's exactly what his father would do? What would he do? He didn't know, and he was far too tired to think about it.

"Fine," he grumbled and found a spot near the fire to curl up as best he could and rest.

It took some time, but sleep eventually claimed him. He'd never been more thankful for its dark embrace.

~

*H*e awoke with the dawn.

His earth talent was incredibly strong and a few hours of sleep was often enough to fully heal and refresh his body. Yet as much as his physical exhaustion had abated, his mind was still a fog and the troubled thoughts of the previous night filled his mind once again.

Cassine wasn't awake. Her mind was still a haze of sleep-confused thoughts, hard to read.

He rose and found the stream she'd bathed in the previous night. He relieved himself then found a spot upstream to drink and splash his face. The chill of the water helped to wake him and bring some faint clarity. This was real. This was living. This was freedom.

He sighed and returned to their fire. He added a few logs and used his fire talent to light them. Then he waited, his gaze turning to Cassine. Her thoughts were strange, probably dreams, for they made no real sense, but her feelings were open. She was at peace, calm and unworried.

He grimaced. Those were certainly emotions he wasn't familiar with. He could feel what they were like within her, but he'd never really felt anything like that before. What must it be like to find that level of serenity? Even his moment of peace the night before had not reached this level of calm.

He wanted to wake her, kick her, shake her, but he knew these were things his father would have done. So he simply waited. Patience had never been a strong suit of his... or perhaps it was...

Blazes! Why was this so difficult?

There was one thought he knew for certain was his own, not his father's. He knew that when he looked at Cassine, he felt stirrings of strong emotions: lust and desire. She was a beautiful woman and his body reacted to simply watching her. Those were immediate feelings and thoughts. They were of this moment, so they had to be his. That at least was something.

Davar knew enough to know he didn't really understand 'love,' not in the way she experienced it. She had a true heart and cared for everyone. She even had some odd notion about caring for her enemies. It was a certain type of love where: if they were hurt, she'd still tend them as opposed to letting them die. He understood it only through her feelings, but the concept was so foreign to him that he couldn't fully accept it. He knew that he didn't love her, his emotions were more physical and sexual. He wasn't sure he could love anything the way she did.

She woke with a start.

There was a hazy instant as he realized that his carnal thoughts of her had infiltrated her dreams as she now remembered them, in that vague way one does upon just waking. She'd been having some rather impure dreams of them together, feeding off of his thoughts of her. She flooded with embarrassment, her face flushing a bright red.

"Stop that," she said, flustered.

He grinned mischievously, flashing all sorts of improper images of them together through his mind. "Why?"

He didn't think it possible, but she went an even deeper shade of red.

He laughed.

She turned away, despite knowing that would do little to hinder their intimate mental connection.

"I need to freshen up," she said rising quickly. She practically ran down the hill to the stream in the woods. Distance dimmed their connection, but before it did he caught a rather odd thought-feeling combination from her. Part of her mind still lingered on her dreams as curiosity built within her, a wondering of 'what would it be like?'

Davar drew in a long breath and found himself laughing again. Perhaps she wasn't as pure and certain in her virginity as she let on. Perhaps they both had some things they needed to figure out.

When she returned, she was all brusque business.

"I can remove your bindings now. Then you can do as you please."

He could sense the conflict within her. There was still a large part of her that wanted to help him, heal him, get rid of the darkness within him, but it was tempered now. She too was uncertain about if she wanted to remain around him. Would he continue to plague her thoughts and wear away at her honor? Could she remain as good as she wished to be if she was around one so evil for as long as it would take to heal him? The thoughts warred in her mind.

Oddly, he was having his own doubts.

"I don't know if I want these things off anymore," he said holding up his bound wrists. He couldn't be certain why he was being so forthright with her. He was trying not to feel that distant spot within him that stung knowing he'd caused this woman pain. He wasn't used to feelings like that.

She looked at him in confusion. "I thought you decided you wanted to be free?"

He grimaced. "As soon as these come off, I give up a part of my freedom."

He showed her what he meant through his thoughts. His sword, Shadowfang, was a creation of the Blacklord just as he was. A corrupted Scion-Blade whose personality was as twisted and dark as Davar had been under this father's control. As soon as the bindings came off he'd be connected with his sword again, be able to call it from wherever it was. But if he really did want to find out who he was without all of that dark influence, then having his sword around wouldn't help.

"You wouldn't have to call it to you, would you?" she asked.

He shrugged. "No, but—"

"Then don't. Keep it away. Let it be a constant reminder of what you wish to walk away from. It may not be easy, but you've already decided you don't want the easy way. If you want real freedom, sometimes you have to fight for it. You can't wear those bindings for the rest of your life, so you're going to have to get used to your sword being with you at some point."

And yet again, she was right. He wondered if she ever got tired of it.

"No," she said. "And I'm not always right."

It seemed she was when it came to him.

He held up his hands. "Fine, get them off."

"How do I do it?" she asked, her thoughts echoing her spoken words.

It will be easier to show you. And he went through the process in his thoughts, every detail.

She drank in his instructions then knelt next to him, laying her hands on the magical manacles and began.

He followed her in her mind as she progressed through each of the steps. The bindings had been made by his father, meant to break the bond between scion and artifact. Without the key, the bindings required a multi-talent wizard, or four wizards, one of each talent, to remove. Davar was a multi-talent, but couldn't free himself, as the magic of the manacles restricted the wearer from freeing himself, a necessary condition. So she worked through each of the elements: earth to feel the metal and manipulate it, see the tiny pipes and weaknesses, water to find the small reservoir inside, fire to heat the water to boiling, bursting the seal on the reservoir, then air to force the steam out in all directions breaking through the tiny fissures in the metal.

The bindings cracked and shattered in a blast of steam and hot air.

Instantly Shadowfang called to him. The voice was faint as if echoing back from a great distance.

Summon me! The shout was barely more than a whisper in Davar's mind. He could live with this, ignore it if he needed to. Shadowfang continued to rail and rant: *Who is this woman? Get her out! Kill her! Call me, Davar. We must be one. You need me!*

"I don't think your sword likes me much," Cassine said.

"He doesn't like anyone much. He only loves killing."

Cassine nodded and rose.

She turned a full circle, seemingly taking in the morning around them, the brisk breeze of the mountains, the bright, warm sunlight, the dew on the grasses, and the birdsong in the trees.

He sensed she was making her own choice in that moment. To go or to stay. In the end, she shook her head, still uncertain, and turned back to him.

"So what will it be?" she asked. "I'm fine to go my own way, but if you really want to be free of the taint of the Blacklord within you, I'll help you."

A great impulse came over him. "Run away with me," he said with a grin. He wasn't sure where that had come from, but right now, he didn't want to face anything, just wanted to be farther away from everything... except her.

Her thoughts jumbled, analyzing the possibility and discarding it, then trying to figure out how to explain.

"You don't need to explain," he said. "It was a rash thought. I don't know how I could've ever thought you might want to be with me. I can see your thoughts, your feelings. There's nothing there for me." *Nothing but pity.* She wanted desperately to help him, to heal him, to bring out the light, the good in him, but beyond that...

He put his head in his hands. "What did you do to me?" he whispered.

You know it wasn't me. You should be asking yourself what the Blacklord did.

"I know what he did." *Years upon years of abuse and pain, molding me into a mirror of his own dark and twisted soul.* Hatred, blind and raging welled within him at the thought. His hatred for his father had always been a palpable thing for him and the Blacklord knew it and used it. Yet with several long breaths, Davar managed to push the anger down. Right now it wasn't going to do him any good.

What would his life be like without that rage and the

eminent darkness within him? It was an odd thought, difficult to even imagine. Did he want to know?

She brushed his mind again, faint and soft, almost a caress. *Let me help you find out,* she whispered through him.

He looked at her. The sun caught her eyes at just the right angle to turn them to gold.

He could feel it, her desire to help fix what was broken within him. And in that moment, with his entire life up in the air, his emotions a confusing whirlwind of uncertainty he reached out her through their connection. He touched her mind as softly as she'd touched his a moment ago. He felt the light within her and in that instant wanted to know what more of that might be like.

He wanted to change.

He felt Shadowfang scream and rage against this line of thought, but he forced the sword's consciousness away. It was time for him to make a decision on his own.

He sent a single word into Cassine's mind, loaded with a myriad of feelings and implications.

Stay.

hat day Cassine began the long process of healing Davar.

There was a lot of darkness in his soul and it couldn't be expelled all at once. A soul was comprised of emotions, past and present, and Cassine could read a person's life through the remembered feelings in their soul. Each emotion was like a thread in a great tapestry which illustrated a life. Davar's was no pretty picture and each fiber was riddled with darkness and not easy for her to touch. Yet this was the process she had to go through. Each strand of evil had to be faced, confronted, and dealt with.

And there were so very many strands.

It didn't help that Davar was over two hundred years old. He didn't look much past his mid-thirties, but he was sustained by his father's magic. She'd known this from their earlier connection, but it hadn't sunk in until now how much work it would be to heal such a long life of darkness.

It would take weeks, months, probably more than a year to cleanse his soul of that which plagued him.

Cassine had always been an exceptional healer, but what she was doing now was far different than anything she'd done before. She knew how to do it, her soul talent was strong enough for her to figure out what needed to be done, but that didn't mean it would be easy... for either of them. She would find a fiber of his soul tainted with the Black-lord's oily darkness. Then, as if it were the string of a lute, she would pluck at it. This would cause Davar to feel that emotion once again, amplifying sometimes long forgotten feelings. The emotion would drag up memories of the events surrounding it and Davar would then relive those moments.

Cassine would soothe a single strand and encourage the stain on it to leave. Yet it was Davar who had to do the truly hard work. For every fiber that was cleansed he needed to come to terms with the events in question. He needed to understand that what he'd done had been wrong, that it had been years of abuse and torture as a child which had driven him to it. He had to forgive himself and empathize with those he'd hurt, feeling their pain to fully understand and come to terms with what he'd done.

What made it worse was he had to accept it from the perspective of someone who actually cared. For an evil man to accept he'd killed a man was no big thing, but for a good man to accept causing a death was a horrid thing.

And Davar had done so much worse than simply killing men.

Dealing with one strand could take them an hour or more. He was the type of man never to admit anything was affecting him, but Cassine could see the way every single remembrance gripped him. He had to deal with a lifetime of moral decay. Accepting things no man should have to deal with. For her part, it wasn't easy simply spending any significant time in the dark and fetid place that was his soul.

They spent three weeks in that clearing in the Silver Mountains and still the process was only in its infancy.

After one particularly grueling session, Cassine withdrew from Davar's soul drenched in sweat and exhausted. She simply lay back on the soft grasses of the mountain field, breathing hard, staring up at a clear blue sky. The sun was near setting. Her stomach rumbled loud enough for him to hear.

He still had some energy for he grunted and said, "I'll find some game. I'll be back in a bit."

She felt him go more than saw it. They weren't connected now like they'd been in the past. Their intense link, which they'd experienced those first few days after the teleportation, had dwindled. Physical contact was necessary for the soul cleansing, but after a few days the connection had almost completely dissipated. Some element remained. Perhaps it was a side effect of all of the work she'd been doing in his soul, or perhaps the teleportation link was something that never fully went away. Yet she could still sense him when he was near. Without looking, she'd know exactly where he was. There were also times of truly intense emotion or thought, which might still travel between them.

As she lay there on the warm earth, gazing up at a pure sky, she spoke to Ehlani, her Goddess.

"Did you mean for this to happen, Lady of Peace? Is this your plan for me? To be connected to this man?"

She let out a long sigh.

Would it be the worst thing, staying so intimately connected with one so dark and broken? Perhaps not. It was the way of her Goddess to love and tend to all beings and truly Cassine was one who followed that doctrine. She loved Davar... in the way her Goddess bid her to love and feel compassion for all things. It wasn't easy and she wondered if she'd be able to maintain that empathy for days or weeks, even months of delving into such a black soul.

She had to have faith in her Goddess that this was for some greater purpose, but... faith didn't always come easy. Doubts were beginning to cloud the edges of her being. Perhaps it was all the work she was doing in such a dark place which caused her to lose faith. It certainly wasn't easy to get the oily feeling of his soul off of her when she finished. She constantly felt dirty, stained, even if she bathed. She honestly couldn't imagine how he must feel.

And yet he'd offered to get her food just now. Was that a sign of him changing?

Perhaps.

She was somewhat recovered from her exhaustion and melancholy when he returned with several small animals in his bare hands.

He skinned and cleaned them wordlessly, but as he was spitting the first to place it over their fire, he looked at her.

"It makes little difference to me," he said, "but if you'd like to be doing this somewhere else, we could." There was something in his gaze, a certain hunger in his eyes. Perhaps he sensed it, for a moment later he turned away. "We could find a town or something. Stay there for a while."

He placed the rabbit he'd spitted over the fire.

Light was fading from the day, but this high up Cassine could still see for some distance. She wondered how her sisters were doing back at St. Antin Abbey. Again, she wondered if this was where she was most needed. There would be legions of wounded back at the abbey.

But Davar had asked her something and she should respond. Did she want a town, a bed? It would be lovely, but she didn't need it. Though eventually summer would fade and the chill of the nights up in these mountains would grow colder still. Perhaps it would be best to go some place where they could spend the winter. If they weren't going to return to the abbey, then any town would do.

She caught his eye. "Yes, I think a town would be nice, thank you for offering."

He gave a fleeting smile, then shook his head and turned away.

After they'd eaten, they did another healing session, then collapsed into an exhausted sleep.

The next day they headed east. Travel was hampered by her healing sessions, which required both of them to be strong and calm and ready. So he carried her, running and bounding over the countryside for part of the day, then they would do a session of healing, then rest.

Even carrying her, Davar could move with incredible speed. One leap from his earth talent-strengthened legs, and using his wind-talent to carry them along through the air, took them over miles of land. They were down out of the mountains and foothills after two days. After that, they moved through thick woodlands for another couple of days.

Cassine reveled in the scent of the pines and cedars around them. Davar said they were passing the western border of Vehndora, a kingdom far to the south and west of Hallania. The end of their second day traveling through the forest brought them close to a small village.

Cassine watched the smoke curling up from a large building near the center of town, most likely a common house. Yes, this had been a good idea. She turned to Davar.

"Let me down please, I can walk from here." He did so. She laid a hand on his arm, feeling the great round muscle beneath the sleeve of his shirt. "Thank you," she said with a soft smile. "A hot bath and warm bed will do us both good."

He gave a faint nod and a soft grunt of acknowledgment.

Soon enough they were down on the muddy road of the small village and at the common house.

Cassine opened the door to a waft of air thick with smoke and smelling of stew and sweat and dirt. It wasn't a grand establishment, but the flushed and rotund matron who greeted them was friendly enough.

"Greetings my lord and lady, shall I send someone to tend your horses?"

Cassine smiled. "We have no horses."

"Oh, well then you must be tired from a long walk. Shall I ready a room?"

"One with two beds please, and a bath and some food," Cassine added.

The matron bobbed a curtsey and hurried off as they sat at one end of a long trestle table close to a glowing brazier. There were three more long tables in the room, another on this side and two on the far side, one of which had a few men drinking and laughing loudly. A great hearth dominated the wall opposite the door. Over its flames and embers roasted a small pig. Several cauldrons and pots bubbled three as well. The matron bustled around the hearth tending the food aided by a young wisp of a woman, probably her daughter.

Cassine let out a long sigh and with it slipped away tensions of which she'd not been aware. It was pleasant to be back indoors with the scent of food other than small game. She hadn't realized how much she'd missed this.

She looked to Davar who took in everything in the room.

Finally, he too seemed to settle, though he did keep an eye on the other men in the room. She could see something different in him now. She couldn't identify the change exactly for a moment, but then she realized what it was and it shocked her. The way he sat, how he'd positioned his body... it was that of a protector. She couldn't be sure what he was thinking, whether this was a friendly concern for her well-being, or a miser clutching at what he thought was his. Either way he was showing concern for someone other than himself. That seemed like progress.

One of the men at the other table called out for more ale. The matron's daughter drew a large pitcher from one of many kegs in the corner and deposited it on the table with the laughing men. A man grabbed her and pulled her onto his lap. The girl let out a short yelp of surprise.

"Common girlie, you'll give Jato a good time, won't ye?" The man clutched at one of her breasts.

"Please, sir, I don't want trouble." The girl tried to get away from him, but he was a burly man and more than strong enough to keep her where she was.

The matron of the house was already hurrying over to the men. "Now please good sirs, let my poor daughter go. She's too young for your tastes, I'm sure."

"Oh she's ripe enough," the one holding her said, emphasizing his point by patting her breast. He then leaned in and pressed his face into her hair. "And she smells a darn sight better than any whore I've had in ages!"

Cassine rose sharply. This had gone far enough. She felt a swell of her fire talent, but stopped uncertain. She wasn't a warrior. She'd never used her magic to harm before and she didn't know how. Yet she couldn't let this continue. She glanced at Davar, but he stared at the conflict across the room unmoving, unmoved. Could she ask him to step in? Should she?

Gods she had to do something but didn't know what.

"Better take her quick, Jato," one of the other men at that table called out, "before she turns to fat like her mum!"

They all roared with laughter and downed more ale.

"Now you see here..." the matron blustered but stopped as Jato drew out a long curved knife.

"No you see, mum. Me and me boys here is gonna have ourselves some fun." He pressed the knife to the girl's throat, tilting her head back. Tears streamed down her cheeks. Jato took out a small purse with his free hand and plopped it on the table. "But we'll pay handsomely for her and the ale so why don't you run off while we go find a room." The matron backed away slowly, then turned and hurried off, hopefully to get someone to help. The men at the table all rose. Jato kept a firm hold on the girl and the knife as they made their way toward the stairs at the back of the room.

Cassine took two steps toward them but felt a strong hand on her shoulder.

"Allow me," Davar said passing her, his tone lethal.

Gods, this wasn't going to end well. "Don't' kill them, just stop them," she said softly, not wanting to alert the men.

But the others must have sensed trouble, which wasn't that difficult. Davar was trouble — over six feet of thick muscle. However one of the men in the group was even larger than Davar, as rare as that might be. That man stepped out to meet Davar all puffed up with bravado.

"Now don't hurt our new friend, Brosto," Jato said, his tone light. He was the obvious leader of the group and Cassine could see how easily the others deferred to him. "Maybe he just wants a piece of this girlie too." Jato's eyes flicked to Cassine then back to Davar. "Maybe he wants to bring along his own wench to join our group. Is that it, friend?"

"Let the girl go," Davar said. This voice was calm, almost cheery. Knowing him... that tone in and of itself was terrifying.

Jato smiled. "I'm not thinking I will, and I'm not thinking you can beat the five of us to make me."

Davar nodded, flashing a grin. He put his hands up in defeat and turned around, taking a step away.

There was a half-heartbeat of reduced tension in the room before Davar swung back around and hit Brosto with a solid backhand to the neck, followed by an even harder punch to the face. The large man crumpled, unconscious.

The other four men froze for an instant in stunned shock, which was enough time for Davar to step in and hammer another man on the side of the head, sending him to the ground with Brosto.

The others sprung into action.

Cassine had been around fighting men most of her life. She could tell these men were used to a tussle, but more... they were used to fighting together.

Jato turned himself and the girl to put her between him and Davar, his knife once again pressed to her throat. The other two spread out drawing weapons of their own, one a short sword, the other a long curved knife, similar to Jato's.

"If you care so much for this girlie, you'd better walk away now, friend, or I'll open her throat." As if to emphasize his point, he pressed the knife higher, drawing a bead of blood.

Cassine suddenly realized what she could do. Her soul talent caught the emotions radiating off of these men. It was almost a palpable thing to her: the fear, anger, and exhilaration. So she sent a wave of calm and peace cascading out to them. Perhaps they might relent once emotions abated. She didn't push as strongly toward Davar, though his emotions were intense as well. She'd wait a moment to see if his feelings escalated.

Jato and his companions relaxed a little, letting down their guard. Jato's blade fell away from the girl's neck by an inch or two.

Faster than anyone expected, Davar rushed in and grabbed Jato's hand and pulled the knife away from the girl's neck. Davar's grip must have been crushing as Jato screamed like a child, face contorted in pain.

One of other two was quick to react and, stepping up behind Davar, plunged his knife into Davar's back, all the way to the hilt.

Davar responded by half turning and elbowing the man in the jaw. That one collapsed as the other rushed in. Davar spun and, using Jato's own hand and knife, blocked the other man's sword, knocking it away. He then kicked the man solidly in the stomach, sending him flying back into one of the tables, breaking it as he went down, groaning.

Davar turned back to Jato, still holding the man's hand. He pried the other hand off of the girl and whispered a harsh, "Run." She did.

Now holding both of Jato's hands, Davar kneed the man hard between his legs. Jato doubled over. Davar released him and brought his elbow down on the back of the man's neck. Jato went limp, splayed on the floor.

Davar plucked Jato up by his neck, holding him easily off the ground with one hand, his limp body dangling. With his free hand, Davar reached behind him and plucked out the knife in his lower back. The wound ran with blood, but only for a moment. He was a strong earth talent and could quickly heal himself. He brought the knife up to Jato's throat and there he paused.

"Davar don't," Cassine said. Killing would only add another stain on his soul and this time it wouldn't have been while under the control of the Blacklord.

Davar's hand shook but didn't move. His knuckles went white on the knife's hand.

Cassine rushed over to him.

"Give me the knife," she said softly. Looking into his face she saw the conflict in his eyes.

Nearly everything in his being told him to kill this man, discard him. But there was something that warred against that impulse.

She watched his face twitch, teeth gritted, hand trembling, as he pulled the knife back and placed in her hands. He was breathing hard.

He tossed Jato's body back to the floor and stalked away.

Cassine turned to the Matron, who was clutching her sobbing daughter. "Is there any sort of lawman in this town?"

The woman shook her head. "Only the local Lord and he's two days east."

"These brutes from around here?" It was Davar who was asking, his voice thick with some restrained emotion.

Another shake of the matron's head. "First time they've been here."

Davar nodded with a grunt. "Allow me to clean this up, then." He hefted two men from the ground, one in each hand, despite one of them being Brosto and larger than him.

He made his way to the door, but Cassine stopped him on his way.

"What are you going to do with them?"

"Dump them someplace far away."

"That's all?"

His eyes met hers steadily. His breathing was easier now and she could see a lot of the tension of the fight had drained from him. "For you yes, that's all."

For her? Perhaps she was making a difference.

"Thank you."

He grunted. "I'll be back for the others in a moment." Then he was out the door.

She thanked any God that would listen that he'd begun to change his ways... even if he had needed a little prompting. She'd seen the conflict within him where before there'd been none. Even how he'd fought the men was a testament to his restraint. If he'd wanted to, he could've easily killed these men instead of incapacitating them. From their time being connected, she knew his impressive strength, speed, and near invulnerability. He'd been pulling his punches... or they'd be dead. He still had a long way to go, but she was impressed. She could only hope things continued to go so well.

CHAPTER 6

*D*avar had never been one to show his emotions. He was quite adept at masking how he felt. Yet he was finding it harder and harder to keep himself in check around Cassine. Perhaps it was her healing, constantly reaching into his soul, or simply that he'd never met anyone so selfless and fascinating. Every emotion seemed amplified when he was near her.

And right now... he didn't want what he was feeling to be amplified any more than it was.

Cassine was attempting one of her healings, touching his soul, filtering through the darkness that lurked there and then bringing it into the light for him to deal with. Yet he couldn't concentrate on the memories and emotions which were being drudged forth within him. He was still slightly agitated from the confrontation in the common room earlier. If that wasn't enough Cassine was nearly naked next to him. They'd both bathed before retiring to their room and not wanting to climb back into dirty clothes they'd given their soiled garments over to the matron who was more than happy to wash them. But since they had no other clothes to wear he was wrapped only in a towel and she was wearing one of the matron's daughter's sleeping shifts. Since Cassine was a much taller and fuller-figured woman than the girl the shift came only to her mid thigh. That and the sheer fabric was so strained and stretched over all her wondrous curves as to be nearly see-through.

Cassine seemed to have no idea of her effect on him.

He was glad she no longer knew his every thought, as she had when they been so deeply connected after the teleportation. That connection dwindled to near nothing.

Yet still she was deep in his emotions and had to be sensing something.

For her, he tried not to think about her round hips and full breasts and instead concentrate on the task at hand.

This time the emotions surging within him from her work in his soul were a mix of hatred, lust, jealousy, and anger. The memory came full force into his mind. The Blacklord's army had just overrun a town in western Noveria, and the defenders were scattered and defeated. The Blacklord's men were enjoying their usual past time of looting and pillaging. Davar burst through the door of a house to find a young man, scared yet determined, protecting his young wife. Davar saw an opportunity. It wasn't that hard to dispatch the man. Shadowfang snaked out and sang with bloodlust as the man's guts were opened and he fell away screaming, eyes wide. Davar then sheathed his sword and moved toward the woman. She was screaming too, but that didn't bother him. He had his way with her, then opened her up like he'd done with her mate.

He felt the hatred and lust turn to shame, pity, and sorrow. He felt their pain as they died. Felt the emotional torment of the woman, seeing her husband cut down then being ravaged. It brought bile to Davar's throat. It was horrible, evil. Then he had to admit to himself that he'd done it. He didn't think anyone could forgive such acts. Yet feeling how Cassine worked with the emotions and memories, she was in her way forgiving him.

"Thank you," she said in the stillness as that strand of his dark past was healed and set to rest.

A rush of... something... like nothing he could explain surged through him. Every time one of those threads of his dark past was exposed and cleaned and dealt with he felt it. The only way he could explain it was like he'd been in a dark room and someone, ever so far away, had lit a match or cracked open a door or window. It was only the faintest slivers of light, but in such a dark place it made so much of a difference.

He could feel the good within him now. It was foreign and often uncomfortable. That evening as he'd held Jato's life in his hands it had been that fledgling light within him which had stayed his hand, that and Cassine's voice.

Yet with the soft whisper of her breath on his cheek that same voice was making him think some very impure thoughts. Now that the memory was fading, put to rest, his emotions roiled and couldn't settle.

"Thank you," she said again. "You could have killed those men tonight and you didn't."

Just a month ago he wouldn't have spared them. By the Gods, he might have joined them! Yet now that other self seemed so distant. Could he really have been like that?

Even he seemed surprised at his progress and yet, it wasn't really him who'd made that change possible.

"No," he said after a moment. "Thank you. I wouldn't be the man I am now if not for you."

His eyes were closed, trying not to look at her, trying to suppress his desire to have her. He couldn't be like that anymore. He could never force himself on her or anyone again.

Silence stretched for a moment before she spoke and when she did her voice was odd, thick. "I think that's enough healing for today." Her hand lifted from his chest above his heart.

Was something wrong? He opened his eyes as she crossed the small room to her bed. He regretted it almost as soon as he did. Seeing her in that nightdress sent waves of heat through him. The way it clung to her buttocks, shifting with each step, caressing the soft flesh, caused him to become very uncomfortable. It was a good thing he was sitting and the towel was wrapped tightly around him. Nothing would show, but it was all the more painful for that fact.

When she turned back to him he could see her skin was flushed, from her forehead down to the abundance of cleavage that the shift exposed. Her breathing was quick, causing her breasts to heave rather noticeably against the taut, sheer cloth.

He had to look away. It was too much. His blood was boiling, his every impulse told him to tear away the two bits of cloth around them and take her in that moment.

He didn't know why she was in such a state. She'd made it clear days ago she didn't feel any attraction toward him. Perhaps she'd sensed his arousal and attraction and that was why she had retreated so quickly.

He knew he shouldn't pry into her thoughts, but couldn't stop himself. It was just a light brushing of her mind to see only her most prominent thoughts. He was so strong in his mind talent and she was weakest in that element, so if he was careful she'd never know.

Images of the two of them naked in a sweaty embrace flashed through her mind.

Gods! Perhaps her feelings had changed?

No that couldn't be right. She must have been having some reaction to his emotions for her. That's what had made her flee from him. She didn't want what she was thinking about.

He wanted it desperately. He wanted to her. A thousand images of them together flashed through his mind as they did all too often. It was a miracle of self-restraint that he hadn't ravished her. He didn't know what it was that had stopped him before, but now he had enough of that faint light within him to know it wasn't right.

He wanted her, but not like this, not now, not yet, not with so much darkness still left in him.

His voice was strained as he said, "Perhaps you should stay in another room tonight." He still couldn't look at her, but his mind still caressed hers and he sensed her dilemma.

I should go, he's right, she thought. An image of him as he was: sitting on the bed, head turned away, naked to the waist lingered in her mind. *No, I'm stronger than this. I can resist. I only want him now because I was so closely connected to him and could feel his desires. Gods, but I hope that's it.* There was yet another quick flash of them entwined in love, quickly dispelled. *Though maybe I should go. Maybe I've been getting too close?*

"I..." she began, but her thoughts were still too much a whirl to finish. *No! Get a hold of yourself Cass, you've slept next to him for many nights now, tonight is no different!*

"I think we'll be fine," she said, her voice calm and even now. "It's not like we haven't been next to each other these past few nights. Unless you really want privacy tonight?"

It was true, they'd been sleeping close together out in the countryside, but that had been fully clothed on chilly nights. He should tell her to go. He should... but he wasn't going to. If she could resist, so could he, though it took all his effort to do so.

"No stay, I'm fine." He even managed to look at her and smile when he said it. He took his mind from hers, not wanting to hear or see anymore, and quickly turned to the lantern in the room, blowing it out.

There was rustling as she climbed into bed and he did the same, removing the towel only after he was covered. He was still far more aroused than he'd like, but he could control himself. He curbed his thoughts in the darkness until his desire abated.

It took him a long time to find peace that night and when he did his dreams were filled with images of Cassine in that flimsy shift... and out of it.

❧

The next day they decided to move on. The matron of the common house had mentioned that the town near the Lord's keep would have access to more amenities, which appealed to both of them. It was two days down the road when walking, but they wouldn't be walking and would probably get there much faster.

Cassine asked if they could walk for a while in the morning instead of being carried as Davar did his running bound across the countryside.

Davar liked this idea. He wasn't sure he wanted to be holding her so tight, even now fully clothed, after the night and the dreams he'd had.

"It's a glorious morning," she said, taking a deep breath of the still misty air.

He was having trouble seeing it. Sure, the sky was clear, the air fresh, the trees green and swaying in the light breeze that was slowly dispelling the fog around them, but his thoughts were elsewhere.

He was having trouble thinking of anything except her. His thoughts and emotions were tumbling and twisting inside of him, which he hoped he hid well.

He had to say something to her but didn't know what. He had feelings for her, but he couldn't really say what they were. He appreciated her desire to help him... and she was certainly attractive...

That was the problem.

Any thoughts and emotions he had were clouded by his lust and desire for her, which burned a bonfire of passion within him. He didn't really know how he felt, nor did he have the words to describe it. He'd come to understand the concept of love when he'd been bonded to her, but wasn't really certain what that felt like nor if this was anything like what 'love' should be. There was something like a tenderness, a desire to protect her and not see her hurt. He wanted to be better... for her. Though he wasn't certain if that last one was just so he wouldn't feel like a stain on the world when he was near her purity and light.

What could he say? Was it even worth it to try if she didn't feel the same way? But perhaps after what had happened last night she did feel the same?

Gods, but these emotions were a massive pain!

"Someone's out there," she said distracting him from his thought.

But it was already too late.

With her words came the *twang* of a bowstring. He should have been able to react faster, but he'd been so befuddled he moved too slowly. It was a moment too late when he reached to grab the arrow, which was now embedded in his neck.

He staggered forward, stumbling to one knee.

The pain was nothing. His mind was trained to shut out pain, but the arrow had hit such a sensitive spot, piercing his throat and the veins in his neck. He would heal soon enough, but until then there was still the shock from loss of air and blood.

The world spun.

Someone called his name.

Hand shaking, he pulled the arrow out, feeling the wound start to close as he did.

But he'd been too slow.

Even as he drew from the element of earth to strengthen and reinforce his muscles and bones, more arrows assailed him. Most were innocuous, hitting in places he could ignore for now, but one hit the side of his head, sticking in his skull just above his left ear. Another, a crossbow bolt from the force of it, blew clean through his abdomen tearing away flesh and organs alike. He could survive it all, could heal nearly anything... given time.

Time, however, was not on his side.

He stood, gritting his teeth to do so, as more arrows planted themselves in his back and legs.

A scream pierced the morning air, clearing his head in an instant.

Turning he saw men all around, several of them grabbing

Cassine. She fought back as only a Multi-talent could, her strength enhanced. She ripped herself away, but they were big men and too many.

Davar felt a push on his emotions and resisted it. She was sending a massive calming wave through them all. For an instant they paused, relaxed, but their emotions were too enflamed and they were on her again.

Davar could only spare a moment for her as he was still under attack.

He leapt high into the air, hearing the shocked exclamations of the men below. He must have been a sight: a pincushion of arrows, his stomach torn open, still able to leap hundreds of feet into the air. Despite air being one of his primary elements he had never learned to fly as Wyllea had, but his leaps were something to behold.

It gave him a moment to take in what was happening and begin to react.

But the more he saw, the less he liked what he saw. The first item that burned him was that five of the thirty or so men assailing him and Cassine were the ones he'd beaten up the night before. That explained a lot, but also revealed something to him as well. Any normal man would still be reeling from the attacks he'd inflicted. They should have been laid up for a day or more, but they were fit and hale. This could mean only one thing, one of them or one of their band, was an earth-wizard, able to heal them. More than that, it meant some of those below might also be unnaturally strengthened and tough as well.

He could deal with that, but two more things were going to hamper him. The first was his injured state. He healed faster than anyone he knew, but it wouldn't be fast enough. By the time he landed, he'd still be disabled, not at full strength from the sheer number of missiles that had hit him. That alone he might have been able to deal with, but it was the last item that concerned him most. Cassine, despite all her struggles, couldn't get away from so many strength-enhanced men. Already she was mostly subdued, three brawny men restraining her. If he tried to free her it would put him at risk for more injury... and too many more hits and he might just go down. Yet if he did try to give himself the time to heal, they would undoubtedly use Cassine against him somehow.

There was one option.

One terrible option.

But he could see no other way.

"Shadowfang!" he called, summoning the sword to him.

The sword materialized in his hands.

And his world spun into darkness...

Kill! Kill them all! I'll kill everyone! The sheer ecstasy of Shadowfang at the prospect of battle overwhelmed him.

Alone he was a multi-talent of incredible strength. Together with his corrupted artifact, he was a force of sheer destruction and darkness.

Using the sword's innate ability of shadow and illusion he split himself. A tangible, illusory double of him fell to earth on the path he'd been on, while his true self, now invisible, pushed at the air and changed the direction of his descent.

As the duplicate landed amidst the mob of attacking bandits, blocking attack after attack in a deadly dance, he alighted behind the three men holding Cassine.

Jato called out a threat: "We'll cut up the woman unless you surrender." Even as he did, the three men holding her died from a rapid series of attacks.

Kill. Die. Slay them all!

Revealing himself to Cassine, dropping the invisibility that hid him, he spoke through gritted teeth. "Run!" It took all his effort to keep Shadowfang from running her through as well.

She was clearly horrified.

He could see himself in her eyes, the bloodlust, his features twisted by the darkness and death he so desired in that moment.

She used her enhanced strength to jump clear of the attackers into the forest.

He grinned as he turned to the rest of the men. "You'll pay for this," he hissed.

They will pay! They will die! Kill them all! The maddened glee of Shadowfang rang through him as he began the slaughter of the men before him.

Their screams are so sweet! And Davar had to agree. Their death-cries rang like chimes, like sweetest birdsong in his ears.

Blood, from a slash that decapitated a man, sprayed his face.

I love the taste of blood! More!

He licked his lips, enjoying the tang of the warm liquid.

Yes, more!

The next man who came at him he punched in the chest. Davar's fist easily broke through bone and reached inside the man to pull out his still-beating heart. He bit into the soft flesh, feeling the rush of blood and gore down his throat.

Some new part of him reviled the act, but it was well repressed and had no say at the moment. Shadowfang was in ecstasy and Davar too was lost in the throes of battle.

The fight was over far too soon.

Davar stood, breathing hard, his body slowly healing

from all the wounds taken previously. He plucked arrows from him where he could reach, feeling the flesh close. Looking around he saw the carnage he'd wreaked upon the bandits and Shadowfang sang in joy at the sight. Yet that new part of him, now straining to get out, saw the dismembered bodies: the blood, the bone, and screamed at the wrongness of this.

"Davar?"

He spun at the voice. Cassine emerged from the forest onto the road.

Kill her! Shadowfang demanded.

He gripped the hilt so tightly his hand turned white.

No, he told the sword sternly. *We will not kill her.*

KILL HER NOW! The call sent him to his knees.

"Cassine, please, go, I can't control myself." His mouth twitched as he spoke, every word a fight to get out. "Please! Go!" Tears streamed from eyes clenched shut as he restrained the sword.

A cool hand touched his cheek. A warm sense of peace filled him, slowly quelling the war within, drowning out the calls of his blade.

Her voice was calm, soft and close. She must have knelt next to him. "Even with the bond we shared, I'd never fully understood the struggle, the darkness you fought against until now. I'm sorry."

Slowly his emotions steadied.

He opened his eyes and looked into hers. There he saw sorrow and pain which mirrored his own struggle.

"I can sense the evil of the sword," she said softly. "If I let you go it will return. You need to fight it."

"How? I've never needed to before. I don't know how to quell the rage."

"Remember your mother."

Those three words struck such a chord within him, the images of the horrific things his father had done to his mother flashing back to him. Yes, he knew how to fight Shadowfang's rage, with a rage of his own.

"No," Cassine said softly, "Not like that." Through her touch, she'd sensed his emotions rise. "Don't think of your mother's pain, think of the good woman she was, the love she would have had for you if you'd been her child under other circumstances. Think of her strength as a scion, her defiance of evil. Let that guide you."

She was right, of course. Rage begot more rage.

He drew in a long breath, nodding.

She removed her hand.

Instantly Shadowfang was back, tearing at him to kill and destroy. But he did as she said, he envisioned the image of his mother, but without the pain, the strong, good woman she'd have been.

Shadowfang had no response for that other than revulsion. The good and evil warred within him, but for now, it was a stalemate.

He regained enough control to stand slowly.

Cassine rose with him.

Davar, not wishing to hold Shadowfang any longer, slung the sword through a loop in his belt, it was where his scabbard would usually have hung. Shadowfang's ranting lessened, but only slightly.

They picked their way out of the mess of blood and bodies.

Cassine laughed a little after they'd walked a ways.

"What?" he asked. He couldn't imagine anything being funny at this moment.

"You bathed only yesterday and already you're a mess."

He let out a short laugh, mostly for her. He hardly felt light-hearted at the moment.

Davar! Where are you? Where have you been? What's happening?

The call, though distant was still intense enough to bring him to his knees. Only now did he recall the other reason he'd not wanted Shadowfang back. It acted like an amplifier for his father's sensing.

Instantly, he was filled with his father's black presence, seeking, knowing.

Davar screamed.

CHAPTER 7

"*D*avar? What's wrong?"

Cassine knelt next to him. Putting a hand to his cheek, she flinched away quickly.

Something was terribly wrong. The darkness within him was complete, black, a void of seething hatred and vile anger.

She stood and took an involuntary step back, fear flooding her. She trembled, terrified. Thoughts flashed through her mind of what she'd learned when they'd been connected. The sword would act like a beacon to the Blacklord. As soon as Davar called it, it would have alerted his father. A sinking dread filled her as she suddenly knew what had taken hold of him.

Davar's head tilted to look at her, his eyes not his own, a disturbingly serene smile on his face.

He stood. Then stepped toward her with alarming speed. His hand jerked up to catch her under the chin. He didn't quite lift her from the ground, but to the tips of her toes, forcing her head up and back if she wished to keep breathing.

"Davar?" She knew the Blacklord had control of him, but hoped that he might still be in there... somewhere.

The Blacklord caught the fear in her eyes and laughed, a grating, harsh noise. His grip tightened, his hold like steel.

"So, you're the one who snatched my prized toy away from me?" The voice was too high for Davar, the eerie tone sending a chill down her spine. She reached up to try and pull his hand from her throat even though she knew the act would prove useless. She had to do something. Panic was starting to overwhelm her. There had to be a way to reach Davar.

"He doesn't even see you as a son, Davar," she said, though it was hard to speak with his hand constricting her breath. She prayed to Ehlani she could reach the man she knew was in there somewhere. "You mean nothing to him. Fight him, Davar."

"He knows that fighting me is futile," the voice hissed, still calm, in control. "This is a lesson you need to learn, sweetling. One I will enjoy teaching you."

She gritted her teeth, determined to do something even if she had no idea what. She had to fight back somehow, despite the dread seeping into her soul. "I'll fight you with everything I have."

"I know you will. That's what will make this so enjoyable." He lifted her from the ground, extending his arm, holding her by her neck, cutting off her air.

"Davar!" she gasped, grasping at his arm.

"Now let's take a look at you." His other hand came to the collar of her dress then ripped it down the front past her hips. Her clothes fell away. She still wore her cloak, but it was pushed back over her shoulders at the moment, not covering her from his sight

The Blacklord observed her form, but with no lust or desire, more like a horse trader inspecting a new acquisition. He poked and prodded here and there. She made no move to cover herself, not ashamed nor willing to let him have the satisfaction of upsetting her. She should have been flushed, embarrassed, but her fear and determination, more primal emotions, overrode anything else. She still didn't know what she could do, but for now, she guessed it would only please the Blacklord if she squirmed and blushed.

Her panic built with each passing heartbeat. She couldn't breathe. Let him kill her. That would be better than the alternative.

"Plump, healthy, ready for childbearing... and according to my son's thoughts of you also a multi-talent. I had only thought to create spawn using a female scion, but a true Multi-talent could produce some intriguing results."

He set her down. His grip, though no less firm, no longer blocked her air. She gasped until her breathing returned to normal.

"Bring her to me!" the Blacklord commanded through Davar's lips.

"He's not the man you created anymore!" she said, though her voice broke and squeaked, not fully recovered from choking.

The Blacklord laughed again, arrogant and dismissive. "You mean your pathetic attempts to heal him of his evil? It's impossible! He's mine and will obey me!" The last was a shout, spittle flying from Davar's lips. "Bring her!" The command was intense. Cassine flinched away despite still being held.

Then something changed.

Through his flesh touching hers she sensed the impenetrable blackness drop away within him.

Davar blinked, a look of horror and shock a mask on his face. He released her chin, his arm falling limp as he staggered a few steps back.

Cassine caught her breath and drew her cloak around herself. "Davar? He let you go?"

"No, not entirely. He's still there. I can feel him compelling me. I can't resist him and not even your touch or the memory of my mother will help me this time. I must bring you to him."

Her dread solidified into a solid lump in her stomach. She touched his cheek and felt the truth of his words. His body was free to move, his mind free to think, but behind it all was a looming presence guiding his overall actions.

"But I won't do it." The defiance in his voice was thick, palpable. Even as he said it he gritted his teeth as if in great pain. "No. I. Won't." He repeated through clenched teeth.

He moved suddenly, spinning away from her and drawing out his sword. He thrust it into the ground, burying the tip of the blade nearly two feet deep. He released it then leapt away suddenly back toward the west.

Cassine was left alone on the road, watching his form grow smaller and smaller as his great leap took him farther and farther away.

Huddling inside her cloak a shiver took her.

That entire experience had left her drained. Fear still trembled within her. She fell to her knees. Her legs like water, weak from lack of air and shock.

She was both eternally grateful and somehow sad that Davar had left. He'd resisted his father, saved her and yet... now she was alone, still dealing with that traumatic moment.

Alone.

She'd never really been alone her entire life. She'd grown up with two loving parents as well as three brothers and two sisters. Then she'd gone directly into service for the Daughters of Ehlani and joined that family, learning their ways. She'd always been around people.

Now, nearly naked, kneeling on this road in the middle of some foreign country, her one companion fled from her, she felt the world press in around her.

Logically she knew she was stronger than this, that simply being along shouldn't bother her. She had control of her emotions... most of the time. But the awe of meeting the Blacklord face to face had still not fully left her. It troubled her... deeply.

It took several long calming breaths, as well as a link to her soul and years of knowing how to calm emotions, before she finally felt ready to deal with what had happened.

And so much had happened.

To start, there were her feelings for Davar. Not that long ago, high up in the Silver Mountains, she'd told him she felt nothing for him, nothing but the love she felt for all humankind. Then last night she'd felt so much more. It had taken her some time to fall asleep, sorting through her emotions, trying to figure out which were after-images of Davar's own desire for her and which were her own true feelings. What she'd found had surprised her.

She did care for him. Apparently, it had developed over her time healing him, being so intimate and close. Yet last night, she had felt... a new type of love. She respected him, his spirit and strength of conviction. He wanted to change. More than that, he was going through with that change, no matter how painful it was. That was more than many people ever did. It would take an incredible man to overcome that much darkness and evil, and she believed he could do it. That made him special and admirable. She had never met any man like him and found herself drawn to him despite his darkness.

Yet what was even more surprising and confusing for her were the physical feelings. She'd seen many attractive men, and given her profession as a healer not all of them had been clothed at the time. The body held no mysticism for her. No man had ever made her feel like she did for Davar.

Last night while looking at his large, perfect body, all hard planes and massive curves of muscle, she'd felt something stir within her. Part of it might have been residual from his thoughts of her, but she'd come to realize that not all of it had come from him.

He made her feel... odd on the inside, her stomach was unsettled and many places a little too warm and... tingly. She wasn't sure what to call it because it was like nothing she'd ever experience before. Was this desire or lust? She didn't know. But whatever it was, these were her emotions. She was certain of that much. Her feelings had always been clear to her.

She loved him, maybe not like a betrothed or bonded, but certainly more than the generic love for all men.

Even after the carnage of what he'd done earlier on the road, even after seeing the true depths of darkness of his 'father', even after he'd abandoned her, this love remained. She knew that the destruction he'd wreaked hadn't been him, not who he wished to be. It had been an effect of his sword. And she knew that he'd left her to protect her from his father, an act of greatest will and sacrifice. This was what she loved about him, such strength.

She understood all of this and still wished he hadn't left.

There was a small emptiness within her now, a hole. Even after all the soothing of her emotions, this remained, unhealed. Yet what could she do about it? She couldn't go after him. That would put them both in danger again.

So finally, after far too much time in rumination, she shook her head and returned to what she needed to do. She was certain that leaving Davar's sword in the middle of a road wasn't a good idea. She knew he hadn't been thinking straight when he'd left it there and didn't blame him, but it needed to be moved.

Yet her hand flinched back as soon as it touched the pommel. She tried again but with the same result. It was too dark, too evil. It wouldn't let her touch it.

Then an idea struck her. It might not work, but it was worth a try. She collected her torn dress from the road and wrapped parts of it around her hands, the rest dangling from her arms. She approached the sword again and grasped the hilt with her thickly covered hands. She pulled hard. It took a great effort of her earth talent, enhancing her strength to its limits, for her to drag it up from the dirt.

She carried it, still straining her strength, into the woods. There, far from the road, she plunged it back into the ground. It was all she could do. She hoped it would be enough.

When she returned to the road, she glanced off to the west, where Davar had disappeared. The mountains stood high and stark.

No sign of Davar.

There was a sting in her heart and she grimaced.

Luckily, she had more to do to distract her. She had no other clothes but her cloak, and that would not do. She walked a little ways back down the road to the men Davar had killed, hoping to find some clothes. It was a gruesome task and part of her reviled searching the torn bodies and the thought of taking anything from anyone, even the dead.

After a short while of searching, it seemed she'd be spared having to steal clothes. Everything was torn to shreds. There was nothing that wasn't either covered in gore or required just as much repair as her dress. If she were going to restore anything her dress would be her first choice. She could use magic to mend it, but it wasn't an easy process. The elements of earth and water could be used on non-living items, but they didn't respond as quickly or easily as people did to such ministrations. It was a delicate operation, requiring more power than it would seem for such a simple task, but it needed to be done.

So she sat by the side of the road, uncertain where to go, or what to do except to begin the slow, tedious process of knitting her dress back together.

CHAPTER 8

*I*n one day of frenzied travel, Davar had covered the ground he and Cassine had traversed since they'd left the mountains. He was back on the plateau where she'd first teleported them.

There he stopped as night fell.

He was tired, drained from the day's myriad events as well as resisting the call of Shadowfang and his father. Leaving the sword behind had been his only thought to escape and it had worked.

There had been a single shining moment when Davar had felt... something... for Cassine.

He shuddered at the remembrance of his father's possession and the way he'd treated her. Despite all his desires to see her nude before him, that had seemed an abomination, something so pure coming in contact with something so foul. He had recoiled from it, hated himself and his father for every second of that encounter.

Seeing Cassine there, exposed, had reminded him of his mother and what the Blacklord had done to her. Another strong, pure woman defiled by the man. But as Cassine had advised him, he didn't dwell on the rage and hatred of that memory, but the love. That, with his feelings for Cassine, was how he'd been able to break his father's command. A single moment of sheer opposition to everything the Blacklord stood for. He'd loved in that moment and the Blacklord hadn't been able to understand, had shrunk back in confusion for only an instant. That had been enough to release the sword, which diminished his father's hold on him. That in turn, had given him the control to flee back to the west and away from the power of the Blacklord.

Love.

That was what had enabled him, for the first time in his life to defy his father.

His love for his mother.

His love for... Cassine?

He gazed up as the first stars emerged.

Was this what it felt like to love?

Was he even worthy of such a love with all the darkness within him?

He sighed heavily.

At least the call of both his sword and his father were quieter now. He was far enough away that they couldn't reach him, control him. After a few more days of travel westward, he might escape them all together.

Then perhaps he could begin to figure out who he really was.

All his life someone had been telling him what to do, who he was, where he belonged. Even Cassine had been intent on him being good. Perhaps he needed to get away from everyone to find out who he was on his own.

That's what he told himself anyway.

The fact remained that he missed Cassine deeply. Missed her angelic smile, the way her long blond hair moved, the way it smelled. It wasn't even the call of her body to his base desires anymore, though that did remain. No, there was something new, some tear in his soul at her loss that was so very unfamiliar to him. It was the remembrance of their time together, the intimacy of her healing, the way she laughed, the approval in her eyes when he hadn't slaughtered those men in the tavern.

Gods, but he missed her.

And he'd never missed anyone before.

He'd known her less than a month, and somehow she'd left a mark on his soul. Actually, there was no 'somehow' about it. She'd helped him heal and discard some small part of the darkness inside himself. That was a very palpable mark on his soul. He just hadn't expected her essence to be such a large part of that.

Yet he couldn't go back to her. To do so would put her in danger. He'd fled to keep her safe...

Hadn't he?

His gaze turned east, over the lands now sinking into night's embrace, toward... her.

He hadn't even said anything to her. He'd just left. What did she think of his abrupt departure? Did she understand he'd done it to save her?

More and more questions circled around in his mind.

I've got a simple solution — just kill her. His guard had come down and Shadowfang had reached him.

Shut up, Shadowfang, he said, clamping his defenses down.

And that was the problem. He couldn't go back east to her, not without coming closer to his blade again, strengthening their connection and that with his father. No, his only course was west, farther away from the darkness in his life... and the one light.

It didn't matter how much he loved her. If he went after her, he'd only be putting her and countless others in danger once again. He couldn't risk it.

A great wave of despair washed over him at the futility of his life. He'd only just begun to see light, and now it would be snuffed out forever. His soul ached for her to be there with him but his mind knew it was impossible.

With a great welling of frustration and desolation, he lifted his head and bellowed a wordless cry of pain into the night.

~

*H*e awoke to the first rays of sun on his face, bright and pure.

He got to his feet slowly, feeling the faint need for food in his belly and ignoring it. He could hunt later, once he was far away from... everything. The ache in his soul still rang through him, but he knew there was no other way but to put more distance between himself and those dark things which called to him.

Yet he found it hard to leave that morning.

He delayed, gazing eastward, trying to think of some last vestige of hope, some shred of a notion as to how he might stay.

Perhaps he could fight his father, but that thought fled as soon as it was hatched. He'd resisted his father but once in his lifetime, yesterday, and he doubted the Blacklord would let such a thing happen twice.

Perhaps if he returned to St. Antin, there might be something they could do for him? Yet still, that meant getting closer to his father's control, even if he took a wide berth around Shadowfang. Once within the confines of the abbey he could resist. There was a magic sealed into the walls of St. Antin which had prevented him from connecting with this father. Yet long before he got there, he'd be well within range of his father's calling and would be plucked from that course.

For most of the morning, ideas played within his head and were discarded. Some came back to him many times in various derivations, but still nothing could be found to work. In the end, it was clear. The east held nothing for him but a return to his father and with that only pain and darkness.

West was his only hope.

So he turned to leap away into the mountains.

"Please don't go."

He halted himself mid-launch but that much energy needed to go somewhere and he staggered forward, arms flailing, legs wobbling, until he fell to his hands and knees in perhaps the silliest and most awkward display in his life.

He was furious and yet wanted to laugh out loud at the same time.

He turned to see who had spoken even though he knew that voice.

Cassine stood, eyes wide with concern, yet with her lips pressed tightly together on the verge of a laugh.

Their gazes met and all the tension in him released in a bout of laughter. She joined him. It was the most beautiful sound he'd ever heard. Not just her laughter, but theirs together. He wasn't sure of the last time he'd laughed in such a pure and light way, perhaps never.

He laughed so hard he fell to his side, rolling on the ground, which only made her laugh harder still.

It was several joyous moments before the laughter slowly died away, returning in fits. By that time she was kneeling next to him. He reached out to her and she took his hand.

"I can't believe you're here, that you're real."

"I am," she said simply. She was just as he remembered her, her dress remade, long hair swaying with every slight movement of her head, eyes golden in the sunlight. "It took me a long time to figure out what I was going to do after you left. In the end, there was no choice. I had to come find you, no matter what that meant for me, or you, or us."

Davar's thoughts whirled. He was about to ask how she'd gotten here so fast when he remembered she could teleport, which led to another question. "How did you find me?"

"I searched for your spirit. Spirit finding isn't as easy for me, but you have a spirit like a beacon. It was quite easy to find something that strong even from that far away. So I teleported, but this time, I tried to focus on your spirit and let that pull me to you. It worked."

He sat up, grinning like a fool. "And I'm glad you did. Gods, but I missed you."

"I missed you too." And with that she leaned in, cupping his face with one hand and kissed him lightly, her lips soft on his. He was so shocked he didn't even have time to react before it was finished. "I couldn't let you go."

His thoughts turned dark. "I didn't want to let you go, but... I could see no way to stay without my father taking control once again." A thought occurred to him now, an extension of one of the ideas he'd mulled over earlier. "Unless..."

"What?"

"Could you teleport us directly back into St. Antin. It would have to be within the walls. It couldn't be outside. That wouldn't work. Do you think you can target your teleport that much?"

She sat back on her heels. "I... don't know. Perhaps. I might need some practice first."

"Then practice. Because if you can get me within the walls of St. Antin, my father can't contact me, and perhaps the monks there know of some way to help me resist him. If they can help me then well, anything is possible."

His soul flooded with hope and joy at her return and the prospect of not having to live his life without her. More than that, he reveled in the faint hope that he might be able to someday resist his father's call.

"Then practice I will." She stood and he with her. "This might take some time, though. I'm only just learning what I can do with teleportation and it's still draining. I wasn't as tired this last time because it wasn't as far as the first time, I'm guessing. If I'm going to practice with great distances, though I may need whole days of rest in between. Tomorrow I'll try teleporting to St. Antin alone and see how well I do. Then I'll need to rest before returning to you. I should be back in a couple of days."

"I can wait," he said placing his hands on her upper arms, then pulling her into a tight embrace, which she returned, as much as that amazed him. "For you, I'll wait as long as it takes," he whispered near her ear.

She drew back and shed the light of one of her angelic smiles upon him. Her gaze met his and he saw how she felt; how her feelings for him matched his for her. It might be young still, but they shared a connection deeper than their bonding had ever been.

"I'll need to regain some energy before I try it. Feel like hunting?"

"You're here with me, I feel like singing or flying, but hunting will have to do."

She laughed at that. "I can't imagine you singing."

He joined her mirth. "Come to think of it, neither can I."

CHAPTER 9

*C*assine found herself standing in someone's private quarters within St. Antin Abbey. If it hadn't been for a faint glow that gave sparse illumination to the small room, it would have been near impossible to tell where she was. She could see a small table with two chairs next to a glowing object, a very large sword. Also in the room were two chests, a bedside table, and a bed... with Senia and Ahrn in it.

Having needed some strong anchor point of spirit to teleport herself back to the abbey, Cassine had focused on Senia, the strongest spirit she knew. She was fairly surprised that she'd hit the mark so close on the first try. She just hadn't expected to find the woman in bed, as... exposed... as she and Ahrn were.

"Oh! Sorry. Ah... Hi?" Cassine said feeling more than a little awkward.

Ahrn was awake. He'd flinched upon seeing her, but other than that just gaped. He composed himself quickly though, seeming to grow calm, smiling at her. He was about to speak with a quick succession of events stopped him.

Senia had been sleeping, her body half over his, head pillowed on his chest. She came awake suddenly and gave a quick cry of alarm, pulling sheets up over herself. A moment later a thick glowing blade appeared at Cassine's neck, lifting her head slightly with its presence.

"Hello, Emberthorn," Cassine said, trying to keep her voice steady. The name of Senia's Aehryn-Gift was well known throughout the abbey.

Senia blinked away her surprise as Ahrn laughed.

"Hello Cass," Ahrn said easily. "Fancy meeting you here. You've been gone for a while. You had a lot of us worried."

Senia slapped him, half-playfully on his arm. "Shut up darling, can't you see she's embarrassed enough as it is?" The blade at her neck fell away and hovered back to its corner of the room. "Sorry about that, gut reaction."

"No worries," Cassine said, breathing easier, though she was then hit by a wave of fatigue and had to put an arm out against the cold stone wall to brace herself. "I didn't mean to... disturb you. I didn't think you'd still be in bed. I thought... well, it's of no matter now. Here I am. My apologies for waking you."

"I can sense your spirit is weary. You've spent yourself. Please sit." Senia rose, wrapping blankets around herself, which left Ahrn uncovered on the bed, naked, an unintended side effect.

"Oh," Cassine said, looking elsewhere. Ahrn was a handsome enough man, if not near as large as Davar. He was very fit as most monks were, with chiseled muscles. She tried not to think about that. His features were pleasant, dark brown hair, long and tousled, vaguely reminiscent of Davar's. His eyes were of a pale brown, like her own, and he had a straight nose and small mouth. In many ways, he could have been her brother, which made what she'd seen just a little more... wrong.

Ahrn laughed. "I'm sure it's nothing you haven't seen before. But let me find some clothes." He rose to dig out some clothes from a chest. Senia helped Cassine to the table with the two chairs.

Senia was the picture of serenity. Her long auburn hair had been tied back for sleeping, now pulled over a shoulder to rest in her lap. Eyes like pristine pools of blue waters regarded Cassine with concern. Senia was nearly as tall as Cass, but mush more slender, willowy some would say.

Cassine sat heavily, tired, but not as wiped out as she'd been that fist time she'd teleported with Davar to the Silver Mountains. She'd still need lots of rest before she tried teleporting again, but she seemed to be growing more adept at it.

"What happened?" Senia asked. "Where have you been? It's been so long. We thought the worst."

Cassine took a moment to regain herself. "I've been in the Silver Mountains."

Senia's eyes went wide. "That's over a thousand leagues from here!"

Cassine nodded. "It's a blazes of a trip, let me tell you. Teleporting is no easy feat."

"Teleporting?" Senia said slowly, sounding out the word.

"Moving from one place to another in an instant, even great distances," Ahrn said slipping on some pants. "It was one of the powers of the most powerful Aehryn-Gifts. It takes all four elements to even think of trying."

"Oh," Senia said still looking slightly confused.

"I'm a multi-talent," Cassine said, knowing she could trust these two. It wasn't something she shared with many. Even among her sisters within the Daughters of Ehlani, she'd told but a few.

"Oh!" Senia said again then laughed at herself. "I see. Well, go on then."

"Actually, I appreciate your help, but I wasn't coming to see you... really."

"Oh?" Senia said, then again laughed at herself. This time Ahrn joined her.

Cassine could tell that the other woman was still a little tired and groggy, not fully awake yet. This was all a little too much information for her so early.

"No, it's a long story, which you're probably going to want to hear, but I need to talk to High Sister Olinda as well, perhaps even the High Abbot. I arrived in your room as you were the strongest spirit I was familiar with. Again, my apologies for waking you."

Senia rose. "Understood. Why don't you wait outside for a moment while Ahrn and I get ready then we can accompany you to the High Sister."

"I'll be fine on my own, I know the way, and I'd rather do this alone if that's alright with you."

"No worries." Senia helped Cassine up then embraced her. "We're just glad you're back. When you disappeared with the Blacklord's son, we feared the worst! I'm glad you are well."

"I am thank you. No need to worry."

Senia nodded. "Then perhaps we can talk later. I'd love to hear what happened to you and how you came to be at the Silver Mountains," Senia said. "I'm sure it's a great story."

"You have no idea," Cassine said then excused herself from the room. Once alone in the dim light of the hall, she took a moment to simply breathe. This helped to steady her and regain some of her strength. She was still a little light-headed and weak from the intensity of the spell that had brought her here, but she dug deep into her earth talent to refresh her body. Though her wind talent wasn't as strong, she used a bit to clear her mind. She felt ready to face the High Sister now. Though in truth she had no idea how she was going to explain any of this.

Cassine made her way through the halls of St. Antin as morning stirred its inhabitants. She met a few bleary-eyed monks as they roused from their rest for another day of war. It occurred to Cassine that the High Sister might not be in her quarters, but out in the bailey helping with healing, but since she was most of the way to the woman's room, she'd check there first.

As it turned out, the High Sister was in her quarters and was more than a little surprised to find Cassine knocking at her door.

"Oh, by all the Gods, girl, you're alive!" the High Sister, tears in her eyes, rushed out and embraced Cassine tightly. After a moment, without releasing her, the other woman asked, "where have you been?" There was great concern in the woman's voice. "When you went missing the same time as the Blacklord's son escaped... and those guards said he'd taken you prisoner. We searched everywhere for you! Gods we thought..." She pressed her lips together for a moment before she calmed and spoke again. "But I can see you are well." She drew in a long breath. "Forgive my concern. It is good to see you."

"And you, High Sister."

Olinda nodded. "So then tell me, where were you?" She ushered Cassine into her chambers and lit a few extra candles.

"Far away... falling in love," she said casually, unsure what prompted her to respond in such a way.

That stopped the high sister. "In love?" Olinda turned to her and grasped her by both shoulders, looking intently into Cassine's eyes. "With a man of darkness?" There was something intense and urgent behind the surprising question.

"Yes, you could say that. Why?"

"But... no... Not..." The high sister's eyes went wide for a moment, then she seemed to come to her own conclusion and shake her head. "No, it couldn't be."

"What do you know?" It was clear to Cassine the High Sister knew more than she should about this.

Olinda smiled and ushered Cassine to a chair. "I'm sorry my girl, I interrupted. Please tell me everything!"

Cassine wasn't sure what she'd expected, but this wasn't it.

So Cassine told the story of her time with Davar.

The high sister's reaction when she found out who Cassine had fallen for was... not unexpected.

"The Blacklord's son! Oh by all the Gods! I didn't think..." The woman sat there for a moment speechless. "This is the man you love?"

"He is. But there's more to the story. He isn't the man he was."

"You best go on then and explain. I'd never imagined the dark one would be..." the high sister was lost for words apparently.

Cassine had to ask. "You speak as if you had expected me to fall in love with someone... dark."

The High Sister only nodded. "There will be time for that later. First tell me your story."

When Cassine had finished, the High Sister sat in

thought for a moment. "This is a most remarkable tale, my child. If I didn't know you better I'd think you were spinning fantasies like a tavern minstrel." The other woman's eyes met Cassine's with a great intensity. "You asked how I knew about all of this. Well, I will say that there's more at stake here than you can imagine. For the whole tale, I think we'll need to gather a few others first."

Within an hour, a whole host of people had gathered in the High Abbot's chambers. There were too many to sit in the area before the hearth, so the members were scattered around the large room.

Cassine, still tired from her magical exertions earlier that day, sat in one of the large chairs. Senia and Ahrn were there, not so surprising as they were some of the leaders, the captains of the defense against the Blacklord's armies. He stood leaning against the wall of bookshelves with Senia in front of him, leaning against him. He had his arm around her, and they looked comfortable together. Emberthorn hovered in a corner.

Wyllea was also there, a hip against the large table strewn with battle plans. Her man was there as well. Tirol wandered the room slowly taking in everything, nothing escaping his keen gaze. He'd seemed surprised to be there, but adjusted quickly.

Master Elia was pacing along one side of the grand table. Her presence was expected, she was second only to the High Abbot among the monks of Embreth. The High Abbot herself was speaking quietly with High Sister Olinda in a corner but came forth as soon as the last person arrived. The one they'd been waiting for was a Scandian girl, wide-eyed and young, seeming very out of place in this counsel.

Again Cassine was prompted to tell her tale and as much

as some of those in attendance displayed great shock and surprise at the notion that Davar might show any signs of benevolence, the High Abbot and Master Elia seemed unfazed. When she finished, she explained that she'd have to rest again today to be able to return to Davar and bring him back.

"In chains, I hope," Tirol said vehemently.

"That won't be needed, he's changed," Cassine said. Some of the others didn't seem convinced.

"I've trouble believing he's changed that much in only a few weeks," Wyllea said with a fire burning behind her green eyes. "He took you hostage less than a month ago!" She pushed herself off from the table and took a solid stance.

"Give him a chance to redeem himself," Cassine urged.

"That he will get," the High Abbot said evenly, silencing further argument. "It's time you all know of a... foreseeing, which involves all of you and... it would seem, Davar as well."

"Let me guess," Tirol quipped. "We trust him, then he betrays and kills us all, is that how this foreseeing goes?" After a stern look from the High Abbot he muttered a quick, "Sorry, go on." Then went back to examining the many books on the shelves around the room.

"This is Ragnalla," the High Abbot said indicating the Scandian girl. The girl curtseyed with a shy smile. "She has the ability of foresight. She's seen two possible futures for us. One where the Blacklord eventually succeeds and darkness covers all the land, and one where he is defeated."

Tirol piped up with, "If it were up to me, I'd take the second option."

Wyllea took a long stride over to where he was and slapped him on the arm with a hissed, "Shut up, lover."

But there was no rebuke from the High Abbot who said simply, "You may get your wish. It may be up to you."

"Uh... oh, really?" he said, otherwise silenced. He was paying full attention now.

Cassine was getting curious as to where this was heading, but her spirit sense of those in the room, mixing with her innate ability to see souls was telling her she wasn't going to like it. The High Abbot and the High Sister were scared. They knew something between them, and yet their emotions were betraying a desperate hope mixed with a distant fear.

As the High Abbot went on, Cassine began to understand why.

"It was seen that six, and only six, individuals will go to face the Blacklord. We have clearly identified some of these: Senia, Wyllea, and Cassine. The others were a bit of a mystery." The High Abbot turned to Ragnalla. "Have you seen anything further on the others, these two men, do they fit your vision?"

The girl, Ragnalla, peered intently at Ahrn and Tirol. Cassine looked to the two men who seemed to be taking the scrutiny with vastly different reactions. Ahrn was calm and unruffled, accepting of this fate. Tirol was visibly dismayed. She could sense the fear and turmoil in his soul.

"Yes. These are two of those who must go. There remains but the dark one."

There was yet another reference to the 'dark one.'

"Thank you Ragnalla, you may go now," the High Abbot said serenely.

The girl nodded and padded softly from the room.

The High Abbot turned to Cassine. "I do not know what great fate put you and Davar together, but it would seem he is to be the last of this six. Ragnalla foresaw one of darkness who would need to go as well. The girl can tell for certain once he returns. So yes, please do bring him to us."

"I will," Cassine, said. "But I'll require rest before I attempt another teleportation. May I be excused?"

The High Abbot nodded. "You're all dismissed. I suggest you prepare yourselves for what is to come."

As she left Cassine could hear Tirol's voice. "Yeah, sure, me against the Blacklord, that'll work." This was followed by a slapping sound then Tirol again, "Ow! You do realize you're stronger than the average woman right?"

"Suck it up lover, you're going. Now let's go back to our rooms and... prepare, shall we?"

Cassine paused in the hall to let Wyllea and Tirol pass. They were close, his arm around her, hers around him. They even shared a quick kiss.

"Oh, I'll prepare you," he said playfully and she laughed.

Cassine sighed. She wasn't sure if her relationship with Davar would ever be that light, that playful, but by all the Gods, she hoped she would have the chance to find out.

CHAPTER 10

*D*avar saw Cassine appear out of the still morning air. With her next gasped breath, she muttered, "I'm not sure I'll ever get used to that."

She'd changed her clothes, now wearing a dress of pale brown, like sand on a beach. He doubted she owned anything vibrant or wild in color or cut. It wasn't who she was and he didn't care. She was still a beautiful sight. The dress set off the gold in her eyes, and the belted waist gave good emphasis to her full bust and hips. She also wore a new cloak of thick wool, which was currently pushed back over her shoulders.

"I think I need to sit," she said taking a few staggering steps toward him. He rose quickly from where he'd been sitting and was at her side, helping her to the ground. He wanted to help her, do things for her, be needed by her. It was still hard for him to understand, but he was learning.

Mostly he was thankful that she was here again. Never before had he sought, or felt so comforted by, anyone's presence as he did with her.

"Thank you," she said. There was a weariness around her eyes, a slouch to her posture. She was working herself hard.

"I can't say I'm used to hearing those words," he said with a grin. "But we can talk more later. You look tired, just rest for now."

She nodded and he helped lay her back on the soft grasses. She wrapped her new cloak about her and closed her eyes. Soon she was resting peacefully.

He sat next to her, watching her sleep and marveling at her incomparable beauty. She woke by late morning and smiled to see him looking at her. She reached up to his face and drew it down to hers. They lingered in a long, tender kiss.

They went for a walk then, through the high mountain forest. While she'd been away, Davar had moved to the forested hill to the south of the plateau. There was better hunting and shelter there. The forest was alive this afternoon as they walked, the trees swaying with in mountain's breeze, the birds adding their high song to the wash of the leaves in motion.

"You may not receive the warmest reception when you get back," she said after a while of silence.

He gave a short laugh. "I don't really expect one." He stopped, turning to her. "You're... an exceptional woman to have seen past all my faults to that speck of light within me. Even now after what happened... on the road... you still see the good in me. I don't know how you do it, but I don't expect that level of sympathy from anyone."

He looked away, ashamed for the first time in his life.

Shame was fairly new for him. An awkward and squirmy feeling inside him, making him feel... like he was sick. His stomach rolled like some heavy lump sat within. He didn't want to feel this way and before he never would have. This was part of what it was to be a better man but it certainly wasn't a pleasant part.

"I wouldn't blame anyone them for hating me. I'm not the most likable fellow."

"They're good people," she said, her soft fingers on his check, pushing his face back toward her until their gazes met. "They'll see the good in you too, given a little time."

"I don't know how you remain so... positive and optimistic."

"It's a gift."

"It must be." He tried to look away again, but she pressed her hand to his cheek, keeping his gaze on hers. For a moment the forest around them, the birdsong and dappled light, all disappeared. He was lost in those golden eyes.

"You've come a long way, Davar. Trust in that. They'll see it too," she said softly.

At the moment with his guilt and shame wriggling inside him, he couldn't see what she must be seeing in him, but he nodded. He trusted her, perhaps she was right.

She smiled, kissed him lightly, then they continued walking, hand in hand.

After a long silence, she spoke again. "There's something else you should know."

He stopped. There was something in her tone that caused the uneasy feeling in his stomach to turn to dread. "What?"

It was her turn to look away, but only for a moment, seeming to find some inspiration or courage from the foliage above them. She turned to look him in the eye as she said, "when I returned I spoke with the High Abbot. She told me of a foreseeing. You were involved, at least that's what they believe. They say you, as well as myself and others, the scions included, will go to face the Blacklord."

Davar had to take a moment to digest that. He blew out a long breath, stepping back to lean against a tree. Now it was his turn to seek wisdom from the sun-speckled leaves above them. He swallowed hard.

"You know I could never..." Where his father was concerned there was so much he could never do. Foremost among them was go back. "I can't even be within five thousand miles of the man without falling under his sway! I don't think I'll ever be free of him."

"I don't believe that."

"Oh?" he arched a brow. "What do you believe?"

She too drew in an extended breath, letting it out slowly. "The future is never set. Things change, this is all that's certain. You've already changed so much. I've faith that we can purge all of the darkness within you. Perhaps then your father would no longer have any hold over you."

He shrugged, seeking her eyes for strength. He didn't truly believe any such thing would be possible, but for her sake, he put on a smile. "Perhaps. But that won't happen overnight."

"No. We'll need time before we leave to face him. Besides, part of the foreseeing was that we would win the battle for St. Antin. I don't know how long that will take, but it probably won't happen overnight either."

"And who's doing all this foretelling? Not even my father, with all his vast powers, has the ability to see the future."

Cassine's tone became light, playful. "A Scandian girl."

"A Scandian girl?" He shook his head. "How...?"

"The Gods are ever mysterious."

"That's true enough."

He looked up to the branches arching over him again.

He knew foretelling wasn't connected to any of the magic

talents: mind, body, soul, or spirit. It was simply a gift of the Gods. To whom the Gods gave their gifts was up to them, yet to think some maid from a rough northern culture had a power his father had never possessed...

Something about that thought gave him hope.

He felt Cassine lean in against him, her body warm and soft, her head resting on his shoulder.

Something about what she'd said a moment ago caught at his mind. "So this girl has seen that my father's armies will be defeated?

He felt more than saw Cassine's nod. "Yes."

"Then what?"

"Then six of us go to the Blacklord and face him."

"Six?" he shook his head again. "And what happens then?"

"Apparently, if the right six people go, your father will be defeated."

"And this girl thinks I'm one of the six?"

"That's still up for debate, but all the other five have been identified and the sixth was known only as the dark one."

"Ah, I see how they could think that might be me, but... Gods, this is a giant mess." The idea that he and Cassine and the scions would go against his father and have any chance of winning was absurd. Did these people even know how powerful the Blacklord was? This was a man who'd lived for nearly a thousand years, accumulated knowledge and power that had once belonged to the Gods themselves. This was the man who caused a permanent bank of clouds to shroud the sun over all the lands he claimed and could make magically enhanced assassins like others made bread. It was crazy to think they would have any chance against him.

"I think you're talking to the right source," Cassine said.

"The Gods sure have made some strange choices in this crazy world."

He barked a sharp laugh. "I'll agree to that."

After a lingering moment of silence, she pushed off from him, slipping her hand into his, tugging slightly. "Come on," she said.

He pushed himself from the tree and they walked again.

"That's all for tomorrow and the future. For now, we're free, together, alone," she said, her voice light and carefree. "What should we do?"

He didn't know what could have shifted within her to be so joyous after what they'd been talking about, but he found it compelling and contagious. He found himself filled him with a similar buoyancy.

Inspired, he spun her around to him, taking her in his arms tightly, and pressing his lips to hers. She was surprised but only for a moment before responding to his advance. Her body melted into his, her arms around him, her lips opening to his passion.

They stayed there, in that warm mutual embrace. One kiss led to another and another, each deeper and more passionate than the last. His hand traced her curves from round hip to a full breast, and there it lingered, caressing through the fabric of her dress. After a moment of this, she pulled away, breathless, light brown eyes catching his. He could see her desire within them. She placed a single finger on his lips, taking a moment.

"Please," she whispered, and he could see the effort it took her to say it, "I'm not ready for this... yet. Can you wait for me?"

Gods, how he wanted her in that moment, his passion a raging flame within him, air caught in his throat. His need was palpable. And though it took a strength of will greater than any he'd ever possessed before, he nodded. His voice was thick when he said, "Yes, Cass, I'll wait. For you, I will wait as long as it takes. For you, I'll do anything." After a moment of reigning in his hunger for her he said, "just so we're clear, though, I'm more than ready when you are."

She gave a light, airy laugh, her eyes darting to his pants. "Oh, I got that feeling." She cupped his face with a soft hand. "Trust that my feelings for you are true and strong. But when I join with a man, I want it to be more than just of the body. I want to join souls and spirits. Do you think your soul is ready to join with mine?"

He recalled how they'd been bonded not so long ago. How awkward and jarring it had felt, his darkness with her light. He shook his head, despite however much he wanted to tell her he was ready. He knew his soul still needed more work before it could truly join with one as pure as hers.

"You're one infuriating woman, do you know that? Wonderful, pure, beautiful, and so very infuriating." He leaned in for a brush of a kiss to demonstrate his restraint.

"And you," she said, her voice turning solemn, "have the potential to be a great man. Did you know that?"

He smiled, amazed yet again by what she saw in him.

"By the way," she said as they began walking again. "I like it when you call me Cass."

They spent the remainder of the day together simply talking. Even though they'd bonded once and had known everything about each other, such deep understanding had faded with time, and they took the time now, to find it once again.

*T*he next day they teleported back east.

Davar grunted as if he'd been punched in the gut as the walls of St. Antin Abbey appeared around him. His head swam, but he took several long deep breaths and slowly steadied himself. Both he and Cass had been prepared for this jump and she'd tapped into some of his strength to make the teleportation a bit smoother.

Instantly, since their hands were already joined, they bonded as they had that first time. This helped them share strength so as not to pass out. Still Davar sat himself down slowly and Cass was leaning heavily on Senia, who again had been the woman's focus to get here.

They were in the great bailey of St. Antin, five hundred feet across and three hundred deep, with the impressive fifty-foot walls surrounding them. The Abbey itself was a squat square structure in front of them, four hundred feet to a side and over eighty feet tall. It had not been built for looks but for function, to house an army of fifty thousand men.

They were surrounded by monks as well as the two scions. Everyone looked a little tense. To ease the tension, Davar gave a tired grin and waved. "I surrender."

Senia stared intently at him, as did Wyllea and they turned to each other at roughly the same time.

"He does seem different. His spirit has changed," Senia said first.

Wyllea shrugged. "He's not thinking of slaughtering us all. That's a start." Wyllea did, however, make several not so subtle glances between Davar and Cassine. Apparently, the mind-reading scion had seen some of his thoughts for the healer. Davar didn't care.

"Now if you'll take me to wherever you're going to keep

me, I really need some rest, so does Cass," Davar said, trying to rise, but only succeeding on the third attempt. In the end, Wyllea helped him along as Senia did Cass.

He was led to a small cell inside the abbey, not the dungeons. Apparently, Cass had really helped his cause when here last. Wyllea deposited him on his bunk where he promptly fell asleep.

When he awoke, there was a different woman in his room. She'd pulled one of the wooden chairs over from the small table in the opposite corner and sat by his bed. She was older, blond hair mixing with white, clear blue eyes met his, a serene smile on an ageless face.

"Hello," she said in a light, friendly tone. "Sleep well?"

Though he'd never seen or met the High Abbot, he'd heard of her, and this woman fit her description. "Yes, High Abbot, thank you."

"So you know who I am. I should have expected that. And I know who you are, but you knew that didn't you? So we're all introduced. Now, down to business."

There was something about her pleasant, straightforward manner that he liked. He could almost imagine her as the grandmother he never knew.

"There are many here who believe you're evil and beyond redemption. Cassine seems to think otherwise. I want to hear from you. What do you have to say for yourself, son of the Blacklord?"

Davar laid there, gaze retreating from her to the ceiling of his chamber. So what did he think of himself? "Had you asked me that a month ago, I would've told you I was evil and past any form of redemption. Well, actually I wouldn't have said that. I'd have killed you."

Out of the corner of his eye, he caught her nod.

"Now," he blew out a long breath, "things are different." He looked over at her, meeting her serene gaze. "I don't really know what right I have to claim any redemption, but Cass seems to think I'm worth saving." He considered that for a moment. "I guess I've come around to her point of view. I know I'm no saint, and still far from the good man she wants me to be. There's still a lot of black in my soul, but there is nowhere I would rather be than with Cass working on removing that darkness.

"You call me the Blacklord's son, but Cass pointed something out to me that I've come to realize is true. He may have created me, but he doesn't see me as a son, only a tool. I'm nothing more to him than an instrument he can use as part of his plan."

A thought occurred to him then. "But, I think I really want to be something to someone. I want to feel that connection, that..." he hesitated to say it, "...love."

"We all want to be loved," she said softly. "Go on."

"I don't know what else there is to say, really. Am I going to betray you all? On my own, no I won't, but if I leave these walls, the Blacklord's influence within me will be too strong and I'll probably turn on you all. Cass has a hope that if she is able to remove all the darkness from my soul, he won't have any sway over me. I've my doubts: first that so much darkness can be removed, second that even if she can get it all out, the Blacklord still won't have some control over me. I'm his creature. I fear for everyone should he take full control of me again. I don't think he'd let go easily."

After several long moments of her penetrating gaze, she nodded to herself. "There will be two guards outside your door. They will accompany you everywhere you go. I've no doubt you could kill them both rather easily if you chose to, but I don't think you will. They're for everyone else's ease of mind. Cassine will continue to see you and work on your healing. We shall see how that progresses and I shall check in from time to time.

"You're free, Davar. You may leave if you like, but I don't think you will. I trust you because Cassine does. Don't let us down. And when the time comes I have faith as she does that you will be able to leave these walls and face the Blacklord without coming under his sway."

She rose and glided to the door. There she turned and bowed slightly. "Be well, Davar." And she left.

Davar was a little stunned at her easy proclamation of his freedom. He wasn't sure he'd be so trusting in her place. But at least he'd see Cass again soon and that thought allowed him to fall back into a deep slumber.

CHAPTER 11

*E*mberthorn blazed with blue fire and Eaglewing was held ready, string pulled taut and nocked with an arrow pointed at Davar. The two scions were ready for a fight...if it came to that.

Cassine held her breath, waiting and hoping.

"Shadowfang," Davar said and the light-sucking blade appeared in his hand. He winced, gritting his teeth, then released the sword. It clattered to the ground and Davar took several steps away from it.

"Take it away," he said harshly. "I don't want to be anywhere near that thing!"

Wyllea released the string slowly, the arrow vanishing as the flames of Emberthorn also disappeared.

"Well, that's certainly a change," Senia said with a shrug. She knelt as a monk handed her a thick blanket in which to wrap the dark blade. She bundled it and hefted it, moving into the keep. Davar came to Cassine and embraced her; his two guards, like twin shadows, not far behind.

She returned the embrace, squeezing his large form as best she could. "I know that wasn't easy for you."

He released her stepping back slightly. "When will I see you today?"

"Soon. I'm almost done my healing rounds with the Daughters. I'll be with you after that."

He smiled at her, his eyes showing concern. "You look tired. Are you sure I'm not working you too much?"

She leaned in kissing him lightly on the cheek. "No, it's my choice. I'll be fine. I can rest... later."

He nodded then returned her kiss, his lips hot on her cheek. "See you soon, then." He left.

She made her rounds of the wounded, most already healed from the injuries taken in last night's combat. Despite Ragnalla's prediction that they would win this war, the fighting was still as intense as ever. That said, fewer of the defenders had been injured in recent days, probably due to the efforts of the two scions who seemed to be everywhere in the night.

Davar hadn't been wrong about how tired Cassine felt. Night after night, she healed the wounded as they fell and continued that work through the morning until the High Sister dismissed her. Then she would go to Davar and work on lifting the darkness from his soul, even more exhausting work. She knew she'd been pushing herself too hard, working for Davar longer than she should, sacrificing her time in the afternoon set aside for sleeping, but she wanted to heal him with all haste. She knew he wanted it as well, which is why she pushed so hard.

By the time she got to his chambers that day, she was so tired she could have fallen asleep on her feet. But when she entered his room to find him in his usual position, lying down, shirt off, ready for her, she perked up. Seeing his chiseled features, the thick rolling muscles of his arms and torso kindled a fire within her.

She knelt next to the bed, kissed him lightly on the cheek, and put her hand over his heart to begin. She delved in, seeking another dark thread, some evil from his past to soothe as he dealt with the darkness in his own way, dispelling it.

~

She started awake, wondering when she'd fallen asleep. She lay on his small bunk with Davar, still shirtless, on his side next to her, gently stroking her hair.

"I told you, you needed more sleep."

"No, you said I looked tired, that's different. When did I fall asleep?"

"Almost as soon as we started. You just kept leaning over me a little more until your head was on my chest and you were asleep. I laid you on the bed figuring that would be more comfortable."

"Oh. How long has it been?"

"The noon watch was called not long ago."

"That's hours! You let me sleep for hours? And what did you do?"

"Watched you. You're so peaceful when you sleep. I wish my dreams were as kind to me." He poked her in the side. "You need more sleep. There, now I've told you. I think we can be done for today."

"Davar, no I..."

His finger moved to her lips, hushing her. "You know how much I want this and I know you want it just as much." He leaned down over her, his lips replacing his finger in a long, deep, sensuous, kiss that left them both a little breathless. When his mouth retreated, taking its sweet warmth with it, he sighed heavily then said, "But I'm not willing to sacrifice you to get what we want. Rest today, come back tomorrow and we'll try again."

He was right. She needed to rest. She kissed him lightly, savoring the moment, then got up from his bed, and smoothed out her skirt.

"Tomorrow, my love," he said.

She smiled, a great warmth filled her to hear those words. "I do like the sound of that. Good-bye, my love." She blew him a kiss and left, returning to her chambers to sleep the afternoon away.

~

She didn't get to her scheduled healing with Davar the next day. She was a little upset, but more curious at the strange summons.

After her rounds with the wounded, she'd been summoned to the High Abbot's chambers. She'd stopped by Davar's cell to tell him she'd been called away and his understanding and patience amazed her. It made her affections for him grow even stronger. She'd kissed him and left, hurrying to the High Abbot's rooms.

There she found several monks she didn't know along with the High Abbot standing around the large table in the room. Laid out on the table was Shadowfang.

"Thank you for coming Cassine," the High Abbot said evenly. "We may have need of your talent with souls. But I'm getting ahead of myself. Sit, we have a story to tell you." The older woman ushered Cassine to one of the large chairs by the fire. The High Abbot also sat and one of the monks an aging man, sat as well, directly across from Cassine. The other younger monks remained standing, silent.

Cassine waited patiently to learn why she was there.

The High Abbot indicated the aged man, who Cassine despite having spent some time in the abbey, had never met. "This is Anar, our High Archivist. He and his team of monks," she said motioning to the others Cassine was unfamiliar with, "spend their days deep within the abbey with the many artifacts we keep here and our vast library of secrets. More-so than even I, these are the keepers of Embreth's knowledge. We sent Shadowfang to them to study in hopes of doing something about the corrupted blade. Anar, tell Cassine what you found."

The man was frail and withered with a fringe of long unkempt hair sprouting from a mostly bald head. His skin was wasted away on face and hands, making him seem drastically emaciated. Yet he still managed to have an air of spritely energy about him at the chance to speak. His dark eyes lit up, and a smile creased his wrinkled face.

"I will tell you a tale, youngling, of a scion of old." He sat on the edge of his chair, leaning forward excitedly. Frail hands shook as they moved in animation of every word. "About two hundred years ago there was a woman, one of the last known scions in all the lands. Her name was Thiona. She stayed here with us for a time, so we have very detailed records of her abilities, her Aehryn-Gift, and her appearance. One young lad even sketched her likeness, but that's no matter now. At that time, the Blacklord was a new but growing threat to the lands, having conquered a third kingdom in the east, expanding his empire out from Nustaria, his homeland. So this scion woman, knowing such a threat could not be allowed to spread set out to fight the Blacklord himself. She never returned and nothing is known of what became of her." The aged man grinned eagerly. "Until now!"

Despite the man's growing excitement at his story, Cassine had a growing sense of dread. She was quite sure she knew where this was going. She might even know part of the story this historian did not. But she'd never tell anyone of such horror.

"This sword," Anar pointed with a trembling hand, "Is hers! Or at least it once was. The details of the blade were explicit and match this blade almost identically except for one thing. The blade of the scion's sword was iridescent silver, glowing with an inner light, where this one, as you know, devours light with its own inner darkness. We believe the Blacklord turned a blade once dedicated to light, into one of shadow the opposing element of magic. And!" His finger jabbed up into the air. "And we think we know how to return it to its former glory!"

"Thank you Anar," the High Abbot said seemingly amused by the old man's excitement. "Cassine, dark magic was used to corrupt this blade, magic of the soul." She paused, checking the room. "What I tell you now is known to only a few, though others might suspect as much. Each Aehryn-Gift contains an ancient soul, one dedicated to an element of magic. This is how Aehryn put such power into her artifacts. She used the souls of once great and powerful men and women. After their death, their souls were some of the most puissant to pass into the Heavens. When Aehryn gave up her life to create these weapons, she infused those souls into them, each with an element that matched their soul. This is how the artifacts were created.

"When the Blacklord took this sword from the scion he twisted that soul. It must have taken him years of work to corrupt a soul of that power and vigor, but he managed to turn it into a vile opposition of what it once was. We believe with your help it can be returned to its former glory."

Cassine sighed heavily. First Davar, now his sword as well, more time taken from working with him exclusively.

The High Abbot continued. "What we are uncertain about is how the Blacklord bonded the sword to Davar if he wasn't a scion to begin with?"

Cassine was torn. There was a secret she knew, one so very personal to Davar. She looked away, uncertain.

"Cassine, are you well?" the High Abbot asked. "Do you think you will be up to healing this sword as well as Davar?"

She nodded. "Yes, I'll do what I must. But that's not what bothers me. There is... I may know how the Blacklord bonded the sword to Davar. But it's his story to tell, not mine."

Something occurred to Cassine then. She sent out her mind talent and found Davar's mental essence alerting him she wished to mind-speak.

Yes? His voice echoed strong in her mind. His mind talent was much stronger than hers.

Can I tell the High Abbot about your mother? We may be able to fix the corruption in Shadowfang, but they need to know the whole story.

He didn't respond right away, though she could feel thoughts racing through his head through their link. Finally, reluctantly, he said, *yes. Tell them what they need to know."*

She sent him a thought-smile. *Thank you, I know how hard this is for you. I will tell you more later, when we have a moment.*

She broke the link and drew a long breath. She spoke to

the others in the room. "May I have a moment alone with the High Abbot?"

The High Abbot gave the others leave to depart and they did, leaving Cassine alone with the elderly woman.

"I have permission from Davar to tell you his story."

The High Abbot raised a brow but did not question how this communication had happened.

"The Blacklord didn't have to bond Davar to the sword. Davar is a scion. The scion woman who went to fight the Blacklord, Thiona...was Davar's mother, or so I believe."

The High Abbot sat back slowly, considering. "That was over two hundred years ago..."

Cassine nodded. "Davar is over two hundred years old. The timing works."

And so she told the High Abbot what she knew of Davar's horrible creation and the death of his mother. It was not a pleasant afternoon.

CHAPTER 12

*T*he memory was deep, long forgotten.

Davar was in a small chapel of Hothar, God of Order and Justice. The priest was using it as a school for the children of a farming community on the fringes of the Kingdom of Kath'Ahan. The priest lay dead on the floor before him, blood pouring from the gaping wound in his belly. The children were screaming. Davar was alone. He could do as he wished. He wished for the kids to stop screaming.

His large hand grabbed one by the top of the head, easily picking the flailing child from the floor. The boy couldn't be more than six years old. It was so easy to crush his skull, Davar's fingers sinking into the goo inside before the rest of the body fell to the floor. He tossed the fragments of bone and gore away and sought his next victim.

He scooped up another boy by the leg, feeling the muscles and bones crush under his grasp. The boy screamed louder. To silence him Davar swung him like a club, smashing the boy's head into a little girl's. Both went silent instantly. There were eight more children, six boys and two girls. They were quiet now, eyes wide with shock. But he was having too much fun to stop. Perhaps he did like their screams after all.

They all died screaming. The last one, an older boy, he took his time with. He crushed one finger after another, then each toe and each foot. He broke every bone in the arms and legs. Then ever so carefully, he used Shadowfang to make a delicate slice over the boy's chest, just breaking the skin and peeling it away. Then pushing his fingers into the boy's chest and through his ribs. In one swift motion, he pulled out the heart. The boy remained alive for a moment, seeing his own heart pulled from his chest, before dying. Davar had smiled, chomping down on the heart as he left the chapel.

The memory was too much. Davar screamed as such a wave of guilt, horror, shock, and shame hit him like a tidal wave and drowned him in remorse.

Davar snapped out of the trance he fell into when Cass did her healings. He pushed Cass aside, rolled off his bed. He searched for the chamber pot as a rush of sickness over-whelmed him. Not able to find the container he scrambled to a corner of the room where he was violently ill for some time.

After a while, he felt a soothing hand on his back. "They're getting worse, aren't they." It wasn't really a question. Cass knew.

He could only nod.

"I could feel the pain, the sorrow in that last one, it was so intense, I... I can't imagine..."

"No," he said, wiping his mouth, still unable to look at her. "You really can't. And I don't want you to try." He spat out more of the bile that burned this throat. "I'm..." No, he couldn't think that way. "...I was... a vile man. I've done unspeakable things." He began trembling and was too weak and tired to stop himself. He began to cry. "I don't know if I can go on. Those memories that remain are the darkest, the most horrific. Even I had blocked them from my memory. I can feel the rest of them, writhing like worms, they'll only get worse from here." He shuddered. He didn't want to delve into them. The revulsion at the mere thought of them nearly made him sick again.

Again, she rubbed his back. "And you're stronger than they are."

He shook his head, full of doubt and fear. The trembling and tears intensified. He wept like a babe, ashamed and relieved at the same time. She held him then as he let all his grief and self-loathing pour out. He couldn't image being this vulnerable in front of anyone else. With her he was an open book. She knew his pain, the filth piled up within him, and still she loved him. There were times, quite often actually, where he didn't know how she did it. It was so easy to love her, she was pure and kind and helpful, but he couldn't imagine what it must be like to love him. He didn't love himself at all at the moment.

After some time the tears stopped and he began to breathe deeply through his mouth to calm himself. He was able to look at her then. What he saw in her eyes, the love and concern, nearly made him weep again. He embraced her and she him, holding each other for some time.

"Things are only going to get worse from here," he said drawing back.

She grimaced. "I don't see what you see, I don't know what you're reliving, but I can feel it. I know it's hard. I know that you're trying to undo hundreds of years of hate and anger and evil. It won't be easy, but I'm here for you."

"Thank you."

"I think we're done for today, though. I need to save some energy for dealing with Shadowfang, or should I say Starsong."

"I still can't believe my sword's real name is Starsong. Not very masculine."

She laughed. "Did you want to come and watch?"

He shook his head. "No, not yet. I don't like getting too close to that sword. Let me know when it starts being... different and I may come along."

She nodded her understanding, then kissed him on the cheek and rose. "I'll check in on you later." She left.

He pulled himself together then asked one of his guards to fetch a bucket with water for him to clean up his mess.

Once that was done, he felt restless. He needed air and decided to go for a walk in the bailey.

His guards kept a respectable distance behind him, which he thanked them for. He didn't want to be around anyone right now. His thoughts were dark, remembering the evil he'd dealt with this morning with Cass. When they'd started, almost two months ago now, it had been easy. She'd started with the minor tarnishes on his soul and he'd accepted and dealt with them usually with little effort. They could get through dozens of memories, hundreds on a good day. This morning they'd only made it past two in so many hours.

He'd reached the bailey. The yard of the abbey was vast so despite there being hundreds of men and monks coming and going or resting and recovering from wounds, there was still lots of room to walk without being too close to others.

It was a bright, warm day, the antithesis of his mood and thoughts.

He shook his head, still feeling the corded, twisting knot

of darkness in him. Soul was the weakest of his talents, but he'd been working with Cass long enough to see and feel his own clearly now. He knew it would still be some time before he was free of the evil that had been bred within him and in which he'd reveled and wallowed for so long. To a degree, he was fine with how long this would take. It meant he was putting off returning to the Blacklord. He didn't think of the man as his father so much these days.

He was not looking forward to that quest. If he was honest with himself, it terrified him. Even with two scions and Cass beside him, he still doubted their chances. So if this darkness within him took a while to undo, perhaps that was for the better.

But how long would it take?

He wondered at this for some time. He had hundreds of years of evil to undo. They were less than half done and already they'd reached some of the more vicious and nasty stains on his soul. Even though he'd been raised by a monster, he'd still had trouble with some of the atrocities he'd been forced to commit. At least he had at first. Then over years of committing worse and worse, he'd become numb to it, even enjoyed it as Shadowfang did. It was then that the worst of the darkness had claimed his soul, not because what he was doing was any worse, but because he'd wanted to do it, even loved doing it.

Unbidden, through the darkness of his thoughts, an image of his mother came to mind. This wasn't the tortured moment he'd seen of her before...no now he had a different image of her to keep. Cass had told him about Thiona, the scion that had possessed Starsong and went to fight the. She'd even brought him an ancient drawing, made by some monk here hundreds of years ago. This image was of a serene and yet strong woman. The artist had captured the beauty and intensity of her soft, smiling face. He'd thanked Cass so much for that. He'd asked if he could keep it, but the archivist wouldn't allow it. The old man had been perfectly willing to have a replica made for him though. It was in his room now on the small table, one of his few possessions and the only truly treasured one.

Senia dropped to the ground next to him. He'd sensed her up on the walls since he'd come out into the bailey, her spirit was a blazing beacon to his own spirit talent.

"I would rather be alone at the moment if you don't mind," he said heavily.

"And I want to run off with Ahrn far away from this wretched war, but we don't always get what we want."

He laughed at that, looking over at her. "There is that." She was an attractive woman if one liked the slender, willowy type. She was nearly as tall as Cass but without the rolling curves. Also, where Cass' eyes were soft, shimmering gold, Senia's were a piercing, intense blue. Yeah, he'd take a woman of softness and water any day over such hard passion and fire.

He waited a moment, letting her say what she'd come to say.

"You've changed."

"So some people tell me. Others have yet to believe it."

"What do you think?"

He stopped. His shoulders fell with a heavy sigh. Despite the black still staining his soul he had to admit, "I've changed, if not as much as I'd like."

"I suppose that's what I'm curious about. You seem to want to change. I can't fathom that. What is it that makes you want to turn from the dark when that's what you've always known?" Before he could answer, she went on, explaining herself. "If we're to be on this quest against your father together I need to trust you and I'll admit, despite the change I feel in your spirit, I'm still not ready to do that, not yet. I need to know this isn't some trick. The wolf concealed amongst the sheep."

This wasn't completely unexpected. "First, the Blacklord isn't my father. He may have created me, but I've since learned that a father is more than just the man who put some of his seed into a woman's womb. A father loves you, raises you. He did none of that for me. There were slave women who raised me...and once I was old enough...he made me kill them. He's the Blacklord. That's all he is to me. The same evil man he is to everyone else. The difference is I know him. I've seen his face. I don't know if that makes him less scary to me or more." He sighed. "But that's getting away from what you asked. How can you trust me? Why do I want to change?" He paused for a moment. "Have you ever met someone who changed your life simply by meeting them?"

She seemed slightly taken aback by the question, but answered anyway. "Yes, Ahrn and Emberthorn changed my life the instant I met them."

"Cassine changed mine." He paused and after a moment continued walking. Senia followed. "An interesting side effect of two multi-talents teleporting together is that they temporarily bond with each other, soul, spirit, and mind. I got to see something truly pure in this world. Not just see, but be immersed in, surrounded by. I understood goodness and purity, even if only briefly. I can't imagine what it must have been like for her filled with my darkness, but for me that shining moment made me see that there was something I was missing. And because I was far enough away from the Black-lord that I could actually fully feel it without having him block it from me; I started to wonder about myself. For the first time in my life, I had own thoughts about something. I started to wonder how in all the blazes of the Void could anyone possibly be so good and pure in a world where everyone I'd ever known was black of heart, devoid of soul. Somewhere along the lines, I'd just assumed the whole world was as befouled and evil as I was and deserved to be conquered and under one rule to tame them. When I saw that wasn't the case..." He shrugged. "I began to wonder what else I was mistaken about."

He walked in silence for a moment, Senia easily keeping pace. She said nothing, perhaps pondering his words.

Another thought occurred to him. "Then there was the moment I met my mother for the first time. Has Cass told any of you about that?"

Senia shook her head. "No."

"She was a scion."

Senia stopped, startled. "What?"

He halted as well, turning to her. "Apparently her name was Thiona."

There was a series of emotions that played over the other woman's face, from surprise to confusion to understanding and something like awe. She spoke, but the words seemed to be some further self-explanation. "Of course. How could I not see that? If you carried her sword, then you would have to be a descendant. Although I guess I thought it had been corrupted beyond the need for such mundane things as blood ties." She looked up at him. "So you're really old aren't you? You don't look it."

He grimaced. "Thanks. I believe that's part of the Black-lord's magic. I'm guessing he thought he might never get another chance to corrupt another scion, so I had to last him for a while."

She thought a moment before saying, "that's why you didn't kill me, why you wanted me and Wyllea alive, so the Blacklord could..." She shuddered. "Gods!"

He grimaced. "I supposed apologies now aren't worth much are they."

She looked at him oddly. "That depends if you mean it."

He looked away, finding the core of benevolence Cass was helping him instill within himself. He found the guilt he felt at trying to bring this woman back to his father. It was one of those minor blotches on his soul already dealt with. Then he looked her in the eyes saying, "I do mean it. I am truly sorry I tried to take you to such a man. No one deserves that fate."

She raised a single brow. "I believe you." She gave a quick "hunh," then an odd smile. "Perhaps I can learn to trust you, Davar...perhaps." She leapt away back to the walls.

"I only hope when you do I'm worthy of it and don't let you all down." That was his deepest fear and his most nagging doubt.

CHAPTER 13

*C*assine collapsed into her bed, exhausted, and almost instantly fell into a deep slumber.

When she awoke, she could feel the tug of nightmares at the fringes of her soul but was glad she could remember nothing of them. She also found the High Sister sitting quietly in her room.

She sat up quickly trying to clear her head. "High Sister, I'm sorry. Have you been waiting long? You should have woken me."

Olinda chuckled. "Gods, girl, calm yourself. You needed the sleep. I didn't wish to wake you. You didn't show up for your evening rounds when the fighting started so I thought I'd come to see how you were."

"Evening rounds have started? I'm sorry, High Sister, I'll be up at once." She threw her legs over the side of the bed. A wave of light-headedness washed over her as she sat up. She put a hand to her head and closed her eyes as the dizziness passed.

"No, I think we can do without you for one night. You

need to rest. You've been working far too hard. You're a great resource to us all Cassine and we'll need you for what is to come. That's another reason I've come."

"Oh?" Cassine couldn't deny the fatigue that plagued her everywhere she went these days. Between healing the wounded at night and working with Davar and Starsong during the day, she was feeling more and more drained even after resting. This was far from the first time she'd been dizzy and disoriented upon waking.

The High Sister moved to sit next to Cassine on the bed. She raised a hand and brushed a few wayward strands of Cassine's blond hair from her face and back over her ear. Where the High Sister's fingers touched her brow, warm healing energy flowed into Cassine.

"You need to save your energy for the wounded, High Sister."

There was an odd concern in Olinda's eyes. "Child, what makes you think you aren't wounded?"

The question struck like a great bell within Cassine. "I..." It was true. She'd been feeling all the symptoms of a mind-weary warrior, traumatized by the wars he'd fought.

She sighed. "But there's still so much to do."

The High sister smiled. "The war goes better for us every night, child. Fewer and fewer of our men are killed or injured and more and more of the enemy fall. Our scouts report that the Blacklord's army has lost so many men the size of our forces are roughly equal now, and we still have our great defenses. We'll need fewer healers on watch each night. You're to be spared that duty from now on."

Cassine considered this. She was one of the best healers of all the Daughters of Ehlani. Yet she was exhausted. "Thank you."

The High Sister wet her lips and drew in a long breath, her air one of apprehension. "There is one other thing I came to tell you."

"Yes?" Cassine fed off the other woman's hesitance, her fear growing.

"Ragnalla has had another vision, or perhaps an addition to her vision about the Blacklord."

"Yes."

"She has seen that the Blacklord is weakest at the high solstice, the beginning of summer when the sun is strongest and days are longest. That is when you must go."

Cassine was confused for a moment as to why this might be worthy of apprehension.

The High Sister set her hands calmly in her lap. Despite this Cassine could sense the worry and fear within her superior. "The autumnal equinox is but a couple of weeks away. That means you have nine months until the next summer solstice. Nine months to free Davar and his sword of his father's taint. Do you think you can do this?"

Now she understood. Lots of work remained to be done with both Davar and Starsong. Davar's progress had slowed dramatically. They hadn't even dealt with a single full strand of emotion this morning.

Then there was Starsong. After more than a month of trying to figure out how to heal such a different type of soul, she'd had very little headway with the blade. Not to mention she still didn't really understand how the Blacklord had corrupted it, which meant she didn't know how to undo what had been done. In one way a year, even nine months, seemed like a long time, but knowing that there was a hard deadline, that no matter what she had to be done by a certain point, did add urgency to her work. She would definitely need the time away from her other healing duties as her days were about to get much longer.

"It will be done."

Olinda smiled. "I'm glad my child. Now rest. Recover. There's time still, but we must all be at our best, yes?"

Cassine nodded again.

The High Sister left, and Cassine laid back down again but found sleep elusive.

After another call of the watch sounded. She rose and left her room. She'd meant simply to walk and get some air, but her steps led her to Davar's room.

She almost laughed when she realized where she was. She doubted anyone one else in the abbey would ever consider coming to this man for comfort, and yet that's what she wanted. Despite all the work they had left to do he'd changed so much. There was a tenderness in his touch and voice now. He cared, not only for her but for others. He was finding out what it meant to love and be loved for the first time in his life. With her especially, he was always so compassionate now. She acknowledged the two guards outside Davar's room. They knew her well and greeted her before she went in.

The room was dark.

She used her fire talent to bring a flame to life in her palm, then she found a candle and lit it.

Davar slept. She sat and watched him as the High Sister had just been watching her sleep.

He shuddered, mumbling. One of his arms struck out smashing the wall next to his bed. It left a small divot, stone chips and dust falling around him. When she peered closer, she could see many such divots in the walls. It was the first time she'd noticed them. His dreams must trouble him greatly. This left her with mixed feelings. It was good that he could recognize the evil in him now and fought against it, but she also knew it wasn't easy for him to keep up that fight on some days. That concerned her. She didn't fear he'd succumb to evil again, but that he'd lose the energy to fight it, which wouldn't help them in their attempts to cleanse his soul.

She pushed some matted hair off of his sweat-soaked brow. For now, at least, he was still fighting, even in his dreams. He gave a clipped cry and sat up suddenly, awake.

He blinked, probably not expecting any light, then looked over at her. "Cass? Is everything well?"

She'd expected him to be upset or confused, but the concern for her in his voice made her heart swell.

She leaned in a kissed him lightly. "Yes, I'm well. I just couldn't sleep and when I thought to go for a walk...I ended up here."

His hand gently caressed her cheek, sliding through her hair. With a sudden urgency, he leaned in to embrace her. She had to use her earth magic to strengthen muscle and bone at how tightly he held her.

"Davar!" she said, air restricted. He released her enough for comfort. His head drew back but remained so close his long dark hair brushed her forehead, his lips near, his breath hot.

"What's wrong?" she asked. It was obvious he needed comfort and she wondered what bothered him so. She touched his soul. Even without having made contact she'd felt a jumble of emotions roiling around within him. When she did seek further, she felt the great swell of passion which rose up amongst his other feelings.

He closed the distance between them, lips seeking hers, intent and needful.

She responded, her own need stoked by being connected to his barely restrained desire. His hands came to her shoulders and pressed her closer. Her hand found his arm, his shoulder. He slept without a shirt and his skin was hot as her fingers traced the heaving mountains of his muscles. A great chasm of passion opened up before her. It would be so easy to fall into its depths and she was dangerously close to doing so. As fatigued as she was, she didn't want to resist. One of her hands moved over the thick muscles of his chest, then down to the sharply cut hills of his abdomen.

His hand slid down her neck then under the loose collar of her sleeping shift. It found a breast and gripped it fiercely. She gasped, a pinch of pain surging with a roar of heat within her, desire mounting to desperate levels. She undid the laces on his breeches and reached within

She was a healer, she knew of the bodies of men and woman with intense detail. She knew of the act of love but had never before committed it. She knew somewhere in the back of her mind that she wasn't ready. He wasn't ready. But her weary body and soul sought greater comfort and closeness with him.

He groaned and pulled her down next to him. The movement was so forceful his cot shifted and knocked the bedside table. The candle fell and clattered on the stone floor, going out. They were left in the dark with only touch to guide them.

She'd fallen. She knew it.

She was lost over the edge that chasm of passion, flying through a torrent of desire. She knew she should stop, but didn't want to any more.

His hand on her thigh made her quiver with an ecstasy of anticipation. He moved his hand higher, pushing her shift up past her hips. He traced a hot line along where her hip met her thigh, moving inward and finding more sensitive flesh.

She let out a low moan from deep within as his lips pressed against the sheer fabric of her shift over a breast.

The room felt far too warm, or perhaps it was just her body radiating a desperate heat.

She closed her eyes tight, crying out again with a shudder as his fingers did wondrous things much lower down. But then he stopped, withdrawing.

"No," he said, his voice choked with passion. "I won't."

She opened her eyes to the darkness but found the room dimly lit. She realized with a shock that she was glowing, a pure white luminescence radiating from her skin.

Davar had pushed himself back, off of her. His skin glistened with a sheen of sweat. His eyes burned with an inner fire. He drew in several long, slow breaths looking down at her. His breeches had been pushed down to his knees so he was mostly naked and magnificent. He reached out a tentative hand to trace delicate patterns on her lower abdomen.

She was so sensitive she responded with a gasp as her desire spiked with that simple touch. The light from her skin intensified where his finger moved, glowing brighter. He withdrew his hand and turned away.

"You wanted to wait," he said, it sounded like his teeth were clenched. "I will respect that. You... we aren't ready for this. Not yet."

She still wanted him. Her body arched up to him as her desire every so slowly cooled. She didn't want to be smart, didn't want to wait. She just wanted him...now. But his words spoke to another part of her and that part fought to reassert control. She dragged in several long breaths and her passion slipped away with a shudder. After several more calming breaths, she covered herself as she came to a sitting position. Her skin slowly dimmed to the faintest of illumination before the room was in darkness once again. She called a fire in her palm, found the candle, and lit it again.

"You're right," she said when she could finally speak. Her throat was parched, her words hoarse. She swallowed, still trembling with the remembrance of her loss of control, the depths of her want for him. "I don't know how you resisted. I... couldn't. I didn't want to."

He stood, pulling up his breeches. "I was going to," he said, his voice still thick with emotion. "But then you began to glow." He swallowed a lump. "The light was so pure. It reminded me of the darkness still within me. After that I couldn't, no matter how much I desperately wanted to." He moved to the far wall, leaning against it. She guessed that for him, as it was for her, the distance separating them helped quell the desire.

All of this had been a little much for her: the swelling of her passion, the odd glow of her skin, his ability to resist when she couldn't. Her emotions were a whirlwind inside her. Fear and doubt about her ability to control herself around him mingled with her love and longing for him. Added to that was the great urgency of their mission and the desperation of all of the things she needed to do before next summer. It was hard to keep it all in. All she knew right now was that he'd saved her from herself.

She rose and went to him, a light kiss on his cheek. "You're truly an amazing man," she whispered. "Thank you."

He drew in a few more steadying breaths as his hand caressed the length of her arm, coming to hold her hand.

"I'm sorry," he said. "I had trouble controlling myself after..." He shuddered at some unsaid thought.

"What?"

"My dreams," he said. "They grow worse. I've never had nightmares before, but now with my soul free from so much darkness, they're getting to be terrible. My only respite from the nightmares is dreams of you, very... intense and intimate dreams of you...and me."

"Oh," she said, understanding. "And when you saw me here..."

He nodded. "I couldn't control myself, not at first anyway."

Her respect and gratefulness at his ability to stop himself only intensified her love. "Thank you." She laughed lightly. "I know I keep saying that, but I mean it." She brought her fingers to his lips and he kissed them lightly. "And know that our time will come. Soon I hope."

"So is my hope as well." He stroked her hair. "You should probably go though. I'll see you in the morning after your rounds."

"No more rounds for me, just you and Starsong."

"Oh?"

She drew back slightly. "High Sister Olinda came to me tonight and told me we have to be ready to attack the Black-lord by the summer solstice, in roughly nine months. You and the sword are my priority now."

"More time with you, I can't complain about that." He smiled briefly, but then it faded. "But things are getting tougher."

"We'll get through it," she said patting his chest. "Then we'll have our time together. Let that thought spur you along."

The smile returned. "I will."

She kissed him lightly and left, returning to her room.

Her body still tingled from her time with Davar. She had to admit she was highly motivated to finish her work with him. She'd never thought she'd want a man like that...now she was quite certain she did. She wanted Davar and she too would use the anticipation of their time together to help get her through the rough time she knew still lay ahead.

CHAPTER 14

*A*nd so the days for Cassine became a blur of Davar, Starsong, and sleep. Weeks could pass without her seeing the light of day. And those weeks turned into months as her work with both man and sword grew more and more challenging. Davar's ancient memories could now take more than a week to cleanse, and still she struggled to unlock the secret of how Starsong had become Shadowfang.

The Winter Solstice came and went.

The monks of Embreth celebrated the solstice differently than Cassine was used to. In her village in northern Hallania the winter solstice was a time for light, celebration, and the giving of small gifts to loved ones. There were ten days of festivities. It was a time to dispel the seemingly ever-present darkness with candles, a time of joy and hope for the coming year and the longer days to come. The monks however, had five days of restriction and seclusion. They ate a diet of only bread and water and every free moment was spent in quiet contemplation of the past year and the year to come. On the sixth day, they all came together for a great feast and bonfire, as if in one great moment of celebration and light they would dispel all darkness and despair.

The Blacklord's army no longer attacked at night, or at all. They sat like a lesion on the plains below St. Antin. Scouts reported that reinforcements arrived daily. Most likely, the army was waiting for better weather and reinforcements before attacking again.

In memory of her old solstice traditions, Cassine gave Davar a gift. It was a small, smooth stone, clear in color. She'd imbued it with a hint of her spirit so that it glowed with an inner light, if faintly. The smiths had forged her a setting for it, which left most of the stone uncovered but allowed for it to be hung on a leather thong.

Davar accepted it gratefully and wore it from that day forth.

He'd been upset, having nothing to give her. She'd told him she wanted only his soul purified. So they worked even harder to cleanse him. Yet he'd insisted on finding some gift for her. He too went to the forges of St. Antin and had some scrap silver formed into a ring, which he'd given to her. She had been very grateful for the gift and wore it always, a reminder of his love.

Yet despite how near they were to releasing all of the darkness from him there remained several bundles of black so tightly woven, so twisted and knotted together, that they had to be dealt with as one. And that was taking some time.

Every day they would labor with a small portion of the knot within him only to have most of their work undone by the next day as the particularly noxious nature of dark strands tainted the previously purified portions.

For a couple of days Cassine left off her work with Starsong entirely to focus on Davar, pushing through the thick tangle of black emotions. This work left them both exhausted, with Davar sweating and in tears half the time from the memories and horrid feelings he was dealing with.

He told her little of what these memories were and in truth she didn't wish to know. He said only that the Blacklord had tried many things to ensure his son's soul would be well and truly stained forever.

Cassine had to believe such vile depths of evil could still be undone with enough time and love and caring.

She'd begun staying with Davar through the nights. She would remain fully clothed, sleeping next to him on his small bed. He held her, trembling and shaking at times through the night. For most people any significant change took time, but he was being forced to endure several lifetimes' worth of change in a matter of months. His nightmares worsened and Davar himself grew more fragile by the day, shaken and weary. She knew he was reaching a breaking point with his emotional and even physical fortitude. Yet still he insisted on pushing onward. His unparalleled strength and will amazed her daily.

This night, a week past the solstice, she lay awake as he twitched and shuddered next to her, tonight's movements worse than any before. He muttered as well, though she couldn't make out his words.

She'd tried a couple of times to soothe his turmoil of emotions, rolling over to touch the skin over his heart. It worked for a while, but then the tremors returned.

She started to form an idea, a way of reaching him through his mother, but she'd need help to do so. When she'd reached back to the time before his birth when he'd been physically connected to his mother, that had been difficult enough. Now she wanted to go even farther back. That would require more spirit talent than she believed she possessed, but there was one person at St. Antin with an abundance of spirit.

Cassine turned toward Davar again, touching his heart and soothing his ragged soul. She pushed a bit more into it this time in hopes he wouldn't notice her leaving. She wanted to do this now, while he slept, feeling it would be easier on him.

She left his room, nodding to the guards outside now used to her presence, and padded along the cold stone floors, following her spirit sense to the massive beacon that was Senia.

It took several knocks on the Senia's door before it was answered by a bleary eyed Ahrn. He blinked a few times looking at her before recognition shone in his gaze.

"Cass? What do you need?"

"Senia."

He grimaced. "Everyone always does."

The tall, slender woman appeared from the darkness behind Ahrn, wrapping her arms around him, kissing his shoulder. "But I always come back to you, my love."

He smiled.

"What do you need?" Senia asked.

"To be blunt, I need your spirit. I wish to try something with Davar, but it will require more spirit than I have."

Senia nodded. "One moment." She slipped back into the room and returned wearing a cloak over her sleeping shift. She kissed Ahrn, told him not to wait up, and left.

"Thank you so much for coming at such an hour," Cassine said as they made their way back to Davar's room.

"I assume it's urgent. At least I'm not out on the battlefield as I've been for so many nights."

Cassine outlined her plan as they walked, finishing as they entered the dark room together. Davar still slept and they remained quiet and cautious so as not to wake him.

"Emberthorn," Senia said, voice low. The large sword appeared in her hand. "Float and Glow," she commanded and the sword hovered in the air with a faint blue light. Senia laughed lightly.

"What is it?" Cassine asked in a whisper.

"Nothing, just something Emberthorn said. He doesn't get tired, but that doesn't stop him from acting all snarky sometimes."

They pulled the two chairs in the room next to the bed, each sitting in one. Then they joined hands and Cassine tapped into the other woman's spirit, nearly overwhelmed by its power at first. She narrowed the connection, siphoning off spirit slowly, then touched Davar's heart once again.

As she had done with him months ago, she following his soul and spirit back into his mother's womb. It still wasn't easy, but having done it before she was able to expend less energy in the process. Once she'd reached the point where she would connect with his mother's spirit she paused. She took a long moment to weave a protective barrier of soul and spirit to block the intense pain and suffering of his mother from both their souls. She drew upon more of Senia's power to do so.

This would be the tricky part, harder than anything she'd tried before. Once connected to Davar's mother's spirit, she traveled back through her essence to a time before Davar was conceived, before Thiona had gone to face the Blacklord. Cassine sought a time of peace and joy in the woman's life. Spirit was the element that created and connected all things, even those who were no longer alive. Even so, pushing so far back into a dead person's spirit was challenging. She had to open up to more of Senia's spirit but there was only so much of the raw, fiery talent that Cassine herself could channel. She pushed her limits to find a perfect moment from Thiona's past.

Then she found one.

It was a part of Thiona's scion training with her father, learning to use Starsong's powers. A time of strength-of-spirit and joy-with-family.

Pulling even more from Senia, pushing beyond her limits to do so, Cassine captured Thiona's essence from that moment. She pulled it forward, past the woman's torture and death and into Davar. Cassine had never pressed her powers so much before. She felt like her spirit talent might burst or burn out.

Almost done, Cassine turned that spirit essence into a bright new thought and feeling within Davar; using her mind, spirit, and soul talents combined.

As she finished Cassine lost herself for a moment. She stood in a dark place. The only light was shed by the woman standing next to her, a being of pearlescent white, glowing brightly. Then Davar was there with them. He blinked as if waking from sleep and looked at the woman.

"Mother?"

She smiled and held out her arms to him. He ran to her, a boy in a large man's body. He hugged her fiercely and she returned the embrace.

The moment passed, the image faded, and Cassine was herself again. She lifted her hand away from Davar's flesh knowing his soul was now being protected by the spirit essence of his mother.

"Gods!" Senia gasped. "I didn't think you'd need that much power! I could sleep for days. That was intense."

Cassine smiled weakly, also drained. "Thank you. This means a lot to me and will to him as well when he wakes."

"You care for him deeply." It wasn't a question. "He's a lucky man to have you."

Cassine nodded. "He tells me that every day."

"I would have never believed..." Senia shrugged and rose.

Cassine rose as well and hugged the other woman. "I'm in your debt."

"Pretty much everyone here is," Senia said lightly. "Luckily I forgive debts easily. Take care of yourself and..." she glanced at Davar. "And him. That will be repayment enough." She left taking Emberthorn with her.

Cassine returned to bed and Davar's warm embrace. He didn't tremble anymore that night and she finally found sleep.

The next morning Davar told her of how his mother had appeared amidst his nightmares to protect him from the darkness.

"I think she'll be there from now on," Cassine said with a grin. She told him what she'd done, finishing with, "You must remember that her spirit is within you and really always has been, along with all the darkness the Blacklord put there."

He thanked her, absentmindedly playing with the jewel she'd given him. It seemed to be glowing brighter today.

After a fortifying breakfast, they got back to work and things started going a lot easier for them. In one full day of effort, they'd reached what Cassine deemed to be the halfway point through one of the last remaining nasty snarls of emotions. The most progress they'd made in one day in weeks.

Again that night, Davar slept soundly and they both woke rested.

The following months had their ups and downs, but by the spring equinox festival, they were working on the last of the great bundles of darkness within him. Only a few more days and they would be finished... if things went well.

CHAPTER 15

*D*avar woke suddenly, warned by what noise or instinct he didn't know. Reacting instantly, he hardened his skin and put his arm up to block the blow aimed for his neck.

The mage-stim-enhanced blow from the assassin still sliced deeply into his toughened arm muscles, cutting to the bone. His mind trapped the pain and he kicked out at the assassin, hearing bones break at the impact. The man crumpled, his sword still in Davar's arm.

Good, now he had a weapon.

He pulled the sword from his arm with his other hand, taking in everything happening around him.

A second assassin came at him. Davar felt more than saw the man. His spirit talent picking out all life around him. To his eyes, the man was barely more than a shadow. There was little light in the room, shed from the open doorway out to the hall, where some distant torch burned. Another assassin carried a body out the door — Cassine. Two more assassins entered the room, as the one with Cassine left.

The guards outside the door were dead, he knew that. He didn't have time to wonder how the Blacklord's assassins had entered the abbey. He needed to save Cass, then he could worry about such details.

Davar called fire. The hand of his wounded arm flared brightly with a ball of flame, which he threw at the nearest assassin. The man shrugged it off, clothes incinerated, flesh burned, but such things meant little to one of enhanced durability. The attack had been more of a distraction than anything else. Davar had trained with assassins like these all his life. The abilities of one were identical to every other, a perfect copy made by the Blacklord. Davar knew their every strength and weakness, and he used all of that knowledge against them.

He surged his earth talent and his arm healed. With his newly acquired sword, he attacked the assassin he'd burned. The man blocked with his own sword, but didn't see Davar's off-hand punch to his face that collapsed his skull. That man fell as the two others attacked.

He let their hits fall, not bothering to block. Instead, he attacked them at the same time. He decapitated one, whose sword slid into Davar's stomach. The other assassin struck at his shoulder, cutting deep. Davar removed that man's sword arm, then ran him through the heart.

Davar plucked the weapons from his body, keeping one. Two weapons were always better than one unless the one was a scion blade, but he wasn't about to call Shadowfang, not yet anyway.

He surged his earth talent yet again, healing the new wounds, then ran.

Dead men lay everywhere, monk and assassin alike.

The assassins must have caught the abbey by surprise after so long with no night raids.

He didn't know which way the assassin with Cassine had gone so he sent his spirit sense out around him. So many were dying, lives flaring out all around him. There was one, still strong despite being unconscious, secondly only to Senia's and his own, which was easy to find.

The assassin had made good time and was reaching the bailey.

Davar pushed everything he had into enhancing his physical abilities and ran, faster than most would have thought possible, after the man with Cass. It was more power than he'd ever used at once, but the need was great. The extra effort strained his earth talent ability to its limits. Yet even as his long strides ate away at the distance between them, Davar knew he'd be too late.

Already the man was leaping up to the top of St. Antin's high walls.

Davar reached the bailey, the chill air of a spring night rushing around him. He jumped to follow the assassin, closing distance with incredible speed, but as he reached the top of the wall, the other man was bounding away.

Davar stopped, hesitating. He couldn't go any farther. One step beyond the walls, and he was the Blacklord's toy once more, which was exactly what the vile wizard wanted.

His heart churned as he watched the assassin land in the hills below St. Antin, then leap again down towards the army on the plains below.

He had to try. If he didn't, he'd loathe himself for being a coward.

He soared out into the night. His one leap alone would

take him to where the assassin would next land. Within less than a minute, he could be back within the walls of St. Antin.

But that would be far too long.

Already the Blacklord was raging around his mind, breaking down his barriers to get in. He put all he had left into bolstering the defenses of mind, soul, and spirit, but he knew the other man's power far exceeded his. It was only a matter of time, a very short matter of time. Again he pushed the limits of his power harder and farther than he ever had before, but he was tiring far too quickly at this rate. He knew it wouldn't be enough.

"No, you don't!" This from a voice nearby.

Senia.

An instant later, the flat of Emberthorn's massive blade hit him hard in the stomach, sending him flying backward. "I'll get her back!" the scion called sailing forward into the night.

He landed hard, his back smashing into the cobblestones in the bailey of St. Antin. The Blacklord shut out once again. His body healed quickly from the harsh landing, bones and sinews knitting together, but he was so exhausted from overextending himself in such a short period of time that even this healing was a strain. He simply lay there, staring up at the stars of a clear spring night. The chill bothered him little, able to call fire or bolster his body's defenses against the cold. But his inability to leave these walls clung to him, cloying and curdling within his belly.

He slammed his fist down into the paving stones, sending fragments flying as he shattered the rock. All of his power and still he was trapped. He couldn't leave the abbey, couldn't save Cass. He wondered if he ever would be able to leave, even after he was fully cleansed.

Senia landed next to him. "One healer as ordered." She

lay Cassine's body down. "There are still assassins around if you wanted to help."

Davar blinked. These were his people now and he should help. He nodded.

Though his strength was dwindling, he reached over and touched Cass. He wasn't trained in healing, but his physical talent was strong and he sent a wave of it into her. He could feel his reserves draining, but it was worth it. The gash on her head closed slightly and she started awake with a gasp.

"Heal and defend yourself. I'm going to help the others," he said and kissed her, seeing the wound on her head now closing from her own efforts.

"I'll be fine," she said, "go."

He smiled and rose to help Senia.

He let his fury at his incompetence fuel his hunt and give him the energy he desperately needed. The assassins seemed to have been after specific targets. He didn't realize he was getting close to Shadowfang until the sword called to him.

Help me! The voice was an odd, twisted echo of the joyously evil sing-song it once had been.

Get out! Davar commanded and reinforced his mental defenses.

He was near the archival vault. He'd never been here before, but he knew it from Cassine's description of the place: a massive room, deep below the abbey, with a great metal door usually locked by several means, mundane and magical.

The door was slightly ajar, more than enough for a person to slip through.

An assassin stepped out with a load of weapons, all Aehryn-Gift artifacts. One of them was Shadowfang.

The hallway was tall and the assassin tried to jump over Davar. A flick of his wrist sent one of his swords flying. The black-clad man died in probably one of the most painful ways possible, the blade buried to the hilt between his legs. The dead man and the weapons he carried crashed to the ground with a loud clanging and clattering.

Four more figures emerged from the vault, all assassins.

Davar picked up the nearest weapon, a long hafted axe. It was incredibly heavy, as was the case with some of the artifacts, too heavy to be wielded effectively by most people, except their scion. With his great strength, he was able to heft the weapon in one hand, even if it strained his waning power to its limits to do so.

The four assassins attacked as one. Two threw daggers. The other two leapt at him. The daggers were a distraction. He knocked one away with the sword still in his off hand, letting the other sink into his shoulder.

He instantly realized he'd made a mistake.

The wound was too much, especially in the shoulder of the arm holding the massively heavy axe. He had to drop the scion weapon to give himself the energy to recover.

He pulled out the dagger with his now free hand, but he'd taken too long to do so; the other two assassins were on him.

He blocked one attack, his sword deflecting the assassin's blade as the man descended on him. The other attack, to his already wounded side, bit deeply into his upper arm. His shoulder wound still hadn't fully healed and his ability to heal himself was slowing as he reached the limits of his endurance. Even the block in his mind that deadened pain was weakening and he grit his teeth at the shock of this most recent hit. The two men near him moved to the sides, flanking him as the other two threw more knives his way, slowly moving in.

They were too many and he was too slow. Davar

managed to take one down, his sword delivering a crushing blow to the base of the neck, nearly decapitating the man. But that left Davar's other side exposed and he felt the burn of a blade sinking deep into his abdomen. He tried to simply evade the knives, but one bit into his leg, hitting a vital spot then falling out with a gush of blood. He kicked the man near him, but it was a feeble strike and despite crushing the assassin against the wall, the man was still up, still going, if dazed.

Davar grasped the wound on his thigh, trying to stop the flow of blood, but he felt the hot liquid oozing through his fingers. He staggered back. He needed more time. He poured every ounce of energy he had left into healing his leg and abdomen. The wounds closed, somewhat, the flow of blood from his leg now only a trickle, but he was spent. His head spun. He knew he was finished if he didn't do something quickly.

"Shadowf—" A dagger bounced off his skull taking a slice of scalp and hair with it. Then a man hit him full force, knocking him down.

Too slow, far too slow, he punched at the assassin. His arm was blocked and in the next instant, a blade opened his throat. His life drained out of him.

Back when he'd belonged to the Blacklord, anytime he'd been overextended in combat, the Blacklord could shunt more energy into him.

But that wouldn't happen this time.

His vision blurred, going dark, and he knew he had failed.

In that instant, before he died, he also knew with a sickening dread that he'd doomed the world. For without him the prophecy of the fall of the Blacklord could not come to pass.

He felt a blade sink into his chest, into his heart. Then he felt no more.

~

*H*is eyes flashed open, his body rejecting the blade in his chest, pushing it out, his wounds closing, raw earth talent-energy rushing into him, filling him.

"No!" A desperate cry, echoed through the hallway. The voice had been Cassine's.

He threw the man on his chest off, bashing him against the wall, shattering bones. That assassin went limp. Davar rolled to his feet with the grace and speed he was so used to.

A surprised assassin stood before him and died before he could react, neck broken. Another leapt at him and he easily dodged to the side knocking the man's weapon away and bringing an elbow down on the back of the man's neck, breaking it.

He swung around, ready for more, but none presented themselves. The only other person around was Cass, down the hall a ways, looking exhausted, leaning against the wall.

She waved a weak, limp arm. "Hi, love."

He ran to her, barely breathing hard. "Was that you that brought me back?"

She nodded.

"I thought you had to touch someone to heal them?"

"So did I," she said with a faint smile. "Until now." She tried pushing herself off the wall, but couldn't do it. "Gods, but that took a lot out of me. I thought you were dead."

"So did I." He turned around slowly again. "I should check in the vault to make sure there are no more."

"Go," she said.

He did.

The vault was massive. There was no way he could search it all quickly. If he did it would still be easy enough for someone to evade his search and slip around him. So he sent his life-sense out. There were several weak essences in the hall, people dying, no others.

He ran back to Cass, pulling her from the wall, supporting her.

"Take back some of your power, there are wounded in there who need healing and you're a lot better at that than I am."

She nodded and he felt some of his earth talent energy slip from him. She perked up, standing on her own.

"Bring them all to one spot. That will make it easier for me to heal them all quickly."

Davar ran off to do so.

He found four monks still alive, if barely, and brought them to her. She was able to heal them all, despite their extensive wounds. Afterward she sat back with a heavy sigh. Even having taken some of her power back, she looked tired and worn.

He took a moment to wonder at the attack. What did this mean? Was it the beginning of a new offensive or some last ditch effort by the Blacklord's armies? Whatever it was it had worked well, if not as well as it could have. They hadn't taken any scion-weapons, but they had nearly killed him and he was certain that dozens, if not hundreds of monks had died tonight. This would be a solid blow against the forces of the abbey.

Yet more intimately, he wondered if he'd brought this all down on his new allies. The assassins had carried Cass away, almost certainly a ploy to get him to leave the abbey and return to this father. When he hadn't they had been doing their best to end him and had almost succeeded. He couldn't shake the feeling that he'd somehow caused this attack with his mere presence. But perhaps that was a bit arrogant.

His thoughts were interrupted by Cass. "Is this all the monks here?" She motioned to the four she'd healed.

He nodded.

Her eyes showed a grave concern. "Gods, I hope some escaped. There were more than a score of monks working down here and if these are all that remain..." She shook her head.

"I'm sorry, Cass."

"You have no need to be. We did all we could." She let out another heavy sigh. "I'm going to take a nap now." And she did, laying her head on her arms on the cold stone floor of the archives. She was asleep within a few heartbeats.

He smiled faintly, also exhausted, but not ready to sleep.

He left the vault, closing the massive door, and swept the area. When he met Wyllea doing the same, he told her of what had happened.

"Gods!" she muttered, shaking her head. "Far too many died tonight."

"Are we clear now?" he asked.

"I believe so."

"Good, if you need me, I'll be in the archives sleeping."

She gave him an odd look at that but said nothing.

He returned to Cass, curled up next to her, and let his body rest.

CHAPTER 16

*C*assine had little chance to recover from her exhaustion.

Hundreds of monks were dead, but more were wounded. There had also been attacks on the western kingdom's armies camped in the hills around St. Antin. Generals and officers killed, many wounded, all in all a devastating blow.

Cassine had been busy for days healing and tending to the wounded. Only a few of the Daughters of Ehlani had survived. The Daughters had been another target of the assassins. It was a strategic move, killing those who could heal. Of the twenty-seven sisters, eighteen had died. High Sister Olinda had survived only through the sheer power of her healing ability. She'd been left for dead with wounds grave enough to ensure any warrior's demise, but she'd drained her earth talent to heal herself as best she could. She still bore a scar on her forehead, which she kept as a reminder to be vigilant. Cassine had no time to work on Davar or Starsong for more than a week. Even once she did, he insisted she rest before they continued.

When she did finally get back to Davar, she found the last vestiges of his darkness had spread once again. It was like a pillar of black marble in his soul, hard and sturdy. She'd need to chip away at it, finding veins within the marble to isolate and eliminate, weakening it until the core could be dealt with. This was the heart of Davar's darkness, the vilest stains on his soul, the worse of his life before.

It took another week, working only in spurts when she had time, to banish enough strands within that massive block to weaken it to the point where Cassine thought she could then deal with that solid core.

Finally she had the time and had regained enough energy to feel she had a chance to eliminate the final blackness for good. She'd slept well the night before as her healing duties had decreased enough to allow for a restful evening off.

She sat next to Davar on his cot as he lay on his back. He too would have to work hard today during the cleansing process. Laying her hand on his chest, she looked him in the eye.

"Ready?"

He nodded. "I've been waiting a long time for this."

She flashed him a smile then drew in a long breath and began.

When she was inside his soul, it was an almost physical place for her. A vast space now filled mostly with light. There was no ground or sky, just light. In this light, there stood the pillar which sucked in all illumination around it. *Stood* was a relative term as there was nothing to stand on. It hung in the space, stretching high and low, as thick around as a great and aged oak. Though it was hard as marble it was riddled with holes and flaws from her work so far on weakening it. Even drawing near it was uncomfortable, it wanted to suck the light out of her soul and fill it with inky, writhing darkness. Yet she drew close enough to connect with it, touch it, for that was the only way to eliminate it.

She felt Davar flinch and tense as she began her work. In some ways this process was like removing a splinter from the skin, only the splinter was a mile long pillar and as such it was that much more painful to remove. Cassine couldn't see the memories Davar was experiencing, but she could feel the emotions associated with them: hate, joy at destruction and violation of innocence, anger and rage, and perhaps the worst of all complacency at deeds which would horrify the most hardened of men.

Ever so slowly, the pillar lost chunks that crumbled into nothing, but the bits were small still and Cassine had no illusions that this was still only the start of a lot of work for them both.

Time was hard to perceive in this place of the soul, but Cassine knew that hours had passed. Davar's body in the real world was a mess of sweat, as he alternated between moaning and screaming as they worked harder and harder. There were great gouges in the column of darkness now, but it was still so vast as to seem impossible to cure. Yet they had to push on. Cassine was certain that if left unfinished it would work itself back to a strong state in the time they took to rest. She was exhausted, and she knew Davar was straining his limits as well, but still she pushed onward.

And she was rewarded with a surprise, even if it wasn't a pleasant one.

Another chunk of blackness fell away, this time revealing a fiery core within the dark pillar.

It was like a vein of blood, but it carried only evil, distributing it to the pillar, feeding it. This was the reason it regenerated so fast, she was certain of it.

She connected with the red, pulsing line and instantly flinched back. It had been too much, too corrupt, too malevolent for her to touch for long. But she forced herself to contact it again and this time it was her screaming out in the real world.

Through that scream, she made a mental connection with Davar and asked, *This, can you feel it? What's here? I think if we can eliminate this, the rest of this evil will fall away.*

Yes, I feel it. And even though it was a mental reply, it sounded like he spoke through gritted teeth. *It's... indescribable evil. I think you're probably right. Do what you must and let's finish this.*

She forced all of her power of soul onto this vile heart of Davar's evil and felt it send a rush of feelings and memories which overwhelmed him for a moment. She sensed his body tense so hard that it arched, his back leaving the cot. Though her eyes were closed she knew his mouth was contorted in a scream, but no sound came out, so extreme was the sensation.

I can't. His mental voice was only a gasp.

You must.

She was being consumed, burning as well, at least her soul was. Every moment in contact with this cord of purest evil defiled and corrupted her. She could feel traces of darkness seep into her soul, thin tendrils now, but the longer she stayed in contact, the stronger she knew they would grow.

This isn't me! He cried out to her mind. *This is him, his evil, I—*

This is you, it's a part of you, even if it was him who instilled it here so very long ago. It's a part of you now, and you need to accept it, deal with it in order to move past it and eliminate it. So do what you must! I can feel it weakening, but it won't go away until you are strong enough to release it.

It's too much!

Nothing is too much for you. You're the most powerful man I know.

She felt his resolve shift and strengthen; some part of his spirit wouldn't allow him to give up. Cassine felt a presence with her, though she saw no other entities within Davar's soul.

Another voice joined them, though it was distant, almost too faint for Cassine to hear.

Fight him, my son, as I did. He didn't win. He never bested me. All he could do was kill me in the end.

Cassine felt Davar pushing through the pain which seared him body and soul. Yet even as he did, she felt the darkness infest more of her soul. This needed to end... before she was too far gone into the Blacklord's evil.

~

*D*avar's body was so tense it trembled, every muscle flexed and taut. His teeth were tight, grinding. His eyes clenched shut. Pain wracked him and billowed like wildfire in his soul.

His mind was a whirlwind of images. Unlike his other healings where there was a single moment in time which played out for him, this was jumbled and most of it wasn't his memory. It was disorienting and confusing. He was seeing and living his mother's pain and at the same time experiencing the twisted, euphoric exhilaration of the Blacklord himself as he tortured the woman. Nine months worth of pain and suffering was being thrown at him in a series of snippets and flickering images, hard enough to understand as it was, harder still while fighting the agony within his body.

Yet he would catch one of these memory fractions and put everything he had into accepting it. That was all he could do. This was an area of his life where he'd had no control at all. All of this had been done to him, and as much as he might have wanted to never imagine such things, he didn't have a choice if he wanted to remove this stain from his soul. He could only accept that this evil had happened, that his mother had endured unimaginable torment for what had seemed like an eternity while carrying him. He knew someday he would face his father and that would be the day when he could do something about this horror, but for now he had to simply acknowledge and accept what had happened as much as it was loathsome and vile.

Slowly he worked, grabbing images, feeling the torment associated with them then moving on. It seemed like hours, days. He grew faint, his energy waning, his resolve fading, but every time he did Cass would be there, spurring him onward.

Because there was no order or logic to the images he couldn't follow them through time, he didn't know how many more there would be. It seemed like there were millions of them.

Time stretched minutes into days.

I don't know how much more of this I can do, he said to Cass through their connection.

She was so strained. She didn't even respond, he just felt her reassurance, though with it there was something else... fear?

Then suddenly there was no more room for thought or communication. His mind exploded with light and pain. It took him a moment to realize he'd reached the moment of his birth, the confluence of so much hatred, pain, and darkness. It was a violent birth, which perhaps was not unexpected. For a moment, he felt the ultimate pain from his mother. Davar knew then, that it hadn't been the Blacklord who had killed his mother, it had been him, his birth. He'd sucked the living energy from the woman and destroyed her, sending her over the edge of pain and agony into death.

For a fraction of a heartbeat that tore at him, breaking him. Knowing he had killed his mother.

Then her voice came to him. *No Davar, do not despair. Don't you see? You saved me! Don't you think the Blacklord would have wanted to keep me alive? He'd have been able to spawn more kin for him? Somehow, even though you were only a babe, you knew this. You took a part of me with you and allowed me finally to rest. You brought me to peace, my son. Thank you.*

Then it was over, and the darkness was gone from him. He'd succeeded and destroyed what the Blacklord had put within him.

His body went slack, exhausted.

～

*C*ass felt the explosion of that fiery line of hatred and evil within Davar.

The blazing vile core vanished and with it, the rest of the black pillar crumbled. What remained was only peace and light.

The fingers of darkness which had reached into her soul begin to recede. They would fade to nothing in time now. She knew that if she had been in contact with that pure evil much longer she might have been tainted herself, but now she'd be saved that fate. She was too exhausted to be happy about that.

She drew herself out of Davar's soul and shuddered once she felt her body once again. Everything ached. Sweat had matted her hair and soaked through her clothes. She was filthy, but again too tired to care.

"It's done," she said, her voice hoarse. She met Davar's gaze — though his eyes were half-shut with fatigue — and smiled. He tried to smile, but he was already fading into sleep. She too felt her eyelids growing ever heavier. Putting her head on his chest, she yielded to sleep.

It must have been some time later when Cassine awoke since she actually felt rested. Davar was laying on his side next to her, playing with the glowing jewel, her gift, an odd look on his face. The stone was the only light in the room.

"What's wrong?" she asked.

"I thought I'd feel different," he said as he held up the smooth oval stone. "I thought I'd feel like this stone, all soft and glowing and smooth, but instead..." he grimaced and waved his head back and forth for a moment, uneasy. "Instead, I still feel like I've got a lot of jagged edges. I thought I'd be pure and perfect, like you."

She had to smile. "I'm not perfect, Davar."

He glanced at her. "Yes, you are."

Her smile turned to a curt laugh. "No, I'm not. I have doubt and fear. I don't always make the right choices. It's called being human."

He sighed. "I've always been more than human."

"No," she said shaking her head slightly. "You're excep-tional in many ways, but as far as your soul goes, you're as human as the rest of us. Your emotions betray you, heaving up when you wish they would quiet, shining through when you wish they'd hide. None of us are perfect when it comes to our feelings."

"Oh."

She looked away for a moment still ashamed. "If you recall, I was the one who wanted to wait to be with you, but then nearly gave myself to you before we were ready. Emotions are unsteady things that take a lifetime to understand, but I don't think anyone ever masters them." She pushed those thoughts away as she brought her gaze back to him.

"Speaking of being together..." he said with a grin spreading across his face.

"Yes?" she asked, blinking her lashes in feigned innocence.

His face turned somber for a moment. "We're both weary still, are you ready for this now?"

She put her hand behind his head and pulled herself up, half-sitting, to bring her lips to his in a deep kiss. When she drew back, she said simply, "Yes. Though I may not be up for too much." With this, she slid off the bed and lifted off her dress.

For a moment, there was a flash of a memory, the last time she'd been naked in front of him. Only it hadn't been him. The Blacklord had been controlling him. She shivered, partly from the cold of the room, partly from that memory. Fear pierced her heart, but then she saw the look in his eyes. It wasn't the cold appraisal the Blacklord had given her, but one of warmth, tenderness, and love.

He brought a ball of flame to life in one hand, then he blew it gently from his hand as if blowing a kiss. It floated in the air, a torch with no handle. Four more times he created such glowing orbs, sending them off to float around them.

"I want to see you in all your splendor," he said, his voice huskier than usual. He smiled softly, simply taking her in for a moment before breathing out a sigh. "You are the most beautiful woman I've ever seen... and I've lived for two hundred years."

Feeling the fire of the floating torches around her, she warmed. In fact, it seemed now the room was growing quite hot. She could see the longing in his eyes. That had always been there, his clear admiration for her, the physical desire. She'd brushed it aside before now. They hadn't been ready. Yet, now with the purity, the light that shone within him she was faced with it at last. She found it mirrored her own desire. Her body was responding, growing warm from more than just the fires around her.

She, too, loved to simply look at him. He was already shirtless, his broad chest, wide shoulders and thick arms exposed. The flickering light of the fires still only served to emphasize his muscles, every ridge and line cast in sharp shadows over his skin.

He rose and removed his breeches. There was even more of him to admire now.

She trembled for a moment a different fear and trepidation filling her.

"This will be my first time."

"I know," he said softly. "I'll be careful."

She shook her head. She wasn't sure if she wanted careful or not. It was more a matter of..." I don't know... anything. I don't know what I want or... I just don't know. I'm unsure of—"

He raised a hand to silence her. "I understand." He stepped in close, his body brushing hers in all manner of enjoyable ways. His hand slid behind her head, strong but still tender and he kissed her delicately.

When they drew apart, their faces were so close that when he spoke his lips brushed hers. "I love you Cassine," he whispered.

The raw emotion in his voice touched her deeply, for it was not desire, not passion, not need or want, but a pure and tender love.

Tears came to her eyes. "I love you too, Davar."

"And I am anything but unsure." He gave her a quick peck. "We'll explore this together, follow each other's lead. Let me know what you like and what you don't and I'll do the same. Don't worry too much." He kissed her again, longer, deeper, pressing his body harder to hers in a heated embrace. "Did you like that?" he asked as his lips left hers.

She gave an exasperated sigh. "Yes, I think you know that."

"Well then, let's see what else you like." He began to explore and she finally relaxed into the pleasant sensations.

The anticipation of the past months and the tension she'd felt for this moment slipped away finally into a glorious exploration and celebration of their love.

∾

*D*uties dragged Cassine away despite a pull to be with Davar. After their exploratory first time together, she was anxious to feel his embrace once more. Throughout the day, she'd have a thrill go down her spine, shaking momentarily with the remembrance of their shared love.

She attended a counsel in the High Abbots chambers, but

her thoughts were elsewhere. They were planning a great strike against the enemy forces on the plains below and she and her sisters would be needed more than ever to help the wounded. She caught that much and that was all. At the end of the meeting, High Sister Olinda pulled her aside.

"Are you well my child? You seem flushed and distracted."

Cassine blinked, a blush blooming on her cheeks. "Oh, very well, just... tired," she said and it was the truth, if not all of it.

The High Sister seemed to accept this, saying nothing further. She did smile faintly, lips pressed as if trying to keep in something. Then she left and Cassine's heart stopped racing or at least raced less from embarrassment and more from anticipation of returning to Davar.

Her session with Starsong was fruitless. She still couldn't understand how to alter the soul within the sword. With Davar, he had wanted to change. He'd been the one who'd faced and dealt with his emotions, she'd simply helped him. Yet Shadowfang didn't want to change and forcing it wasn't working as she'd hoped. She gave up early and retreated to Davar's chambers.

As she arrived, Wyllea was leaving. The scion stopped and greeted her as a slow, mischievous grin spread over the other woman's face.

"Wyllea? What are you doing here?"

"I think I might have a way to keep the Blacklord from getting into his head again. We're going to give it a try tomorrow." She kept a straight face as she spoke, but couldn't help but breathe a few laughs at something when she finished.

"What?"

"I read minds remember. I try not to out of habit, but sometimes when people are having really strong thoughts it's hard to ignore." She patted Cassine's shoulder. "I wish you and Davar all the happiness Tirol and I have found. Now get in there and be with your man before you make me blush." Wyllea smiled and hurried off.

Blushing herself, Cassine entered the room.

"Great news!" Davar said leaping up from his bunk. "Wyllea thinks there may be a way to keep the Blacklord out."

"Yes, I just spoke with her. You're going to try it tomorrow," she said lifting off her dress.

He raised a brow. "Aren't we eager?"

"Yes," she said, her heart pounding with excitement to be with him again. "I haven't been able to stop thinking about you all day." She'd closed the distance between them and was undoing the laces of his shirt. He lifted it off and her hands then went down to his breeches, unlacing them. They slid to the floor.

"What have you been thinking of?" she asked playfully.

"Whatever it was, I've forgotten now," he said pulling her close for a hard, deep kiss.

She didn't feel unsure this time. She knew from their previous time together he was a caring lover and had learned just how wonderful he could be. He showed her even more of his patience and passion as they came together again.

She let herself go, feeling all of the wonderful sensations of their joining as he pleasured her for what seems like hours, a timelessness of paradise. Her passion, like waves crashing on a shore, built to greater and greater peaks until she could take no more and she opened her soul to Davar.

She felt his ecstasy and pleasure, reveling in their joining. But he was holding back, restraining himself to ensure their time lasted as long as it could. When her own bliss poured into him from the connection she'd made and he suddenly felt everything she was, that all ended.

Together they cried out, wordless. They shared one perfect moment of harmony in a culmination and explosion of their passion.

Her eyes, which had been clenched shut for that heavenly instant, opened to find the room lit nearly as bright as day. It took her a moment to realize it was her. Golden light emanated from her skin, similar to the time long ago when she'd nearly given herself to him. Only this time it was ten times brighter, near to blinding. This was how she manifested her elation: as a combined joy of mind, soul, body, and spirit. It was beautiful.

It was a little while later, as they lay exhausted next to each other, when Davar asked, "What was that, at the end? You did something."

"I opened up my soul to you. You felt what I was feeling."

"Gods Cass, truly?" he whispered, a grin spreading on his face. "I... I would have never imagined." He brushed his lips on hers and she responded, playing for a moment. When he drew back, he grinned. "You nearly blinded me at the end there."

She giggled and squirmed a little, remembering. "I think that's just how I show my pleasure. I'm guessing it's a multi-talent thing. When I'm feeling really good in all four elements, I guess... I glow." She couldn't help another little laugh. "It's just that no one's ever made me feel that good on all levels before. That's what you do to me. You're amazing."

He joined her laughter for a moment. When it had died down, he simply said, "We're amazing."

"I like that." She snuggled closer to him. Her skin was

cooling and the room was starting to feel less... hot than it had. "We're amazing." She kissed him.

As their lips separated, he ran a hand up her side and she felt a thrill run through her. He smiled mischievously. "And we can be again."

That sounded like an amazing idea. She once again relaxed into his tender ministrations, fairly certain she'd be glowing again before long.

CHAPTER 17

*D*avar checked the knife. It was as sharp as any he'd known. He nodded and handed it back to Wyllea. "Go ahead."

Wyllea looked over to Cass who stood close, next to Davar, her body pressed to his arm. He was sitting and Cass standing, which would make the procedure to come easier for all. He grabbed her thigh with a hand and gave it a squeeze to reassure her.

They were in a small room with a window letting in the blazing sun and warming air of an early spring day.

"It'll be fine," he said turning his head to look up at her. The sight of her round bosom right there above his shoulders sent a thrill through him as he remembered their time together the previous night. Gods, but he was a lucky man.

She smiled faintly but didn't seem much reassured. Then she let out a breath of a laugh and grimaced. "This probably won't hurt you at all, but I can't seem to make my feelings understand that."

"I could squirm a little if you like; to make it look like it hurts," he said, his tone playful, teasing.

"No, don't. I couldn't handle that."

"Fine."

"Are you two done now?" Wyllea said with a half grin. "I know you certainly didn't get done with each other last night until late."

Davar watched Cass blush furiously, the deep red blooming over her face and sinking into the collar of her dress.

"Sorry," Wyllea said with a chuckle. "I can be a bit crass. I'll stop with the mind reading."

"Yes, please," Cass said intently.

Davar just chuckled lightly. He didn't much mind anyone reading his thoughts now. His soul and his mind were clean, for the first time ever. As for his thoughts about Cass, they were pure too, borne out of his love and desire for her. Everything he wanted to do with her was for her benefit and pleasure, and he didn't see anything wrong with that. He could see how Cass could get embarrassed by such thoughts, however, so he'd keep as much as he could to himself.

Wyllea tapped the dull side of the knife against her hand. She spoke to Cass. "There's something you should probably know. After today, I'm going to have a link to your man's mind. I won't even have to try. I'll know what he's thinking. In fact, I'll probably have to work at keeping him tuned out. Are you good with that?"

"Oh, really? Ah..." Cass seemed a bit taken aback by this.

"It will be fine Cass," Davar said. "Besides, it's not like we have many other options."

Cass pursed her lips then sighed. "You're right. I guess I can live with that if you can."

"I can."

"Fine, then," Wyllea said preparing the knife. "Let's begin."

The procedure was simple... in theory. Wyllea had come up with it after Davar had told everyone about how the abbey itself blocked the Blacklord from contacting him. Wyllea had done a little research into the spells that had been carved into the walls of the abbey with the help from old Anar from the archives, before his death in the raid. She'd found that some of the runes contained mind magic specific to keeping mental communication out.

So they were going to try to use her mind talent to raise a shield around his mind. But to make it permanent, they needed to carve those same runes into his skull.

Davar was only slightly concerned. The pain of someone carving into the bone around his head he could block, but to make sure he didn't heal the bone instantly, he'd had to completely shut down his earth talent. The healing would be done by Cass, carefully healing the skin, but not the bone. Actually, she would heal the bone too, but in a special way that would leave the carving intact. This way his body wouldn't try to heal the bone when he put his talent back up again. It was beyond his ability to do such delicate healing work, so he was thankful to have her there.

Wyllea began, digging the knife into his forehead. There was a moment of sharp pain before his mind blocked it out. After that, he was left with the odd sensation of the knife in his skin, digging into bone, but no pain. Blood ran down along his nose, and he absent-mindedly wiped it away.

His hand, still on Cass' thigh felt her tremble slightly. She could see what was happening and despite all the war wounds she might have witnessed in her time, he didn't doubt it was altogether different to watch someone you love being intentionally harmed. Yet she stayed strong and said nothing.

"Done. Three to go," Wyllea said, moving to Davar's side.

Cass moved in front and placed warm fingers next to the wound. Davar could feel the skin knitting together once again, and an odd sensation like an intense headache washed over him for a moment then vanished.

Cass knelt before him, her smile forced. "I feel better now. Hang in there. We still have three more to do." Her words sounded as if they were meant to reassure him, but he didn't need it. He guessed they were more for her benefit than his.

He smiled back, not wanting to speak for fear the movement of his head might throw off Wyllea where she carved into him above his ear.

And so it went with Wyllea carving and Cass healing until the last rune over his left ear. When Wyllea had finished carving, before Cass came to heal, she pressed two fingers into the wound onto the bone of his head and crashed through into his mind.

Davar screamed, not from the intrusion, but because when she'd broken through he'd lost his protection from pain. So he felt the full glory of a rather nasty open wound on the side of his head into which she was poking her fingers.

This will only take a moment. I'm sorry for the pain, Wyllea said into his mind. I need to set up the barrier and fuse it to the runes. Please lower all of your mental defenses.

It was hard. He rarely had all his defenses down. With the intense pain over his ear he wanted nothing more than to throw up his mental shields and block everything out, but he knew this wouldn't work if he did. So he dropped all his mental defenses, feeling bare and exposed to the world physically and mentally. The only time before he'd ever been this open, this vulnerable, was when he'd been bonded to Cass after teleporting.

He focused on that memory, those moments, the pleasure and joy he felt. The angel who'd chosen him and everything she'd done for him since.

All done. Wyllea left his mind, taking her fingers from his head.

Cass moved into heal quickly.

Davar raised his defenses as soon as she was done.

"Try putting your mental defenses back up again," Wyllea said

"They are up."

"Oh." *And can you hear me?*

Yes.

Wow, that was easy. Are you sure your defenses are all the way up, I can't feel any resistance at all.

They're fully in place. Glad to know you can slip by them so easily now.

Don't worry. I won't do it often. I'll let you have your privacy... most of the time.

Can he hear me, too? This from a new voice in his head.

Who's that? Davar asked.

That's Eaglewing, apparently being connected to me means being connected to her.

Oh. Great. Now he had a bow in his head too.

Not just any bow! Eaglewing said indignantly. *Also, sorry about nearly killing you all those months ago.*

It's ok. Can we stop now? This is getting weird.

Done. Blocking you out.

"Thanks."

"Any time," Wyllea said. "I'll leave you two alone now. Try

not to have any thoughts that are too intense right away, I'm still new at this connection and may have trouble blocking them out."

"Noted."

Wyllea stopped at the door. "Tomorrow morning come up to the bailey. Senia and I will be waiting. We need to see if this really works and if you can go beyond the wall now."

He nodded and she left.

Cass sat sideways in his lap, throwing her arms around his neck and hugging him close. His head was cradled on her breasts, soft and yielding. He felt a spike of arousal but ignored it to simply embrace her in return.

The door opened. "What did I say about intense thoughts?" Wyllea yelled.

"Sorry. My fault I think," Cass said sheepishly.

Wyllea shook her head. "Can't you two keep your hands off each other for one minute?" She sighed. "Well, try to keep *it* down, will you." She pointed to Davar then slammed the door leaving again.

Cass laughed. "Oh, the things I could do right now to get you into trouble."

Davar was trying really, really hard not to imagine those things, but the effort seemed ridiculous. He couldn't stop laughter from bubbling up from within. He steadied himself slowly thinking of nice calm thoughts, a pleasant meal, a sunset. "Please don't," he said. "Wyllea would never forgive us."

Cass slid off his lap. "Fine. I should continue my work with Starsong anyway."

Davar knew she was still having trouble with the soul in the sword. "Perhaps I could come down and help some time, just probably not today, if I'm supposed to stay away from intense thoughts. I don't think Wyllea wants to hear about my loathing for that thing. Though that might be preferable to my thoughts about you."

"And what are these intense thoughts about me?"

"I…" He grimaced. "You little troublemaker. Do you want her to know everything about us?"

Cass laughed. "Something tells me she already does. But I love you, and I don't care what people know. It won't affect how I feel."

"You don't mind her knowing the details of what we did last night? Every… little… detail?"

Cass flushed again. It spread from her cheeks to her entire face and down into her cleavage. "Well, perhaps not."

"I didn't think so. Now, go do your work before I start remembering things."

She smiled, came back to him for a quick kiss, then left.

❧

The next morning Davar stood on the wall of St. Antin, fear and doubt plaguing him. The day was dark, thick clouds overhead seeming to emulate his mood. The weather had turned colder too, but he could block that out. A strong wind buffeted him atop the wall and he tried to use the cold on his face to blow away his fear, but it wouldn't go.

"How goes the war?" He asked in hopes of distracting himself and perhaps them, from what was to come.

Senia and Wyllea stood on either side of him. It was Senia who responded. "Well enough. They've done little since the raid, as have we. We're planning a strike soon. We can no longer just let them sit and wait for more reinforcements.

With our forces depleted of healers and leaders after that raid, we need to strike fast and eliminate them as a threat."

"Enough stalling, you ready big guy?" Wyllea asked bluntly.

He nodded.

"Remember jump down to the base of the wall, don't go too far," Senia said. Of all of them, she was most restricted in how far and how fast she could move.

He nodded again, walked to the edge, vaulted over the crenellations, and fell the fifty feet to the ground.

He waited, expecting the Blacklord to sense him, break through his barriers, but nothing happened.

The two scions landed beside him, weapons ready.

"Seems to be working," he said cautiously.

"How do we know?" Wyllea asked.

"You're the one who can get into my head whenever she wants."

She grimaced. "Right." He felt her inside his mind, looking around. "Looks clean-ish in there."

"I think the wards must be working." Davar nodded. "I haven't even felt him try to reach me. I don't think he knows I've left the abbey, which means I'm invisible to him. It worked."

Wyllea relaxed a little, but Senia not seeing his mind was skeptical. "How can we know for sure?"

Davar smiled. "Because I'm about to willingly go back." He pointed at the walls of St. Antin. "If the Blacklord had any sway over me, there would be no way he'd let me do that and lose control of me again."

Senia cocked her head to one side. "Understood. Let's go then."

All three of them leapt back up to the top of the wall, then down into the Bailey. There was a mutual feeling between them, like some great sigh of relief.

"Well it seems we're good to go. Now we just need to win the war," Wyllea said.

"That and I'd like to get my sword back before we leave. A scion without their bonded weapon is—"

"Still a very powerful multi-talent, at least in your case." Wyllea finished for him. "But I understand your point. And we'll want every advantage going up against the Blacklord."

Davar nodded. "Cass hasn't been having a lot of luck with the sword so far and with only two and a half months left before we go, I'm starting to worry... a little."

"Win a war, undo the curse on a sword, defeat the most powerful wizard of all time, I'm glad we're not overburdened or anything," Wyllea said acidly.

"I don't know how much Wyllea and I will be involved in the planning for the upcoming attack, but perhaps we can help Cass with the sword?" Senia offered.

"Perhaps. I'll ask her what she needs," Davar said. "Good-day ladies."

He found Cass in the archives working with Shadowfang. He still thought of the blade as Shadowfang despite knowing its proper name was Starsong. There was far too much evil in the blade for Davar to acknowledge the new name yet.

She looked up as he entered and a smile spread across her weary face. His heart bloomed whenever he saw her happy. She was everything to him now.

It occurred to him that the purpose of Cass healing him had been to him figure out who he was without the Blacklord's influence. Well, he knew now. He was a man who loved Cass with every fiber of his being. Her joy was his joy, and her pain was his sorrow as well. He had lived to destroy and inflict pain before. Now he lived to serve her and to grow as a man to be more like the ideal she set as a person.

She ran over to him, embracing him intensely. "It's so good to see you," she said, then released him, falling a little to stand before him. "How did it go today?"

"I'm free," he said with a grin.

She hugged him again, her voice slightly muffled from her face being pressed into his shoulder as she said, "I'm so happy for you!"

"How do things progress with... that?" he asked motioning to the sword when she'd disengaged again.

She grimaced, sighing. "More of the same. You've heard it all before."

He approached the large marble table on which the sword lay. It seemed different to him, but only slightly. Cass had the area lit with several balls of intense light and even with the light-drinking black blade the intricate detailing on the blade, guard, and hilt were clear.

He reached out to the rounded pommel, noticing the starburst pattern inlaid there.

"Was this here before?" he asked.

She came over to look. "Yes, I think so, why? Don't you remember it?"

"No. Odd." His hand hovered over the hilt. A sudden realization hit him and he drew his arm back sharply. He blinked, looking from his hand to the blade then inward to his thoughts. He couldn't sense Shadowfang at all. Could Wyllea's shield be keeping the sword out as well?

"What is it? Is the sword calling to you?" Cass asked.

"No just the opposite actually. I can't hear it at all. Usually if I'm this close it's screaming at me." He tentatively reached out and touched the pommel, retracting his hand quickly.

There had been a moment of connection with the sword when he'd touched it, but after that, there was nothing.

The moment had been more than enough, though. "You must be doing something right. The sword is in pain. It doesn't like what's happening. I'm thinking that's a good sign."

She shook her head. "You got all that from the barest of touches and I still have yet to even really connect with the soul in this sword. That's my real problem. I'm trying to change something I don't even understand."

He could see the frustration plainly on her face, hear the defeat in her voice. "It's been months, and I've yet to make any real progress."

He stepped in to hold her close, her disappointment and concern pricking him, his pain echoing hers.

"I could help." The words were out before could stop them. He didn't want to help. He didn't want to be anywhere near this sword as it was. Yet he now knew that love meant sometimes doing things you really didn't want to do. Besides he couldn't stand by and watch her suffering if there was something he could do. "If you connect to the sword through me that might make things easier."

She looked at him, her eyes softening. "You would do that? I know how much it pains you to deal with the sword. Thank you." After a moment she added, "Is there any risk you'll..."

"Go evil? I don't think so. Shadowfang could control me last time because I was still very far gone to darkness. Now I have a lot of light in me to resist his call for slaughter. Also with Wyllea's block in my head, I think that also limits the connection. I think I could allow someone in or in this case *something*, but put the walls back up if I need to." He put a hand on her cheek, caressing it. "As for my willingness to help, you know I'd do anything for you. So here I am, doing something."

She threw herself at him in another embrace and he returned it. "Thank you," she whispered close to his ear. Her hot breath and soft voice caused memories of their time together to flash to mind. Yes, he'd do anything for this amazing woman. She was everything to him.

Wow! That was intense, Wyllea said into his mind. *Remember to keep things down for awhile, will you?*

Actually, I'm about to do something that will probably get some pretty strong thoughts going, just to warn you. They won't be pleasant.

Do you have to?

Yes, I promised Cass.

Fine, I'll try to block it out.

"Let's give this a try, shall we?" He held out his left hand to Cass. She took it. He laid his other hand on Shadowfang's hilt and tentatively let down his newfound mental defenses.

Help, she's trying to destroy me! Again, the voice seemed distorted, sometimes high in pitch, sometimes low, fluctuating as if on some unseen wave.

So am I, he said to the blade. He connected with Cass' soul and let her join in his link with the sword.

Noooooo! Shadowfang let out a long wail as Cass touched him.

I'm not here to harm you, she said through the connection to the sword.

Yes, you are, you're too pure, full of light, your touch hurts, go away! The sword wailed in its wild variations in voice.

My touch hurts? What of Davar, he is purer now too, does his touch hurt?

The question seemed to stun the sword, who stopped his wailing to consider this. *Yes, yes it does. He's not the same. He is pain too, both of you go away!*

I can take away your pain, Cass said soothingly.

Yes, by leaving, go now!

There's another way.

No, you must leave!

I know what was done to you. I can see it now. All of those dark rituals, the blooding, the torture. I can see what you endured, how you changed. Let me help you.

No! That's who I am. I'm the darkness! Don't touch that!

I must.

No! This wail was so loud and piercing within Davar that he nearly let go. Yet he could sense Cass starting to touch the darkest parts of Shadowfang's twisted soul, to sooth and heal the pain and black memories.

The wail continued, nearly all Davar could bear, as Cass worked.

Davar felt a hand on the bare skin of his neck. Then a voice boomed into his mind.

WHAT IN ALL THE BLAZES OF THE DEEPEST VOID ARE YOU DOING! Wyllea was furious. *I had to come down to the archives just to get through to you. You're driving me crazy!*

Sorry, but I warned you. This is apparently what it's going to take for Cass to heal my sword.

Really? Wyllea seemed skeptical. Oddly the scion reached through his connection with Shadowfang to Cass, still speaking in his mind. *Hey there, healer, can you come out and talk for a minute?*

A moment later Davar had released Shadowfang and Cass. He stood, slightly disoriented. The sword's call still rang in his mind, dizzying him.

Wyllea was rubbing her temples as well. She found a chair and sunk into it.

"I'd hoped that putting the barrier up in your mind wouldn't impact me this much," the scion said slowly, voice tense. "I was in the middle of target practice when that... sword screeched into my mind. I flinched and nearly killed a guard on the wall." She looked up at both of them. "How much longer is this going to take?"

Cass was leaning on the table with the sword. "I was only just getting started. There's a lot of evil there to root out. Even with Davar's help, I fear this will still take weeks."

"Weeks! Burn Me!" Wyllea heaved a deep breath to calm herself. "No, not like this, not for that long."

"We have to," Cass said evenly. "You know we must. If I don't do it with Davar's help, it will take as many months if not more, and you know we don't have that time. I'm trying to undo what the greatest wizard alive has done, that's not going to be easy or quick."

Wyllea grit her teeth. "What if you had more help? Would it go quicker?"

"What help?" Davar asked.

"Me. What if I were here with you, keeping all of our minds sane against the cries of that thing? Might that make things go quicker?"

"Actually, you might have something there." Cass rose from where she'd been leaning against the table and began pacing. Davar could see the woman's mind working, considering, developing a plan. "Do you think Senia might help as well?"

"If it gets this done quicker, then I'll convince her. If you had all of us here, how long might it take then?"

"It's hard to say for certain without trying it, but perhaps a couple of weeks."

Davar looked from the one woman to the other as that hung in the air. Wyllea seemed stuck but finally shook her head with a sigh.

"I'll take that. Leave off for now. Senia and I will be here by the call of the eighth watch tomorrow morning. We'll see how things work then, okay?"

She nodded. "Understood."

"Great." Wyllea got up and left.

Davar put his arm around Cass. "So," he said with mock innocence. "What could we possibly do until tomorrow?"

She raised a brow and leaned in to kiss him. "I'm sure we can come up with something."

Wyllea's voice slipped into his mind. *Really?*

CHAPTER 18

*C*assine took in the other three around the table.
Davar was smiling, his eyes full of love. Their 'day
off' the previous day had been a luxurious day of love making
and relaxation, taking their time, teasing and pleasuring each
other, exploring desires and deepening their connection.

Next to him was Senia, looking a bit uncertain as to why
she was here. Then there was Wyllea, looking upset and
eager all at the same time, very obviously not wanting to be
here, but knowing the sooner this was over the sooner she
could get on with her life.

Cassine was very glad to have all of the others here. She'd
been working with the blade for months and had made so
little progress until yesterday. Her brief time connected
through Davar to the sword had been nearly as productive as
all the previous months combined. With the help of these
three and a little luck, things would be so much faster and
easier.

"When I was connected to the sword yesterday, I could
see what the Blacklord had done to it and as you might

expect, it was far from pleasant. Months of rituals and being forced to slay so many innocent people, children, and babies. It was horrific. It affected the essence within the blade in more ways than just as a soul. It affected the mind and spirit as well. That's why I wanted both of you here. If we can all work on this at once, mind, soul, and spirit, I think we'll undo the darkness three times as fast as I could, working alone."

The plan had its risks and uncertainties of course. Cassine's only real experience with anything like this was her work with Davar. How exactly they would need to deal with the mind and spirit elements wasn't as clear to her. The main risk was having all of them 'inside' the blade with Davar being their only link connecting their essences to their bodies. If anything were to happen to Davar, they might all be lost inside the sword.

"The quicker, the better," Wyllea muttered.

Senia shrugged. "Glad to help, but there's a war to fight as well. In three days we'll probably all be needed elsewhere when our forces attack those on the plains."

Cassine nodded. "I understand and I want to thank you all once again for helping with this. Shall we begin?"

"What exactly do you need me to do?" Senia asked. "I'm not really used to working in these hidden worlds on people's souls and minds."

"I'll guide you once we're inside. You'll catch on quick enough, I'm sure."

The young scion shrugged again. "As you say. Let's begin."

They all joined hands. Cass held Davar's and Senia's. Senia in turn held Wyllea's hand and Wyllea was touching the side of Davar's head as his other hand would be on the sword. They stood in a circle around the table. Once connected, Davar touched the blade and Cassine guided them all inside. It was an odd sensation using all of her talents, spirit to connect to the others, as well as mind and soul to help them find their way into the sword, and then earth to keep herself steady and strong during all of this other taxing work.

Having connected to Senia and Davar before, even if Davar had been unconscious at the time, Cassine was able to bring them together as glowing representations of themselves within the darkness that was Shadowfang. Then she sought out Wyllea's spirit and brought her in as well, though it took her drawing on Senia's spirit talent to do so. Senia appeared wreathed in blue flame, Wyllea with an aura of brilliant green, Davar shone with white light, and Cassine herself appeared surrounded by a nimbus of gold.

Even before she'd begun, Shadowfang began his resistance, wailing and screaming in his warbling, inconsistent tone. Cassine clamped down on this, she couldn't shut it out completely, but it was reduced to the level of a whisper.

"This seemed the easiest way to get everyone together and explain things." Cassine shifted her perceptions to the realm of spirit and the darkness around them shifted. It became a writhing, twisting thing, dark forms appearing and disappearing within the darkness. "This is Starsong's spirit. Senia, I need you to work here. This darkness represents the wounds and pain inflicted on the sword to corrupt it."

Senia's spirit form suddenly held a great blade, Emberthorn. "I'll rip them to shreds."

"No!" Cassine said, her spirit holding up a translucent hand. "Wounds can't be healed by inflicting more wounds."

"Oh," Senia said, the sword vanishing. "What must I do, then?"

"Since all four elements of the body are intricately

connected, when I start working on a part of the soul, you'll see a part of the spirit beginning to change as well. It will start to shine with light, whatever color Starsong's spirit was originally. I think it was pure white, so look for that. Go to that area, see within the torrent of spirit, sooth it, and let it reconnect to what it once was. I've heard that you can use your spirit power to inspire others, connecting with the living essence inside of others to uplift them. Essentially you'll be doing that only to a specific strand of spirit within a sword."

"Ah." She shrugged. "I think I can manage that."

"Now a warning," Cassine said, "I'm about to enter the realm of Shadowfang's mind. There will be a lot of disturbing images. Be prepared."

Cassine shifted the perception again and the raging darkness turned into a thousand images of the dark rites and rituals, the recounting of so many slaughtered innocents playing over and over again.

Through their connection to each other, Cassine could feel the mutual revulsion they shared at the sight.

"Gods," Senia breathed. "I'm going to need a bath after this."

"Sounds like a great idea," Wyllea said, her spirit form looking a little pallid.

Cassine agreed. "Wyllea, you'll work here and when I begin, you'll see one or a series of these images come to life above the others. You need to work within the mind of the sword reminding it that it was forced to do these things. That these acts do not define the sword, yet it must accept these happened to it to release these memories and move past them. Can you do that?"

"I'll try."

"Thank you." Cassine's spirit form turned to Davar. "Lend us what strength you can."

He nodded.

Next, she had to do something very difficult, splintering her own perceptions such that Wyllea stayed with the mind, Senia with the spirit and she herself with the soul. It was a great effort, but she separated them all out. Then she began her work.

Choosing a thick, knotted cord of hate and anger, she began soothing it, seeing the depths of the emotions and helping them relax and let go.

~

When they all emerged back into the real world, exhaustion was written on everyone's face and in their posture.

"Gods, that was rough," Senia said letting go of their hands. She leaned against the small table, arms supporting her as she simply drew in long deep breaths for a moment. Her hair was damp with sweat and her face drawn.

"Yeah," was all Wyllea could manage, looking just as tired.

"But we got a lot done today, more than I thought we would," Cass said hopeful, despite the gnawing fatigue in body and soul. "At this pace, we should be done in less than a week."

"Thanks to all the Gods for that," Senia said with a long sigh. "Now for that bath."

CHAPTER 19

Three days later the abbey and its allies attacked the Blacklord's forces. As midday neared, Davar stood on the wall of the abbey watching a great battle rage below him.

He'd been denied permission to join the fight despite his knowledge of the enemy and many martial abilities. The High Abbot had been skeptical about his newfound ability to resist the Blacklord, and since his scion weapon wasn't yet ready to use, he'd been told to stay behind.

He'd received but one concession. If the battle was going poorly or if Cassine herself was in danger, he could join the fray. The High Abbot knew she wouldn't be able to stop him in this case. That and Cass was too important, needed as one of the six to go against the Blacklord.

So Davar kept a careful watch on the events below.

He had a detailed view of the battle despite the great distance. He used an earth talent trick of enhancing the acuteness of his vision a hundred times over. It meant he could only watch a small part of the battle, but he could see it very well. He focused on Cassine. She was well behind the front lines with the few remaining Daughters of Ehlani, healing those they could. A steady stream of wounded was being ferried back from the fighting and she looked harried and weary, tending to one man after another. Some she couldn't help except to ease their souls and suffering as they passed from this world to the void or the heavens.

He was concerned for her, but as of yet she'd been put in no danger.

He changed the focus on his eyes such that Cassine was now much smaller, but he had a wider view of the area around her.

A dark, black-clad shape dropped in near the healers, having somehow evaded the main battle. Then another one joined it... and more were on the way. His heart skipped a beat, fear and concern flooding him.

"Assassins at the healers," he said to the others watching on the walls nearby, then he leapt off the wall in a great jump which would take him directly to Cass and the others. He kept his gaze on them, though it became more and more difficult as he drew closer. Finally he let go of the enhanced sight altogether.

He only hoped he'd arrive in time. More and more assassins were arriving and sneaking up on the healers.

He landed hard, right behind Cass.

She started, so intent on her work that she hadn't noticed anything amiss.

"Protect yourself! Get the healers to safety!" Davar called as the first assassin rushed him.

He was still fresh and aching for a fight. The first one sliced at him and he spun out of the way, catching the man's sword hand and crushing it, then snatching the sword from the limp grip as he elbowed the attacker in the throat. The man dropped, eyes wide. Davar decapitated him before he hit the ground, ensuring he was dead.

More were coming from all directions.

He couldn't protect everyone at once. He tossed his newly acquired sword hard. It slid cleanly into the head of an assassin who was about to slit the throat of another healer. Three more reached Davar, attacking him together. He slapped the flat of one sword such that it blocked a second attack, then grabbed the arm of the last man pulling him closer. He snapped that man's neck then used him as a shield against the other two as they attacked again. He threw the dead man into one of them and dodged the attack of the other, crouching then coming up hard with a blow to the man's chin that broke his jaw and snapped his head back so hard it broke his spine. Davar plucked the sword from the newly dead man's hand and thrust it into the last one.

A quick spin showed only bad news. There were at least a score more assassins. One healer was down, bleeding heavily if not already dead.

"Davar, jump!" he heard Cass call. Without knowing what she was planning, he did as commanded. He launched himself into the air as he heard her shout, "Sleep!"

In a wave around her, people fell. Not all of the assassins were affected, but those closest to her staggered and fell. Several assassins, with their enhanced senses and reflexes, had heard Cass's warning and had also been able to jump, avoiding the spell. Davar used his wind talent to push himself through the air at two who had leapt. Both were dead by the time he came down.

It wasn't hard to finish off the remaining ones, as most were dazed if not dozing.

He found Cass next to the wounded healer, helping the girl to sit. The wound closed. The girl looked wan and weak though. She'd lost a lot of blood.

Cass turned to Davar. "Take her back to the abbey. She's in no shape to keep working here."

"I won't leave you," he said, still hot from battle.

"Yes you will, lover. It will take you hardly any time to get there and back and we're safe for now." Her tone was commanding, not to be disobeyed.

He grinned. "As you say. Give me one moment, though." He wanted to be sure for himself and did a quick scan around the area. Indeed as far as he could tell there would be no more threats for the near future.

He plucked up the waif of a girl, told her to hold on, then leapt back to the abbey. Landing in the bailey, he handed her over to two attendants, two young men not yet trained well enough to be out in the fight. Then he leapt back.

He arrived to find the healers swamped with a new wave of wounded.

"What happened?" he asked one of the stretcher carriers.

The young man was covered in blood, not his own, and was near exhaustion. "The enemy broke through the northern flank and hit some unprotected archers from Fjoria. It was a slaughter, but the flank has closed again, and the enemy is dealt with."

Cass called to him over the din of the crowd. "If you want to make yourself useful, lover, use your earth talent and heal some of these people. I don't care if it's pretty, just save their blazing lives!" Again, her tone left little room for debate.

He knelt next to a wounded man. The soldier was unconscious and had a great gash in his thigh. He was near death.

Not knowing the finer points of healing, Davar put his hand over the wound and filled the man with his earth talent.

The man gasped, waking, eyes wide.

Davar checked the wound, and it was indeed closed. "You're welcome," he said with a grin. It seemed this healing thing wasn't so hard after all. The man lay back blinking, then his eyes rolled up in his head and he went limp. Well, perhaps it wasn't so easy after all.

Davar swore, he checked the man over, but there were no more wounds he could see.

Cass arrived next to him. "Go help someone else, this man's body is whole. It's his spirit that needs help now."

"How do you know that?" Davar asked.

"You see enough wounds and wounded and you just know."

"Ah." He leaned over to kiss her dirty, blood-spattered cheek then did as she'd instructed and moved to another man.

She spent the afternoon healing and learned a lot in that short time, learning as he went.

Assassins attacked twice more that day, but these were smaller, last-ditch efforts by the enemy to hit a weak spot. Davar turned them all back, with some help from Cass.

By sunset the battle was decided, the tattered Blacklord's armies fled across the plains of Hallania. They were but rabble now. When Senia and Wyllea arrived to help ferry the wounded and weary back to the abbey, Davar got the full report. The scions had ensured that the commanders and wizards were dead and that most, if not all, of the assassins were also eliminated. This army would be no threat for some time.

CHAPTER 20

*C*assine woke in the darkness. The screams of pained and dying men echoing around her from dreams as fresh as an open wound. Tears streamed from her eyes, filled with sorrow for those who would never see loved ones again. Gods, how she hated this war.

A large, warm hand stroked her arm. "Hush now." Then a strong arm enfolded her, Davar's warmth surrounding her. "You're safe here."

The visions of the dead lingered, dancing before her in a morbid display of blood and death.

She nodded and worked within her own soul, soothing and healing herself. She had to keep telling herself that she'd done everything she could for as many as she could. Some she would never have saved.

The war itself was over. That's what they'd fought for. Still, she didn't feel good about any of it.

She snuggled in close to Davar, her crying abated as weariness overtook her again.

When she woke the next day, Davar was leaning against

the wall of their room watching her with kind eyes. He'd bathed and dressed and even brought her some breakfast. Beside the bed was a tray with warm bread smothered with melted butter as well as dried fruit: cranberries, blueberries, and slices of pear. She ate in bed, greedily, famished, having had little time or energy to eat the previous day.

"I spoke to Senia and Wyllea in the kitchens," he said. "They won't be available to work on Starsong today, they're too exhausted and need some time before something so strenuous. You can rest more if you like."

She sighed heavily, feeling tension flow out of her. Her shoulders slumped in relief and she gave him a weary smile. "I would like that."

He sat next to her on the bed and rubbed her back lightly. "Whatever you wish. I hadn't thought healing to be so exhausting. You have amazing energy to help as many as you do."

She leaned into him, her head on the rolling muscle of his shoulder. His arm slid around her, warm and comforting. "Thank you for all your help yesterday. Many men would surely have died had you not been there." She gave a half-hearted laugh. "We all would have died in that first raid if you hadn't been there."

She felt his kiss on the top of her head. "Anytime, my love."

She drew in a refreshing breath and pushed away from him. "I'm feeling well enough at the moment and I could do with a bath, then some fresh air. Would you like to go for a walk in the bailey?"

"This is your day. I'll do whatever you want unless you want to be alone."

"Let me have that bath and get dressed. Then we'll take a walk."

He was waiting in the room when she returned from the hot springs.

"I like this part," he said leaning back on the bed, watching intently as she stripped off her robe and towel. She gave her body a little shake to tease him then found a sturdy gray dress and cloak, as well as her stockings and boots.

As they left, he put his arm around her. "You know if you have that much energy I can think of some other ways to spend our time."

"I bet you can." She gave him a playful elbow to his ribs.

As they made their way out to the bailey Davar asked, "That was something new you did yesterday, that sleep spell."

The memory kindled joy and sadness within her. "It was far more effective than I'd imagined."

"Where did you learn it? I've seen you calm emotions before, but never anything like that."

"The archives." The tinge of sadness deepened, swelling to a dull ache in her stomach and forming a tear in her eye. The memory that went with the feeling was just as melancholy. "On days when my work with Starsong wasn't going well, I would take breaks and wander the archives. Old Anar usually found me. He had a preternatural sense for people among his stacks of books. He was the one who showed me the small section on multi-talent magic. I read some of the books on how to mix talents with various effects. I'd never thought to try it in practice, but yesterday I felt desperate enough to try. It's a mixture of soul, body, and spirit, dulling emotions and filling the body with fatigue, then using spirit to reach those around you and connect to them more effectively."

"Quite the trick. Was there more in that book?"

"So much more." She shook her head. "I know Anar had been so eager for me to try something. I wish he could have seen yesterday." But the old man had died in the raid on the Abbey months ago, the day Davar had nearly died.

"We should look into those books further. There may be some other useful tricks for when we attack the Blacklord."

"I'll show them to you tomorrow when we go down to work on Starsong."

They had reached the bailey. Despite how spring was progressing there was a crisp chill to the morning air, but the day was bright and clear, the sun strong and warming the earth slowly. They made their way up the many steps to the top of the wall, and Cassine took in the amazing sight of the plains of Hallania stretched below the walls and hills on which they stood. With the armies having been camped below for so long, she'd not seen the plains in some time. Even from this distance, the scars of the army's presence and the recent battle were clear to see, but also evident was the vast green expanse that surrounded the torn up areas. The plains would reclaim themselves soon enough. Life would prevail. That thought filled her with joy. She hugged Davar close beside her.

"We will win," she said confident in her words.

"I wish I had your faith," Davar said.

The hand that was not around Davar touched her belly, rubbing it slowly.

She hadn't wanted to say anything before now as she hadn't been certain of this new sensation within her, but she was sure she knew what it was now. There was the spark of a soul forming deep within her.

"Life will prevail," she said slowly. She turned to him,

pressing close in the cool morning air. "We must win for the sake of life. For the sake of new life." She looked intently into his eyes. "For the new life I carry."

He blinked. "Wha...? Are you...? Are we...?" He grinned, a large silly, lopsided, grin.

"Yes, you're going to be a father."

His surprised joy turned dark suddenly. "A father? What do I know of being a father? What if..."

She knew his fear. She could read it clearly in his dark eyes. "Do you really think you'd be anything like the Blacklord?"

"I..." He pulled away from her, turning to look out over the bailey. "I know he wasn't a true father to me, but... Cass, you don't understand, I... He..."

"You're nothing like him." She said and laid a reassuring hand on his shoulder. "And you know your mother now. You know who she was, what she was like. One of your parents was pure and loving. Carry that with you. Use that to be the father I know you can be. You love me and I know you'll love this child."

He took several long breaths, blowing them out through his mouth. "I'm going to be a father." He seemed to be testing out the words. "A father... me."

She put her arm around him and leaned into him. She couldn't be more excited. Before she'd met Davar, she hadn't thought she'd have children. She'd never found the right man. Yet she'd always wanted children. This was something she'd been dreaming of since she was a girl.

She kissed his cheek. "You've lots of time to get used to the idea. It will be many months before this child comes."

"My child." He was still staring out over the bailey though she had the feeling he saw nothing below and was seeing possibilities instead. "My child. I will have a child. We'll have a child." He looked at her, a smile spreading on his face. "Of all of the things I'd envisioned for my life, a child was never one of them, but now that I'm faced with it, I realize I want one. I want to be the father I never had. Thank you." He kissed her with a sudden passion.

She laughed when he drew back. "You really don't need to thank me, we both did this."

"Right," he said. "We should celebrate!"

"Yes, we should. But why don't we wait a little? A few more days of working on Starsong and she'll be whole again. Then we can celebrate that as well."

"I'm going to be a father," he repeated. "You're right, we will win. We have to."

⚬

Five days passed and their work with Starsong resumed in full force. Cassine was certain they were nearing the end of that work and grew ever more excited. As they'd gone to work in the archives on that fifth day, they'd all been anxious to get to work and free this sword from the darkness within it.

Once again, Senia and Wyllea were there to help her and Davar, but it was Cassine who was doing all the hard work.

A pure white light and an intense deep darkness warred for dominance with Starsong. This was so very different from the final battle within Davar. That had been a push against pure evil. This was more a whirlwind of confusion and identities. That which was Shadowfang clung desperately to existence, while the now greater part of the blade known as Starsong battled against it.

Yet this wasn't what was supposed to happen. Well, the truth was Cassine had no clue how this was supposed to work, but this didn't feel right at all.

No, don't fight against the darkness Starsong, you need to... how to describe this? *Fighting is what Shadowfang wants, more dismay and conflict. You need to accept that this was a part of you and let it go. That is how you defeat it.*

No. The cry from the sword was vehement. *There's no way I could ever be any part of that filth. It's disgusting and evil. I can't accept that's what I was!*

But it is what you were. Don't you see? Shadowfang is what you became, what you have the potential to become if you submit to everything evil and dark within you. But that doesn't mean it's who you are or who you're going to be. But you need to admit that it's a part of you to move past it, to get back to being the radiant light you know you are.

You'll never be rid of me, Shadowfang taunted. Somehow, the last vestiges of the black blade were stronger, held on longer than any before. Perhaps this was like Davar's healing. For him as well there had been that last solid core of evil which had been so very hard to dispel. It just hadn't had its own voice to express its displeasure. *If you fight me I win, and if you accept me I win. You can never again be as pure as you were. I will always be a stain on your soul.*

You're a vile corruption and I will defeat you. I'll destroy you! And yet again, the cycle of battle between light and dark ensued while Cassine could only watch.

Though, perhaps there was something Cassine could do. She'd been focusing on trying to soothe and eliminate the last of the darkness, but with Starsong constantly interrupting and trying to fight it, that had proven a near impossible task. So she changed her tactic. She grabbed the light instead, pulling it from the fight. Up until now, she'd only tried talking reason to Starsong, hoping the light side of the blade would help her, but that had garnered little. Now she calmed and soothed the light.

What are you doing? I'm not the one who needs fixing, Starsong said, the bright soul squirming in her grasp. *Let me go.*

No. You may be a weapon, but that doesn't mean all you know how to do is fight.

Well of course not.

What else can you do?

I'm a beacon of light. I can blaze forth like the sun. I can create walls and orbs of light. I see the truth in all things dispelling shadows and deceptions. I'm not as strong in either talent, but I have access to both soul and spirit talents. I can bolster my wielder and heal their wounds. I am Starsong!

You know of the soul and how it works, right?

Yes, of course.

And if you were helping someone try to heal and expunge the darkness and evil from their soul, how would you do it?

I would... but that's different, I'm... different...

No, you're not. You're a soul like any other. You just happen to be a part of a great weapon instead of in a human body.

But...

Really, are you still going to fight me? Cassine's soothing of the light was working. She could feel it relaxing, calming, finding peace.

No. You're right. But you can't know what it's like to live with that slimy... thing inside you for hundreds of years! She felt the equivalent of a shudder in this place of soul.

No I can't, but if you resist any more than you'll never be rid of it. So what do you say, are you going to help me, or fight against it and me?

I'll help.

Thank all the Gods! Finally!

Cassine let out a great sigh. *Then follow my lead. Watch what I'm doing with the soul and do the same.* Cassine turned her attention back to the cloud that was Shadowfang. Another difference in this healing versus Davar's was that the remaining bit of black was more amorphous and harder to get a hold of, where Davar's had been a solid thing.

You'll never cleanse me. I'm the purest distillation of evil you'll ever see! I will fight you and evade you forever, Shadowfang yelled. Cass could imagine spittle and froth at the intensity of the sword's vehemence.

You know, Starsong said casually, *I'd forgotten that shadow is the element of deception and lies. I don't think anything Shadowfang says is true.*

Now you're catching on, Cassine said and with a great bubble of soul-magic fully encapsulated the writhing mass that was Shadowfang. She could feel Starsong helping, lending energy. Then the essence within the blade began the arduous task of finally accepting that it had been corrupted and changed by the evil of the Blacklord.

Shadowfang fought back with lies and threats, but ultimately with Cassine and Starsong working on the soul together and with Senia and Wyllea helping in their respective realms, it was only a matter of time.

Though time was hard to gage in this place, it seemed to still take hours to dwindle the venomous essence which was Shadowfang. Then with a great and final push, Starsong grudgingly accepted the worst Shadowfang had done and let it go. The darkness within the blade was finally and ultimately destroyed.

Hands fell apart as Cassine, Davar, and the two scions emerged from within the blade.

"I can't believe it," Senia said slowly. "We're done."

Wyllea sighed heavily. "I won't say it was easy, but that sure was a lot quicker than I thought it would be."

Cassine smiled. "This is what we can accomplish when we work together. I'm certain now that we can defeat the Blacklord."

The two other women smiled, but Davar was distracted. He stood, one trembling hand hovering over the hilt of Starsong. There were tears in his eyes. He'd been lending the others energy, connecting them to the sword and been aware of the changes, but he seemed unable to touch the sword now.

"This is my mother's sword... my sword." His hand raised a little, drawing back. "What if it... What if she doesn't...?" He swallowed hard.

Cass took his outstretched hand in hers. "I've been working very close with her for some time now. She's been waiting for this moment Davar."

Slowly Cass pushed his hand onto the hilt. She hoped this, like the day not long ago when she'd told him about their child, would be a transition, a healing moment for him.

Davar's eyes went wide and he gasped. "Oh."

Senia laughed. "I remember my first moment with Emberthorn. It was rather..." She searched for a word. "...awakening."

Wyllea laughed. "Mine was in the middle of a fight and more like a cold bucket of water or a slap to the face."

Davar picked the blade up, holding it tentatively. He let out a long, slow, shuddering breath. His features fell, eyes tearing, mouth trembling, lips pressed.

He laid the sword down then bent over the table, half falling over the weapon and weeping like a babe.

"Well, that's different," Senia said, taken aback.

Cass laid a comforting hand on his back, connecting to his soul to see what was wrong. She was flooded with light and love and realized that nothing was wrong at all. This was a joyful reunion. Starsong was sharing all her memories of Davar's mother with him. Two souls, perhaps even three, coming together in the perfect mingling of love and unity. This is what Shadowfang had never been able to give him.

She withdrew her hand. "He's going to need a moment or two. There are a whole lot of emotions flowing between the two of them, some happy, some sad. It's as if he's meeting his mother for the first time, as well as bonding with Starsong."

The two scions nodded their understanding.

"Thank you both for your hard work and help. Davar and I will be celebrating tomorrow in the grand commons. You're both invited of course." Cass hesitated then added. "We're celebrating many things including my pregnancy."

The two other women looked at each other, sharing a knowing smile. Wyllea spoke, "We knew, it was sort of all through your thoughts."

"And I could sense the new spirit," Senia said. "Even as new as it is, it's very strong, that will be one powerful child."

Cassine laughed. "I should have known. Thank you again." She hugged them both. They left and Cassine returned to Davar, staying with him as he connected with Starsong.

CHAPTER 21

*D*ays vanished and the summer solstice drew near.
Davar alternated between fear and doubt about the coming attack, and joy at his time spent with Cass. He just couldn't bring himself to accept that the Blacklord could be defeated. So he spent every moment he could with Cass, whether they were planning their attack on the Blacklord's palace with the High Abbot and the scions, or searching through the books on multi-talent magic in the archives, or celebrating their love in bed at night. Any time with her was so very precious now.

She wasn't showing any signs of the pregnancy except for the great radiant spirit that grew within her. Every day when he woke, he'd open his spirit talent up and sense the great strength of Cass' spirit as well as the newer, ever so strong spirit essence within her. Cass had used her earth magic to resist morning sickness and was a joyous, radiant, glowing beauty as the pregnancy progressed.

Sometimes during the day, at moments when her heart was light and her joy overflowing, she'd start to glow like she did when impassioned, her skin giving off a faint aura of golden light around her. Others commented on this and joked in a friendly manner about her pregnant 'glow.'

Davar glowed as well, if not actually giving off light. He felt a certain inner peace he'd never known before. He had everything a man could want, a loving woman, a child on the way, his darkness purged from him, and a newfound bond with a powerful weapon.

He'd been spending a lot of time with Starsong and loved every moment of it. She was amazing, light and cheery and full of vigor and joy. She loved to tell Davar stories of his mother, who'd apparently done much in her few years as a scion. Not so long ago Davar would have been repulsed by the thought of his bonded weapon being imbued with a bubbly, chatty, far too optimistic, woman's soul. But he found her somehow perfect for him. Where Cass was the unconditional love he'd never thought he'd have, Starsong was the unconditional friend he had never thought he'd have.

Some evenings in bed he found himself telling Cass of all of the funny and strange things Starsong had said that day, or of some tale she'd told. Cass would laugh, full of love and not the least bit jealous of his relationship with the sword. Probably because she could do things with him that Starsong would never dream of.

His life was perfect, save but one thing, the threat of the Blacklord still hanging over them all. Yet as the day of their departure drew near, he found himself drawn into Starsong's and Cass' optimistic view of events. They would prevail. His fear and doubt diminished...

But never fully disappeared.

One night as they lay together, with Starsong hovering in

a corner of the room shedding a dim white light, Davar knew he needed to address the concerns which still plagued him.

They had just finished making love. All of their emotions tumbled out into a hectic desperation of desire leaving them both spent after the first round of passion. They lay holding each other, breathing hard. Their bodies were still covered in a sheen of sweat despite the chill of the room, which held out the late spring heat well enough, leaving it cool in the night.

Davar knew if he didn't say anything now he never would. He moved from where he lay, half on her, and she squirmed making soft noises of complaint as he propped himself on his side next to her.

"Cass," he whispered. "There's something you should know."

She stopped her playful movements at the tone in his voice and looked at him, curious.

"I've told you all about the strength of the Blacklord, but... I just wanted to emphasize, he's an incredible mind talent. Even if my mind is blocked to him, he'll have filtered through everything in the rest of your minds within moments of knowing we're there. He'll know everything you know, everything about us."

Her brows furrowed in concern. "You've said all this before."

His deepest fear bubbled to the surface and he shivered, the room far to chill now. He swallowed hard, hoping to get across to her the severity of his words. "He'll know about our child." He let that sit in the silence of their room as she looked away, considering this. After a moment he went on, "He'll use that knowledge to hurt us if he can."

"How can he hurt us? We know each other too well.

There's nothing he can say or do to break us apart. We have no secrets."

Davar knew she spoke the truth. He had no secrets from her. Moreover, he was more than willing to die for her and their child. He knew it would make things difficult for her and the baby, having no father, but if it meant winning this war for them, he'd give everything he had. "Still, the child is a weakness, a soft spot in our defenses. Given what happened to my mother I—" He couldn't go on.

"I know. If the Blacklord gets a hold of me, I'll probably suffer the same fate. But you can't think that way. We have two scions with us. That's a lot more than your mother had. If the Blacklord does take me, that probably means we've lost anyway. I would prefer to think that we have a much greater chance of success and hence that outcome isn't possible. And frankly, if we're defeated I'd rather die, taking our child with me than have myself or our daughter succumb to such a fate."

He sighed. She was right of course, but that didn't stop him from being concerned. "Just, be careful. I'd rather you didn't die. I'd rather none of us died, but... none of that is certain."

"Trust me, I'll be careful," she said bringing a hand to the side of his face then kissing him in a long soft embrace of their lips. "But for now, let's forget such thoughts. We're safe and together and there are far more pleasurable things to think on."

That was true enough. Looking at her in the dim light of Starsong's glow, as well as Cass' own lingering radiance, he couldn't think of anything more wonderful than the woman with him. She was perfect. He reached up and brushed a hand over the sensitive skin of her belly. She gasped, smiling.

He'd learned that, while pregnant she was quite tender and sensitive over her belly and bosom and used that to full effect in their love-making.

After another round of passion, Cass lay on him, drowsing and running playful fingers over his skin.

"Whatever else may happen," she said dreamily. "The Blacklord can't take this from us."

Davar smiled, hugged her close and kissed her forehead. She was right and his soul finally relented and relaxed.

∼

*D*avar stabbed a finger onto the map. "Here."

A large group crowded around the large table in the High Abbot's chambers. There were the six who were going against the Blacklord on the summer solstice as well as the High Abbot, High Sister Olinda, and Master Elia. This was their final meeting. All the details were set and this was to confirm they all knew the plan. No fire lit the great hearth today, it was quite warm, but the two small windows in the room had the shutters open to let in a spring breeze and oil lamps hung around the room giving light.

Davar ran the meeting as he was the only one with intimate knowledge of the Blacklord's Castle and surrounding areas. "There was a woodsman's village here long ago. It's within a day's walk of the castle and puts us near the Blackheart Forest, but not within it. We'll need to skirt the forest to reach the castle. Trust me, you don't want to be in the forest... though being out in the open isn't much better."

"I don't know," Cass said with a concerned sigh. "Always before, when teleporting, I've had a strong spirit to point me in the right direction, I'm guessing there won't be much if any significant spirit in that village."

"No," Davar said, "but you can link into my mind and memories. Use that to teleport. I know the place well, and I'm assuming teleporting to a place you know well, is easier."

"I would assume so too, but I've never tried it." Cassine frowned. "That's not entirely true. When I teleported accidentally as a child I went to my loft in our house, a place I knew so well it was just instinctual to go there. So perhaps that would work."

Davar nodded. In their previous meetings, he'd outlined some of the specific creatures they might face, so he glossed over that a little now. "There are supernatural predators all around the castle, as I've discussed previously. We'll have to avoid or deal with each in turn. But given our combined prowess, I'm thinking none should pose that much of a threat." Davar shrugged that off and was about to go on when he heard.

"Not to you, perhaps," Tirol muttered.

He's not very positive, is he? Starsong said into Davar's mind.

Not really, no. Not everyone can be as cheery as you all the time.

Why not?

He didn't answer.

"You'll be fine, lover." Wyllea grinned. "You're quite the warrior now and if there's anything you can't handle the rest of us will be there to help. You're fairly adept at avoiding trouble as well, if I recall."

Davar had to admit the man certainly looked far more ready for combat than he had over a year ago when Wyllea had brought him to the abbey. He was now broad of shoulder, having filled out through his chest and arms. Apparently, he'd spent nearly every waking moment training with the monks and anyone else who'd teach him combat. He'd even fought in the last battle. Davar didn't miss the way Wyllea looked at him and could tell she was quite happy with how Tirol had turned out.

Davar tapped the map again, bringing them back to their plans. "The castle itself, like most, was created to keep people out. The wall is oddly shaped, the inner side of the wall is vertical, but from the outside, it leans inward just a touch, such that it angles to a sharp point at the top. Anyone trying to scale the wall from the outside would find it an easier climb than most walls but then would have to face a sheer drop on the other side. It actually makes it harder to climb over because you can't rest at the top, nor can you pull up any ropes or ladders to use on the inside because you need to stay on them, there's no place to stand. For us it shouldn't be an issue, we can all jump it well enough." He grimaced, reconsidering that statement. "Or we have someone who can carry us over. From there we have to find the correct way in then navigate the inside without dying."

"Sounds fun." This from Tirol again.

"Can you elaborate at all on 'the correct way in'? Do you know exactly where to go?" Master Elia asked.

Davar nodded. "The palace is a great maze of halls, some of which lead nowhere, most of which lead to traps and dangers you don't want to think of. The correct path through isn't easy to follow, but I know the way. Similarly, there are many false entrances with halls that go deep inside, always ending in traps or dead-ends. There is only one right way in and only one path that will get you to the throne room."

"Can you show us at all? Draw it out, so we know what to expect?" Ahrn asked.

This wasn't the first time someone had asked. Davar sighed. "I could, but I fear that would confuse you more than help. The keep is massive and there are myriad twists and turns and not just on a level plane. There are shafts straight up or down. It would be hard to truly comprehend on paper. I've already told you about some of the specific chambers and traps we'll come across. As long as we stay together and you follow me carefully through we'll be fine."

Ahrn grimaced and said nothing further.

Davar continued. "In some of those chambers are the magical guards. Each is a formidable foe and the best way by them is to not spend too much time or energy fighting them." Again, he'd gone over the details of each of the beasts they might face in previous meetings.

It was Wyllea who questioned this. "So we don't fight them?"

"Not if we don't have to, no. Chances are we'll have to face a few, but the fewer the better. The last thing we want is to be drained by the time we reach the Blacklord."

They all agreed to that.

"Even once we reach the Blacklord himself, he has two abominations of magic he keeps in his throne room that we'll have to deal with while we're fighting him. Trust me when I say they are powerful. I used to spar against them and at my best I was equal to one of them, but I could never take both at the same time."

Through his connection with Starsong, he felt a mind-shudder. The sword remembered those 'old days' even though she'd been Shadowfang at the time. They were not pleasant memories.

"That's what we're for," Senia said with a grin that wasn't entirely genuine. He could tell there was some fear behind the jovial facade. But that was good. Fear would help them where they were going, keep them alive, this wasn't any place to be over-confident.

"And this is all assuming the Blacklord hasn't created any new nasty things since I've lost contact with him. That's a definite possibility."

The faces around the table were grim.

"One last thing," he said.

"Of course there is because the rest of this isn't bad enough," Tirol said.

Would it kill him to look on the bright side? Starsong asked.

Probably.

"The Blacklord knows everything that goes on within those walls. Once we're in, we have to assume he'll know we're there. There will be no element of surprise. We have to hope we have everything we need to beat him within us."

There was silence around the table as that sank in.

It was the High Abbot who finally spoke into the quiet. "I have faith that the six of you, together, can defeat the Blacklord. He may be a powerful wizard, but the Guardians of Aehryn were created specifically to defeat men like him. We have three guardians and two powerful wizards in their own right, and two great warriors. That should be more than enough to eliminate this curse on our lands once and for all."

It was a strong point. Davar could see others around the table come to the same conclusion.

They could win this. Something in his heart, which had been clenching and contracting as he'd gone more and more into detail about their plans released and he sighed it out quietly.

It was some time later when the meeting was done and they were all breaking up to go their separate ways that the High Sister pulled Davar and Cass aside. The older woman's face slid through a myriad of emotions before she spoke, from fear and concern to doubt and uncertainty. Her voice was low, a whisper. She spoke to Cass. "I know that Ragnalla's vision says you must go, but I'm concerned... for the baby."

Davar glanced at Cass. It had become second nature for her to have a hand on her abdomen, rubbing slowly over the area. She wasn't showing, but it was obvious enough to anyone who watched her long enough that she was either really hungry or pregnant, most likely both.

Cass answered, her voice also low. "I appreciate your concern, Olinda. I wouldn't have chosen this timing for a pregnancy, but we can do little about it now. I must go and so this child must go with me. To stay would be to break the foretelling and risk the lives of everyone else who went."

The High sister nodded, but still seemed unconvinced. "And you feel strong enough to carry this through?"

"I do."

If Davar knew but one thing about Cass it was that she was a trooper, she'd do what she must. Their child was also something special as well. Every time Davar opened his spirit talent to the still-as-yet-unborn being, he had to be careful. He could only create the smallest of connections for the spirit that blazed out from the womb was an incredible force, stronger than any spirit he'd ever known with the possible exception of Senia. Over the weeks as the child had developed, the spirit had grown stronger and stronger. It certainly matched Senia's now, if not exceeded the scion. Even Senia thought this odd. Usually, magic was passed from parents to children and certainly Cass and he were powerful multi-talents, but oddly spirit wasn't a strong ability for either of them.

Yet even now, as he connected with the child, that intense spirit seemed to ease his thoughts and feelings.

He wrapped an arm around Cass. "I get the feeling we'll be fine, even with this child tagging along." He wasn't sure where the words had come from nor this peace in his soul which seemed to sooth all doubt and fear, but for the moment, that's how he felt. "Cass is strong and together, as the High Abbot says, we're the most powerful team in a thousand years."

The High Sister finally relented and wished them luck.

As they walked the halls of the abbey back to their room, Cass said, "You seem calmer than usual."

Yeah, you're feeling sort of strange at the moment. This from Starsong.

Davar shrugged off the sword's comment and laughed, not even knowing where the levity for a laugh had come from, which made him laugh a little more. His heart was light and free at the moment and he didn't mind at all. He nodded as he replied. "Yes, I am."

They departed two days later.

But he wasn't feeling so confident then.

CHAPTER 22

"Well that's not intimidating at all," Wyllea said, sarcasm dripping from her voice as they stared at the Blacklord's palace.

It was the morning of the summer solstice, not that Cassine could tell. Dark roiling clouds blocked out the sun for hundreds of miles around. The land was dead from lack of light, the earth brown and desolate. They hid in a small copse of what had once been trees, branches overhead bare and rotting, with massive obsidian walls looming before them.

Cassine had to agree with Wyllea's assessment. The walls were as high as St. Antin, but the area the palace occupied dwarfed the abbey in scale. These outer walls stretched more than a mile in either direction. Apparently, the square compound was roughly three miles per side according to Davar. This had once been the summer palace of the King of Nustaria, a grand place with great gardens. The Blacklord had claimed it as his home, erecting massive walls and the even more massive structure within by the use of magic and a great many slaves. Now it was a place of looming evil.

They had teleported to the abandoned town several miles away two days ago, then had rested for a day and slowly made their way to the castle, mostly avoiding the many mystical creatures prowling these lands to keep unexpected visitors out.

Davar had led the way, everyone else following his explicit instructions. Only he knew how to make it through these lands alive. They had faced one... thing... which looked like some twisted amalgamation of a bear and a wolf and an eagle, with great wings, two heads and claws as long as daggers. Luckily, as tough as its hide was, it still couldn't take the flurry of arrows from Eaglewing that Wyllea sent at it.

It helped that they had been preparing for this for some time, training together back at the abbey. They were well equipped and as ready as they could be. Cassine was a little uncomfortable in her new acquired leather leggings and soft leather overcoat, which served as light armor. She would have preferred a dress, but the others had all opted for similar outfits and she'd taken the hint that such accouterments would be well advised.

Wyllea, a veteran soldier, was in full studded leather armor with a steel breastplate. Senia, no stranger to battle, was similarly attired, but without the heavy metal front piece. Tirol and Ahrn were in light armor, preferring to retain mobility while still garnering some protection. Only Davar wore no armor at all. It wasn't a show of bravado, but simply that he'd never worn any in the past and felt too restricted in anything but his shirt and breeches. They all wore darker colors to blend in with their surroundings as much as possible.

They were well provision and prepared. Cassine hoped it would be enough.

Everything about this place spoke of death and decay. Evil was in the air and tainted the water. It seeped into the soul and fouled one's mood. As sensitive as she was with the element of soul, Cassine could sense the effect on her feelings and she'd been using a small bit of her magic to help the others resist the effect to keep their moods as positive as possible.

"This is it. From here, we'll want to keep moving as much as we can. Follow me. Do as I do and we'll all hopefully get to the Blacklord alive. Every other time I've been here the Blacklord has protected me, kept the guards from attacking me, but I get the feeling I won't be so lucky this time," Davar whispered just loud enough for all to hear.

"Great pep-talk," Tirol muttered.

"Let's go," Davar said and began his sprint to the wall. They had nearly a mile of open ground to cover, but they were all fit enough to make the run quickly. At the base of the wall Senia grabbed Ahrn, Wyllea took Tirol, and they leapt up and over.

Davar stopped long enough to give Cassine a quick peck on the cheek before they launched over the wall. Cassine, though not strong in the element of wind, had learned how to enhance her leaping by infusing her legs with greater energy from her spirit then using the element of wind to help her along. She could now jump at least as far as Senia if not the distances Davar traversed. One of many long-forgotten tricks she'd picked up from the multi-talent tomes in the archives.

Cassine and Davar landed as the others were spreading out slightly, ready for a fight. Emberthorn and Eaglewing were out and ready, Ahrn had a staff he spun lazily, and Tirol held two slender long-swords.

Davar called out a hushed, "This way."

They followed him across the half-mile wide bailey toward the stark black walls of the main keep, which jutted up hundreds of feet into the low rolling clouds.

The inner keep was a lesson in structural horror. No wall was smooth. There were no curves or square edges. The outer surface was a crisscrossing of jagged stone, sharp and haphazard. There were no doors only dark maws with ragged stone teeth that gaped in various spots along the walls, none on ground level. Odd protuberances and stone spikes clawed out from the walls all over, like some giant armored and deformed porcupine.

Cassine shuddered from the feel of despair and horror the walls gave off and she bolstered her soul-soothing to the others and continued on.

As it turned out the jagged edges of the wall were functional as well as ugly. Davar came to one spot in the wall and began to climb the rough stone to a dark opening fifty feet up. The climbing was easy with the all the large and small uneven stonework, and they were all quickly at the entrance, standing just inside an unlit tunnel.

The flames on Emberthorn's blade and Starsong' soft white luminescence lit the hallway, and Cassine created a small ball of fire to float ahead of them as they started deeper into the keep.

Inside there were no windows, no torches, and no magical light other than their own. This was the heart of the Black-lord's realm and here darkness reigned. Without light, these passages would be treacherous. Holes gaped in the floor, tunnels tilted down or up suddenly. Sometimes a hall would end and the only way to go was straight up, perhaps hundreds of feet.

At these points, Wyllea or Davar would ferry them up the long shafts. Wyllea flew smoothly up the tunnel, while Davar made a great leap to throw himself up the vertical hallways.

There was little sound in the keep, the floor absorbed their footfalls into an oppressive silence.

After what seemed like hours of careful stalking through eerie narrow halls, they came to a room so large their light sources penetrated only partway into the quiet darkness

"This is the first of the galleries. There are guards here, stone statues that move as fast and as quiet as the wind. Most likely they're already on their way here to slay us," Davar said with a hushed, intense tone. "Try not to engage too many of them. If possible, we want to get around these guys, not fight them. Though I'm itching for a bit of action right now."

"You're one crazy man, you know that," Tirol said.

A whisper of sound, that was all it was, and Davar pulled Tirol out of the way of a massive stone blade swept through the air to decapitate him.

"You said they were big, but Gods!" Wyllea called as one lumbered into their light, a thirty-foot tall man of stone with a stone sword just as long.

Ahrn and Tirol fell back since they wouldn't do much good in this fight. Cassine dropped a bright ball of fire above them to let them see farther then joined the three scions in combat. She had no weapon as they did, but these were creations of stone and that she had power over.

She stood behind the wall of bodies the scions created and sent her senses into the darkness, feeling for more of the moving statues.

Gods, but there were a lot of them!

A dozen more were closing fast and even more flooded I behind them. There was no way they could fight them all, or if they did they'd be exhausted afterwards. They needed to end this initial fight quickly and move on before the rest got here.

Cass steadied her heart, calming her fears, and acted. She sent her earth sense into the closest dozen. She felt the stone, the flaws and weaknesses within every moving block. These things had no spirit to connect to, so if she was going to do anything to them it would require raw earth talent and lots of it. She thrust her energy out, pushing and pulling with all her considerable earth talent, exploiting each flaw.

Stone ground on stone as she forced it harder still. Then with a great crash and creak, the statues crumbled to piles of thick stone blocks and dust. She'd pushed harder than she wanted, but the threat around them had been eliminated.

"What was that?" Senia asked.

"Me," Cassine said breathing hard. "But there are many more coming. Davar, what's our route out of here, this will have to be a moving fight, or we'll be stopped here far too long."

Davar grunted his acknowledgment. "This way," he said, skirting along the wall to their left.

"I sure hope he knows where he's going," Tirol said, as he and Ahrn began running.

"Don't we all." Senia jogged along with long strides beside them.

Wyllea flew above them, facing backward, guarding the rear.

Cass used her earth talent to strengthen her muscles and bones, rejuvenating her for the sprint to come. She also continued to keep track of the stone guards. The constructs must have had some way to see in the dark or perhaps didn't need to see at all and simply knew where intruders were. They adjusted their course to purse Cass and the others.

"Davar, look out!" she called

Davar launched himself upward. The guard was close, sword sweeping underneath Davar as the big man sliced cleanly through the thing's neck. Its stone head crashed to the ground and shattered. That did nothing to stop it.

Its blade slashed again. This time at Ahrn. He narrowly ducked under it. Senia, close behind him, leapt and sliced through the guardian's sword arm. It crashed to the ground in front of Tirol and Cassine.

Cassine grabbed the tall rogue, surging her earth talent to increase her strength and carry him while jumping over the debris.

"Thanks," he gasped.

"I'm sure you'll get a chance to repay me later," she said, feeling the incredible drain on her body from so much earth talent used.

They ducked into a smaller side tunnel before the next guardian could reach them, pausing to catch their breath once they were safely out of the gallery.

Cassine moved up next to Davar. "I've used a lot of earth talent so far. I don't know how much more I've got."

He brushed back some hair from her face and with the touch came a surge of his own energy. "Here's a little for now," he said softly. "And remember that spell we learned. You can drain your spirit talent to fuel any other talent. It's a last ditch thing, but at least it's something."

She was grateful and tried to smile, but succeeded only in a tired, lopsided grimace.

Once again, Davar led them through a maze of passages

and finally stopped them when they came to a sheer drop. Even before he spoke, a noise filled the tunnel, as if they were surrounded by a great hive of bees.

"Hear that?" Davar asked.

There were nods all around. "What is it?" Wyllea asked.

"That, or more precisely, *those* are the Raging Disciples."

In one of their gatherings to prepare for this assault, Davar had told them all of the Raging Disciples. These were men and women who'd come to the Blacklord willingly to undergo the magical transformation that would turn them into his dark assassins. Yet the magic needed to imbue a person with such power did not always flow smoothly into a body. For every dozen assassins created, there was a Raging Disciple made. Deformed, crazed, and seeking only death, they would fight anyone who came near them with all the terrible power of an assassin, but none of the training or control. They'd been known to eat their victims, or rend them limb from limb, usually while the person was still alive. Why they didn't attack each other was a mystery, probably some mind-infused spell from the Blacklord.

"How many are there? It sounds like thousands down there?" Ahrn asked.

"The gallery is massive," Davar said, grim. "You're right. There are thousands, perhaps tens or hundreds of thousands, I don't know. The only way past them is to fly. But we still must land to pass through the locked door on the far side of the chamber. This will take all of us working in tandem to survive. Everyone clear on the plan?"

"Remind me what's on the other side of that door?" Senia asked.

"The room of fire."

"Right, the one with the lava."

"Yes."

"Great," Tirol sighed with a grimace.

Davar took a moment to glance at each of them. "We all know what to do. Let's make sure we all survive this." Then he turned to Wyllea. "You're up."

CHAPTER 23

*D*avar watched the dark-haired scion concentrate for a moment before stepping out over the shaft. She didn't fall but seemed instead to be walking on nothing.

"This isn't easy to maintain so let's make this quick," Wyllea said, a hint of strain in her voice. "Everyone on."

Davar had no fear of the fall below and was the first to step out into the hardened air Wyllea was creating. It was odd. He expected to fall but didn't. They'd practiced this at the abbey, but it was still an odd sensation. The others gathered onto the invisible platform quickly, even if a few looked a little uncertain.

Then Wyllea lowered them down the shaft. Davar's stomach lurched at the speed of the drop. The effect was clear on the faces of the others as well.

"Could we go a little slower, perhaps?" Tirol asked, his face an odd shade of green.

"No lover, we can't, so suck it up. I want to get this over with as soon as possible. This isn't easy." Wyllea's voice was clipped, strain more than audible now.

Quickly enough they were below the roof level of the massive chamber and began to move laterally, following the curve of the high-arching ceiling.

I think we could use more light, Davar said to Starsong.

Done! The blade gleamed, a clear bright light, reflecting off the sheer, smooth black surface not far above them. As Shadowfang had been attached to the sub-element of shadow, Starsong was of the sub-element of light and she could blaze forth like the sun itself when needed. The room below was now clearly illuminated. The Raging Disciples on the ground were also used to darkness and many cried out and covered their eyes from the new star soaring above them.

Below them was a sea of sea of crazed humanity — if indeed there was any humanity left in those poor souls. They surged and moved, like waves upon the ocean, screaming jeering and discordant song of madness.

Uncertainty sunk its dark claws into Davar's heart. He'd been through these halls many times before, but on those journeys, he'd been protected by the Blacklord's magic. This time would be much different. Not only would there be no protection, but he was sure he'd be targeted specifically. The Blacklord would want to keep the scion women and Cassine alive if possible, but Davar himself was a lost cause to his once 'father.' He was fine with that. It meant he was no longer redeemable in his father's eyes, and he was a threat to be eliminated. That was a good thing.

Now he just had to survive.

He turned to the others. "Don't worry. There may be a lot of them down there, but we'll be fighting in a small area, only a few will be able to get to us at one time. We can handle this." They knew it, but he'd wanted to reassure himself as well.

"So what you're saying is that we don't have to kill all seven million of them?" Tirol asked grimacing as he stared at the seething horde.

"There aren't that many," Ahrn said stoically.

"Exactly." Davar tried to put on a smile, but truth be told he had no clue how many there were. The room was hundreds of feet across and so tightly packed that it was impossible to tell how many there were. There could be millions... he didn't know.

And it was coming time to drop down into that crowd.

There was a great double door at the far side of the room. To get to it, they'd need to deal with at least some of the raging disciples. He and Senia would go down first and clear an area. The others would follow, Wyllea and Ahrn would help enlarge the area around the door while Tirol and Cass opened it.

They reached the far wall and Wyllea lowered them a little.

Are you ready to free some tortured souls? He asked Starsong. *More than ready. Let's go.*

He dropped a ball of light below him to clear a small spot then allowed himself to fall.

Some of the maddened throng below threw themselves at him before he even reached the ground, but he was ready and Starsong sang with light and fury. He cut through their toughened flesh with ease, freeing them from their eternal suffering.

Landing right on top of the ball of light he began laying about him with Starsong. With a few quick, aggressive swipes of his sword, he'd cleared enough area for Senia to drop down behind him.

She came out swinging, her longer blade clearing an even

larger area than he could with Starsong. But it would still take them a moment to create enough room for the others.

Dealing with the Raging Disciples was in some ways easier than dealing with Blacklord's assassins, and in some ways harder. The disciples had no focus, no training, and no discipline. They came at him in a horde and with one great swipe of his blade he could often take four or more at once. Also, they didn't coordinate their attacks and could get in each other's way, which helped him. Yet they were far more intent on their target, their fury a constant beating wave against his defenses. This is what made them deadly. Their sheer numbers and unrelenting ferocity. Assassins would take stock, plan, coordinate and in doing so give him time to plan, but this was purely slaughter on both sides. Either he slew them or they him.

The constant need to infuse his muscles with immense strength to slice through the hard hides of these once human foes wore on him, draining his earth talent. It didn't help that he'd lent some of his strength to Cass. He hadn't thought it would be an issue, but he'd underestimated how tough these foes would be.

Once he and Senia coordinated their attacks, falling into a rhythm which cut up the disciples, they finally managed to take that step or two forward, creating room for the others. Cass and Tirol went to work on the door as Ahrn and Wyllea joined the fight. The monk used his staff, even his bare hands, bashing skulls and breaking necks. Wyllea hovered above them, picking off anyone who threatened to break through their lines.

It was up to Cass and Tirol now. He had to pick the lock and she was to detect any traps within the door or the lock to keep Tirol alive while he opened it for them.

Time expanded and stretched. It was probably only minutes, but it felt like hours. Davar felt himself slowing, his strength waning against the constant onslaught of malignant flesh intent on killing him.

Starsong, I need some energy. Give me some of that spirit.

Sure! Starsong said still somehow cheery, and he felt a rush of life and energy renewing him.

Thanks, he said, his focus restored.

It was one of Starsong's abilities. Since light was the sub-element of fire and water, of spirit and soul, the sword could essentially give him an infusion of pure light. It was an interesting effect, using spirit to take some of the sword's soul energy and re-energize Davar's body. In addition, it boosted his soul and spirit at the same time, uplifting him more than just physically.

How often can you do that?

Not often. Maybe three to five times depending on how much energy you need.

Good, I may need it later. He used some of his newfound spirit energy to restore his earth talent using the spell he'd discovered with Cass.

"Got it!" Tirol shouted, followed by the creaking of great hinges as the door swung open behind him. There was a great blast of heat on his back and a stench of sulfur. "Let's get out of here!" Tirol added.

"Go!" Senia said. "Ahrn and I can keep them at bay until the rest of you are through."

"Will do," Davar said and took several steps back, as did the other two, closing their radius of control to a smaller area she and Ahrn could manage. Then Davar turned and fled through the great double doors into the Gallery of Fire.

Cass and Tirol had been smart. They'd only opened one

of the two great doors between the rooms, which opened into the chamber with the Raging Disciples. The two of them had pried the one open far enough for a person to slip through, not much more.

Wyllea came hot on Davar's heels as Davar grabbed the door and braced himself. This was going to take some strength.

"Senia! Now," he shouted and instantly the two still in the room broke and ran, Ahrn first, followed closely by Senia. The trick was to have as few of the disciples reach the door by the time everyone was through. If those madmen began prying it open their combined strength would be hard to overcome.

Davar began closing the door even as Senia slipped through. Only a few of the disciples had enough clarity to try to pull the door open. They were in the minority as the press of thousands behind them practically closed the door for Davar.

Tirol went to work on the lock once again as the rest of them took a moment to catch their breath.

Davar glanced around the chamber of fire to see if it had changed much since his last visit. It was the only place so far with its own light. Yet the light was a dim red glow from the bubbling lava that covered the floor of most of the room. There was a narrow ledge around the sides of the room, but that was a trap, the stone walls were alive and able to envelop anyone trying to go around. The only true way across the room was flying or across the scattered stepping-stones. The problem with the stepping-stones was they sank almost as soon as any pressure was put on them. Everything seemed the same here.

"That should do it." Tirol stood back from the door. The

rogue smiled. "I had my doubts about this plan. I really didn't think we'd make it this far, but now that we have... well, it's fairly smooth sailing from here, right?"

"Straight to the Blacklord, yes," Wyllea said.

"Still," Tirol said taking several steps over to the edge of the pool of lava. He seemed to be getting a sense for the fiery liquid and the few stepping stone across the lake of molten rock. "We're mostly in one piece and haven't strained ourselves too much."

The lava jumped up and attacked Tirol.

It was only the man's incredible agility which saved him and the fact that he'd been looking intently at the lake of fire. Tirol leapt to the side in a dive-roll and came up running.

"Don't get too close to the walls." Davar reminded them all as Tirol came to a quick halt several feet away from the rough stone. The small man turned back, swords out and ready.

"What's that?" he called pointing to a shape emerging from the lava.

But Davar had no clue. This was new.

The shape took form, roughly that of a man with two arms and two legs, and seemed to be made of the molten rock. It had no head and the arms and legs were thick, two feet in diameter. The whole monstrosity was over ten feet tall, nearly as high as the low ceiling in this room.

Even as it emerged fully and came to stand on the rocky shore, dripping fiery liquid rock, two more began crawling from the lava as well... and the stepping-stones all began sinking into the lake. There would be no way across but flying at this point.

"They're beings of earth and fire!" Cass called out. She must have used her abilities to assess their makeup. Davar kicked himself and did the same, using all of his talents to give these new monsters a once over.

They were indeed as Cass said. Made of spirit and body, fire and earth, they were yet another demonstration of the Blacklord's power. Combining opposing elements like that was not easy.

"What do we do?" Senia asked.

"I don't know. These are new. Kill them however we can."

Arrows began peppering one of them only to burst into flames and fall away. "This isn't working!" Wyllea's voice was a pitch too high, strained. The three lava creatures were pushing forward as even more climbed from the lake. There was precious little room left for the allies, especially if they couldn't get close to the walls.

Senia stepped forward as flames blazed to life on Emberthorn, but every slash she took at the giants seemed to do little damage, her fire only adding to their own. She stepped back. "We need to get out of here."

Davar agreed.

"I can't rip them apart like I did with the stone giants," Cass yelled. "They're more fire than rock, and I'm not as strong in spirit."

That was it.

"Senia, don't attack them, use your spirit talent to hold them, stop them. If they are mostly fire, you should be able to affect them."

The willowy young woman threw her hands out in front of her, an intense look of concentration on her face.

The monsters stopped.

"I can't force them back," Senia said through gritted teeth. "They may be mostly fire, but there's enough earth in them for them to resist me as well. Stopping them is the best I can do."

"It'll do." Wyllea plucked Tirol up and flew over the burning forms. If they'd been able to move their arms, they could have bashed at her, so low was the ceiling of this long room. Wyllea flew as fast as she could to the far side, setting Tirol down, then returning with all haste.

"I can feel something or someone opposing me," Senia said. "I don't know how much longer I can hold these things."

"Cass, can you teleport us across? It's not that far." Davar called out.

"Yes, everyone join hands."

They all met up around Senia. Touching her as she kept the lava forms as bay.

Then in an instant, everything shifted and they were on the far side of the long chamber.

Tirol was shouting at them, pointing at more of the things crawling out of the lava on this end.

The way out of this chamber was a shaft directly upward for several hundred feet. Wyllea or Davar would have to ferry them all up, and they didn't have time for that.

"Join us!" Cass called out, and Tirol didn't need any more incentive, he was already there with them.

Davar, Cass spoke into his mind, *I need to know what the landing up above us looks like now!*

He sent here a mental image of the antechamber they would arrive in. Then the lava chamber vanished and that's where they were.

Cass cried out from the exertion and collapsed to the floor, tremors wracking her body.

Davar knelt next to her, laying a hand on her shoulder, checking her eyes. She was staring off into space, mouth slightly agape, shudder after shudder wracking her body, unresponsive. He focused inward, using his talents to assess her and find out what was wrong. He wasn't the healer she was, but he could try.

He tried with mind first, as that was one of his strongest talents. Yet as soon as his mind touched hers, it reeled back as if struck. He'd gotten only a glimpse of the chaos within her. Thoughts jumbled together in a cacophony of images and sounds playing over one another.

Next, he tried his earth talent to *feel* through her body and instantly found the problem. She was exhausted. That made sense, he should have realized that. Two teleports back to back, even at such short range would drain her. He funneled earth-energy into her, but he soon had to reign in the transfer. Her body was so fatigued it acted like a sponge, sucking the energy from him faster and faster. Even after only a moment of this, he had to stop or he too would be drained as much as she. Yet it wasn't that easy to cut the flow and took a near inhuman level of power to finally break the connection.

He grunted and sat back heavily, but he saw Cass blink and stop shaking, gasping in air. He'd overextended himself, but she was alive and no longer thrashing about. It was worth it.

After several gulps of air, Cass finally looked around. Her gaze met Davar's and a tear slipped from her eyes.

"You shouldn't have done that. Now we're both nearly drained."

"I had to do something. You were dying. Your body was consuming itself."

"We're all alive, that's what matters," Tirol said. "All of us have to face the Blacklord, remember."

Wyllea spoke up. "But it looks like it's coming at too high

a price. If we're this exhausted, do we even have a chance against him? He's still fresh."

Davar dug into his reserves of strength, as shallow as they might be at the moment and pushed himself to stand. "It will be enough because it must be enough."

Ahrn knelt next to Cass, laying a hand on her shoulder. "Thank you." He looked up at Senia then. Cass had saved them all.

Cass raised a hand and waved at him before the hand fell back to the rocky floor. "Anytime." Davar could tell she was trying to be light about this, but the toll it had taken on her was clear.

Do you need more energy? Starsong asked.

Yes, how much can you give?

The usually cheery voice grew somber for a moment. *How's this?* Energy flooded into Davar and he channeled it into his earth talent, feeling his body renew itself.

Thanks.

Perhaps we can rest a bit before we go on? That was a lot of spirit I just gave you. I might only have one more like that left in me.

I don't think we can rest. Not here.

Starsong gave the impression of a nod.

Even with the infusion of energy, Davar still felt tired and worn. The others looked similarly as exhausted, but time was drawing short and they had to move on.

Cass especially looked haggard, working to drag herself to her feet. It looked like they'd all be fighting fatigue as much as the Blacklord.

But there was little choice.

"Let's go," Davar said.

At the far side of this antechamber was a door. It was a

false door, opening it would reveal only a great pit filled with razor spikes and a sucking wind to draw you in.

The real door was in the rough stone wall beside the fake door. Davar found the secret spot to push and the wall swung inward.

Beyond was the Blacklord's throne room.

Starsong was still blazing bright and the room, though massive, was mostly illuminated. A great expanse of black floor led to several steps. Atop the final dais was a great chair of blackened bones and in it was a shriveled man in black robes, his skin drawn tight over a shrunken skeleton, with barely any flesh or muscle. The skin itself looked charred and scarred, desiccated and half decomposed. His eyes were empty black sockets, his teeth gone. There was a soft scraping-slapping sound echoing through the room to meet them.

The Blacklord was clapping.

CHAPTER 24

"*B*ravo!" he called out in a rich, commanding voice belying his physical appearance. "I had hoped some of you might survive my trials so I might play with you myself. Well done!"

"He'll only deceive and betray. Trust nothing he says and remember to be wary for the final guards," Davar hissed.

Scanning the room, Davar couldn't see either of the two demonic guards. These were the pinnacles of the Blacklord's work, animating raw elements to protect him. Both constructs had been created and imbued with all four elements and talents. Their bodies were stone and could regenerate and heal themselves like someone with the earth talent. Their eyes burned with red flames and liquid fire — like a physical manifestation of their spirit — flowed through the stone like blood. Their wings were made of air and their speed was like the wind. More, they had cunning minds capable of intricate thought and deduction. Their souls radiated with despair and hopelessness and it manifested physically as a miasma which wept from their joints and gaping mouth. One breath could dishearten the most stalwart of foes. Finally, they could cloak themselves in shadow or reveal themselves in blinding light. They were the masterwork of all the Blacklord's creations.

"What have they done to you, my son?" The Blacklord called across the great room. There was a mixture of curiosity and mock dismay in the resonant yet rasping voice. "I can't sense you. Your mind is blocked to me, your spirit protected, your soul entwined with your whore of a mother. Are you lost to me?"

Davar did not deign to respond.

The six of them stalked slowly into the room, ready and cautious. Starsong blazed a bit brighter and the far walls were revealed. The room was truly colossal in scale, perhaps five hundred feet across and twice that long. Wyllea took to the air, spinning slowly, arrow notched.

"And you brought me a pair of scion beauties as well as your multi-talent lover. I shall enjoy breaking them as I did your mother. You've even started a child for me. Corrupting the unborn is one of my favorite past-times."

Davar shuddered. Unbidden, one of the memories of his distant past — or perhaps it wasn't his memory at all, but his mother's — came to mind. It wasn't an image so much as a mixture of sensations, intense pain and sorrow, and over it all was the gleeful cackling of the Blacklord. Davar knew exactly how much the Blacklord loved to corrupt and defile babies, even those as yet unborn. It was a truly horrid thought.

"Chatty isn't he," Tirol said.

"Ignore him and watch for the guards," Davar warned. Yet they were nowhere to be seen. That meant that they were cloaking themselves in shadow and invisible. They could be anywhere.

"Cass," Davar said softly. "These things reek of a rotten soul. Can you sense them?"

She paused in her slow pacing forward and looked around. "Yes. They're waiting, unmoving... over there." She pointed.

"Oh!" The Blacklord cried in feigned terror. "Oh no, did you find my pets? Very well, then I will let you play with them."

And they appeared. Towering monstrosities of evil.

"Gods!" Wyllea breathed and immediately began filling one with arrows. It didn't seem to notice.

"Entertain me!" the Blacklord shouted gleefully.

The two abominations moved with incredible speed, one flying up to Wyllea, the other charging in at the rest. Davar hoped Wyllea could deal with hers and concentrated on the one before him. It spun, one translucent wing of air knocking Cass down, sending her sliding across the floor.

Davar's heart lurched, but he knew Cass could take a hit or two and he didn't have time to think about it now. The creature completed its spin with a rake of its claws at Davar. Davar blocked with Starsong and spun into the creature, knowing proximity would be a hindrance to the larger foe. He sliced into the thing's leg and it bled lava, but the wound did not hinder it.

It kicked at Davar.

He blocked the blow with Starsong, but the force of it sent him tumbling backward.

He was up quickly, but the demon had moved on to attacking Tirol who was doing an amazing job at blocking slash after slash with his dual blades. That was until the creature completely sliced through one of Tirol's blades, severing it just above the guard. The next swipe was blocked by Tirol's other sword, but he could only block one at a time now and the creature's other hand followed quickly.

Senia not only blocked the blow aimed for Tirol, but Emberthorn cut cleanly through the abomination's wrist.

The creation flailed wildly, the opened arm now gushing lava and black smoke that sprayed over Senia who screamed and staggered back.

Tirol stood stunned for a moment, staring at Senia, but the demon wasn't long distracted and came for the rogue once more.

Davar was up and moving. He stepped in the way of the attack, blocking the oozing wrist with Starsong. A wash of burning stone splashed over him as well as a wave of heart-tearing despair.

The force of the blow knocked him back several steps. The liquid fire on his face and torso seared away skin and ate at bone, but Davar felt no pain. He pushed his spirit and body talents: the fire to burn away the lava in a rush of flame and the earth talent to heal and remake his body.

Davar stalked back in and took a quick assessment of the situation as he did. The Blacklord sat on this throne laughing. Wyllea was using her incredible speed and agility in flight to dodge the one creature that pursued her. Tirol was doing the same on the ground, tumbling with incredible coordination to avoid the blows from the one relentless going after him. The rogue was evading most of the attacks, blocking some with this remaining sword but he'd soon have his back to a wall and be able to go no further. Cass was healing Senia, though both women looked strained. Ahrn was... nowhere to be seen and Davar didn't have time to look.

Davar charged. As he did, he sent a thought to Cass. *I*

don't know how much strength you have left, but do you think you can rip these things apart like you did with the stone giants earlier?

I don't know. I can try.

Please do. I'm too busy trying to keep myself and everyone else alive.

Davar ran up behind the demon and, leaping, sliced deep into its back in a long scoring hit across the top of its shoulders. Again, there was no reaction, only the ooze of lava. It clapped its wings together in a torrent of wind behind it and buffeted Davar out of the air. He only just managed to land on his feet, his head spinning, vision blurred from the force of the blow. That gave the thing time to lash out backward with a leg and once again send him flying across the room.

He rose, forcing his body to heal the many cracked and fractured bones, then leapt back at it. It had Tirol against the wall now, its last slash with its claws rending the stone of the wall itself as Tirol ducked and tried to roll underneath it. It was too quick for that and before Davar could reach it, it slammed its legs together, catching one of Tirol's legs, completely crushing it. The man screamed, trapped.

The abomination released him, turning nimbly and lifting a leg to stomp on Tirol and finish him.

Davar added a great gust of wind to his flying leap and slid Starsong home in its chest, hitting with all the force he could, trying to knock it off balance or at least backward.

He succeeded only in stalling the deathblow on Tirol as the creature's forward momentum was halted, not knocked back.

Cass must have used her earth talent to lift the stone under the creature's feet. That finally sent it off balance, falling backward. Davar pulled Starsong free, leaping away as the demon crashed into the wall.

Tirol was trying to crawl away, shattered leg dragging behind him. Davar had to give the man credit, for someone who couldn't block pain he was handling the injury admirably.

The creature recovered quickly pushing itself off from the wall with its wings. It bellowed a cloud of noxious gas at Davar that ate at his soul. Soul wasn't his strong suit, but he'd learned a lot from Cass, and he fortified himself. He managed to not fall prey to the fear and hopelessness. However, that had only been a distraction.

Davar managed to only just get Starsong up in time to block the massive clawed hand raking at him. He surged his earth talent, not wanting to be knocked away yet again and instead was only pushed back a few feet by the great strength behind the attack. But that few feet made all the difference.

The demon was now within stomping distance of Tirol. It lifted a foot to crush the man and Davar did the first thing that came to mind, he threw himself down over Tirol as the creature's foot fell. He reinforced his bones and muscles to their max, managing to stop the great stone foot from crushing him and the man under him.

He was nearly tapped out of earth-magic, but with one last great effort heaved upward, hoping to throw the abomination off balance again, but it simply lifted its foot and remained standing.

Davar spun and thrust Starsong up into the bottom of the thing's foot.

I have an idea! Starsong said.

You don't need to tell me, just do it!

The demon's foot exploded in a great blast of light. Davar turned and covered Tirol, feeling the searing lava pour over his back.

"I have it!" he heard Cass cry out and a moment later, another great explosion rocked the room.

Davar was dazed and partially deafened. Blinking, he tried to look around and focus on what had happened. His body was healing, but it was slow, sluggish. He saw Cass on her hands and knees nearby, shaking her head as if to clear it. Tirol was still alive if only barely, tears in his eyes and his teeth gritted against the pain of his crushed leg.

Behind him, Davar saw the remains of the guard, stone and lava spread over a great area.

Slowly Davar got to his feet.

Wyllea was still battling with her own guard. How she'd managed to stay alive this long on her own against the thing Davar had no idea. But she seemed to be evading the creature with her amazing aerial speed and agility. Meanwhile, it was a virtual porcupine of arrows, dripping lava all over the room.

That's when a great blazing... something... passed through Davar's field of vision.

He blinked and when he opened his eyes again, Emberthorn was embedded in the chest of the Blacklord, sunk to the hilt. The wizard wore a surprised look, gave a rasping cough, and slumped over.

The demon Wyllea was fighting screeched and plummeted from the sky, crashing to the ground, digging a deep trench in the stonework.

No, this wasn't right. Davar staggered a few steps forward, closer to Cass, as silence sunk heavy over the room like a smothering blanket. Davar was certain the Blacklord would not die so easily.

Wyllea landed nearby, a stunned look on her face as she stared at the limp form of the Blacklord. "I really didn't think it would be that easy."

"Oh, it isn't. Senia call Emberthorn back now!" Davar shouted.

"What? But…"

They all watched as the Blacklord's head rose from where it had fallen against his chest, a rictus grin on his face as a frail hand reached for the hilt of Emberthorn.

"Emberthorn!" Senia called, and the blade vanished from the small man's chest, appearing back in her hand.

The Blacklord stood slowly, his grating laugh growing louder.

"Oh, what sports you are!" he cried out as if watching a pet doing tricks. Then the mirth faded from his voice. "But I think it is time to end this, don't you?"

Cass had crawled over next to Tirol and, pouring healing energies into him, had almost nearly restored his leg.

"I'm nearly spent," Tirol whispered. Davar checked. None of them looked good. Senia seemed mostly well, and Wyllea was only starting to tire, but the rest of them were weary. Once again, he couldn't find Ahrn. Why had the monk avoided the fight? Where had he gone?

"I think you are all nearly spent," the Blacklord called out. "Why don't you all rest." He reached out a hand, and a great black wave flowed from him, quickly washing over them all. Davar felt a sense of futility, despair, and the desire to simply give up, lie down, and die. It took nearly everything he had of his soul magic to resist the urge to stop and surrender.

"No!" Cass shouted and instantly Davar was filled with hope and inspiration as she dispelled the Blacklord's magic.

"Oh she's a strong one, isn't she?" the Blacklord said, his playful tone returning. "I'll have so much fun defiling her."

"Is that all you have? Words?" Wyllea shouted.

"I have far more than that!" His hand sprung up in a

clutching motion, and the stone floor around Wyllea erupted up forming a spiky cage. "Does the little bird like her cage?"

"Do you have enough earth talent left to undo that?" Cass asked in a hushed voice. "Because I don't think I do. I spent myself blowing that guard up."

"How did you do that anyway?"

"It took all four elements, but that drained me. How's your strength?"

Davar knew he didn't have much left either. Everything he had was going into slowly healing his back from the spray of rock and lava when the guard had exploded. "Not good enough."

A sound distracted them. Senia was hacking away at the stone around Wyllea with Emberthorn. It was doing little.

Suddenly another cage of stone sprung up around Senia as the Blacklord laughed a high-pitched giggle "Two birdies with one stone!" he said and laughed louder. "Oh, how I had hoped you wouldn't force me to kill you. I really do want to keep you. I'll spawn more of my dark scions!" The high grating voice instantly dropped to a dark and menacing tone. "Only this time I'll make sure they don't betray me."

"Looks like it's up to us," Davar whispered to Cass and Tirol.

"Where's Ahrn?" Tirol asked, and Davar shrugged.

But it seemed the mere speaking aloud of the question had warned the Blacklord.

"Yes, where is the little monk?" the Blacklord asked, then with mock surprise. "There he is!"

Davar finally spotted him. With all the commotions around everyone else, Ahrn had been using the distraction to sneak around the sides of the chamber and had nearly reached the Blacklord.

"If you wanted to see my up close, all you had to do was ask." The Blacklord made a lifting motion with his hand and Ahrn was plucked from the ground by some large invisible force. The Blacklord made a motion with his hand as if to come closer and Ahrn was whisked across the rest of the room to float before the Blacklord.

Ahrn swung with his staff. It passed inches before the Blacklord's face. The dark wizard didn't flinch. Ahrn threw his staff. It bounced off the Blacklord's head with a hollow *thunk*.

"Normal weapons cannot hurt me, monk, but I can hurt you!" A great grin spread across the skeletal face as the Blacklord raised both hands and closed them into fists before him. Ahrn grunted as if being squeezed. Then the Blacklord began pulling his fists apart and Ahrn was stretched, arms and legs pulled to the side. The warrior monk screamed a horrible sound as bones popped and muscles tore. Senia screamed as well, reaching out from her cage, useless. Beneath both screams was the joyous laughter of the Blacklord.

Arrows began hammering into the side of the Blacklord. He looked around, hollow eyes tight, annoyed. Wyllea was shooting a long stream of projectiles through her cage. A great wall sprung up from the floor to block the remaining bolts, and the Blacklord turned back to his work with Ahrn. The arrows that had landed were pushed out from his body after a moment as his earth talent healed him.

The Blacklord stretched Ahrn out a little more then released one of his fists and with the other made a motion as if to toss him aside. He flew like a doll through the air, crashing hard into a wall and falling, limp, to the floor.

"Who's next!" the Blacklord asked gleefully. "This is getting fun!"

"What can we do?" The terror in Cass's voice clear, tearing at Davar's heart and shredding his tenuous faith that they could still, somehow, prevail. Wyllea was trapped, her arrows useless, Senia was similarly useless, raging against the stone spikes which held her in place, but achieving little. Ahrn was most likely dead and Tirol only just healed and nearly spent. Things did not look good.

"We do everything we can," he said, grimly. "Even if it means our death."

Cass met his eyes and they shared a single pure moment between then. She nodded.

.

ell Starsong, this is it. Whatever you've got left, I need now. Spare nothing.

I know Davar, and... She paused as if drawing a breath, yet she needed no air. *Be careful*

Not blazing likely, he said with grim determination.

Right, sorry, what was I thinking? Go all out and kill this bastard!

He laughed quietly. *That's more like it.*

He felt another great surge within him, this one more powerful than anything before. Flooded with spirit and hope, his nearly expended earth talent was infused with new energy. He felt the wounds on his back close instantly.

He turned to Cass. "Let's do this."

Tirol still lay between them. "What about me?"

"Stay out of the way and you might live."

A wild grin spread on his face. "Screw living, that's no fun. I've got an idea. Follow my lead."

"I know what you're all thinking. You can't surprise me," the Blacklord said, but Davar thought he could detect a hint of uncertainty. In fact, Davar knew for certain the Blacklord couldn't detect his thoughts. That gave him an idea as well.

Tirol sprung to his feet and dashed over to Wyllea. "Hello, my love. How're things? Mind if I go kill this mad man?"

"What are you doing?" she hissed.

"You'll see." Then he turned to the Blacklord. "Oh yes, you thought I was a normal human, didn't you? You can't see my powers, can you? Oh, you're in for a surprise!"

Davar contacted Wyllea through their mind-link.

What is Tirol doing? Wyllea demanded.

I have no clue, but I think he's providing a distraction. Now let me make his effort worth something, send me all the mind talent you can spare.

Here you go. Davar felt a rush of awareness and memories, her memories, flood into him.

He knew the Blacklord was an amazing mind talent. Davar was as well, but with Wyllea's help he might be more powerful than the Blacklord! He had such control, such finesse over mind and air even his vision changed slightly. It was as if he could see the currents of air in the room.

He touched Cass on the hand. The contact made it possible for him to create a blocked spot in her mind, so tiny the Blacklord would have to dig through her thoughts to find it.

Get close, be ready, the Blacklord can't sense these thoughts, be prepared for my move, he said into her mind.

"What is this?" The Blacklord took a step forward. There was something in the ancient man's voice Davar had never heard before. Could it be a hint of uncertainty? "What are you doing? I know you have no power little man. You can't fool me!" The Blacklord puffed himself up a little, again another thing Davar had never seen. Such posturing wasn't needed when you were as powerful as he was. "You can't defeat me!"

"Ha! You're a fool!" Tirol called with a confident grin.

The Blacklord's head tilted to the side. "Your thoughts make no sense. You're nothing but a puny mortal."

Davar didn't know what in all the blazes of the Void Tirol was thinking to confuse the Blacklord, but it seemed to be working. He paced slowly forward keeping in line with Tirol who strode toward the Blacklord with confidence.

With his newfound ability to see the currents of wind, Davar saw the Blacklord reach for Tirol, to pick him up. Davar created an ever so slight variance in the wind that caused the dark wizard's unseen hand to miss Tirol.

"What?" the Blacklord hissed.

Tirol began to glow with a soft white light.

What's that? Davar asked Wyllea through their mind link.

I created a safe spot in Senia's mind and told her Tirol was going to try a ruse and asked her to play along. She's using her spirit to add to it.

Nice.

Again, the Blacklord reached out with wind to crush Tirol and again Davar deflected the attack.

"Impossible!" the Blacklord screeched.

"You can't defeat me!" Tirol's voice boomed through the hall — an ability one could do with spirit magic, Senia's work. "I'm your ultimate nemesis. You never saw me coming. Scions are nothing. For I am..." Tirol paused for effect. "The Whitelord!"

"There is no such person!" The Blacklord sputtered, quivering with rage. He sent a thousand tendrils of wind-borne magic to clutch and rend the hapless rogue, but Davar placed a wind-shield around Tirol. The Blacklord's magic raged around the man but could go no farther. "Who are you?"

Even Tirol seemed a bit surprised at the Blacklord's reaction. But the man couldn't see the war of winds happening around him.

Tirol pressed on with his diversion. "Yes, I'm the Whitelord and I'm here to defeat you once and for all!"

"No, you lie. Your mind is slippery, unfocused, but I know you lie!"

Davar contacted Wyllea again. *The Blacklord should have opened Tirol's mind and read all his secrets by now. Are you protecting him?*

Of course. I put a shield up around his mind months ago, reinforcing it daily for weeks. I wanted to make sure my man was safe.

That explains it.

"Do I?" The certainty in Tirol's voice was impressive. "I don't need this to defeat you!" Tirol threw away his remaining sword. "My magic has grown for as long as yours in lands far removed. Yet I was called here to restore order to this land."

The fury of the Blacklord's unseen, wind-based attacks on Tirol pressed Davar's shield to its limits.

"I will know the truth!" the Blacklord screamed and suddenly the wind attacks stopped.

For a moment, Davar didn't know what was happening, it looked like the Blacklord was just standing there. Then he saw it, a thin line of mind magic, so fine and yet so powerful, meant to crack into Tirol's head and read his deception. Davar saw it too late to stop it, however, and Tirol staggered back as if hit.

By all the Gods! That was powerful. I don't think I can protect Tirol's mind much longer. Wyllea's voice was urgent in Davar's mind. *If you're going to do something, do it now!*

"Your mind is mine," the Blacklord cried, still focused on Tirol.

Davar summoned all of his and Wyllea's wind talent and launched himself at the Blacklord.

Luck was on his side. The Blacklord didn't notice the attack until the last moment. He tried to evade it, but Davar succeeded in slicing off one of his frail, bony arms, Starsong shining bright.

Like Davar, the dark wizard's mental prowess would prevent him from feeling pain. Yet even as Davar turned to strike again, the Blacklord's rage became palpable. A dark, noxious cloud seeped from his skin. When Starsong hit the black smoke, it stopped as if striking hardest stone.

"Well done, my son. Of all here, I expected as much from you. But that is as far as you will get." The wizard's remaining hand waved before him and suddenly Davar couldn't move.

He tried to see how the Blacklord was holding him, but it was not use of wind. He could have stopped that, fought it off. He knew he was just as powerful as the Blacklord with his and Wyllea's mind talent at the moment.

No, this was something else.

The Blacklord laughed a crazed cackle, his voice arching high and tight. "Your mind is strong, boy, and your spirit protected by that of your mother. Your soul I can't reach, but your body is mine to command!"

So that was it. The Blacklord was using earth talent and probably a little spirit to control Davar's body. He knew he was too weak to resist. He'd spent far too much of this earth talent already.

Davar would have shouted if his mouth had worked. His mind whirled, his emotions ran wild. Fear and the horrid dread of failure seeped into him. Would this be as far as they got?

The Blacklord backed away a couple of steps, the miasma of foul smoke oozing from his wound sinking to spread out across the floor of the dais.

"I control you now, my son. Your body is my toy. Now where is that woman of yours so that I might make you kill her?"

Davar knew where Cass was.

No, it won't work! He called out to her mind, but she was committed to her course.

A moment later the tip of a dagger punched through the front of the Blacklord's chest, through his heart. Cass, standing behind the man, had made a valiant attack, but Davar knew the man no longer had a heart. There wasn't even a surge of hope within him. He knew this could only end badly for Cass and his heart tightened at the thought, pain stabbing the tender organ.

The Blacklord spun and his remaining hand caught Cass under her chin. It was what he'd done to her when he'd inhabited Davar's body those many months ago. Despite being a small man, he was still tall enough to lift her off her feet, if only just. She gasped, beating at his arm, but it held fast.

Davar reached out with his enhanced mind magic, trying to use it to pry away the Blacklord's hand, but he felt the ancient wizard rebuff his attempts. He was a match for the Blacklord, but no stronger.

So he was forced to watch, unable to do anything to help. He struggled against the Blacklord's control of his body, but to no avail. Even with all the energy Starsong had given him, he was nothing, a helpless puppy against the storm that was the Blacklord. A tear leaked from his eye.

The Blacklord turned, bringing Cass closer to Davar. "Oh, the things I will do with you, my lovely." His tongue like dried, cracked leather, black as pitch, snaked out of him mouth to an impossible length and pressed to her check. It slid across her mouth to the other cheek, then retracted.

"You are quite sweet, aren't you," the Blacklord crooned. "Shall I do to you what my son has done? Will you scream as loudly when I am inside you, sweetling?"

"I'll never let you touch me!" Cass croaked despite the hold on her throat. It was a vain threat, but she remained defiant to the last.

"I think you forgot someone!" Tirol said as his sword sliced through the Blacklord's neck. The Blacklord's head tumbled to the ground, landing with the sound of stone on stone.

Then the severed head laughed.

"What does it take to kill you?" Tirol breathed.

Davar struggled harder, hoping perhaps the attack might have distracted the wizard, weakened the Blacklord's hold him, but no, he was still held.

The Blacklord's head floated up and sat back on his neck. "So very much more than that! I'm invincible!" Without any movement at all by the Blacklord, Tirol was flung hard against the wall, collapsing to a heap on the ground.

Davar heard Wyllea's scream but barely registered it. He was too busy trying to extricate himself.

"Now, where were we?" the Blacklord asked smugly. "Oh, yes, I was getting to the good part. Perhaps I will defile your woman right here in front of you before I have you kill her. What do you think of that, Davar?"

Davar's mind was reeling, searching for something to help, some desperate idea to free them.

"Yes, I think I shall!" The Blacklord laughed a high-pitched noise of gleeful evil.

Cass was lifted higher still, away from the Blacklord's hand, still choking, some invisible force holding her. Now that she was out of the wizard's physical grip, perhaps Davar could do something. With his still enhanced mind-sense, Davar could see the wind patterns holding her. He tore at them with his and Wyllea's combined powers.

He broke the Blacklord's hold!

Cass fell to the floor, gasping for air.

The Blacklord reached for her again and Davar deflected the wind-hand, giving Cass more time to recover. Twice more, harder and harder still the vile wizard attempted to grab at Cass but was blocked by Davar. Again, they were a match now and neither would win this fight easily.

"Enough of this!" the Blacklord cried out. "There's another way." With a flick of his wrist, Davar moved with amazing speed.

Cass, watch out, move! he said into her mind.

Davar? No! Too late she understood.

Davar, manipulated and animated by the Blacklord, hit her hard with the flat of Starsong's blade. She was knocked to the floor, dazed though still conscious.

Then the Blacklord had him reverse his grip on Starsong and thrust it down into her belly, driving through her into the stone of the dais below as he dropped to one knee.

No! Davar yelled, even if only in his mind as Cass screamed in pain.

The Blacklord had known exactly where to place the

blow. Their child was dead, and Cass would be mortally wounded.

Davar trembled with rage, forcing as much earth talent as he could through his body to escape the Blacklord's hold on him, but still he could not free himself. Tears streamed from his eyes as Cass squirmed in pain. Perhaps she'd put up her mind-shield against pain for she no long screamed, but she wept, knowing what they'd lost. Knowing her life was now measured in minutes.

The Blacklord knelt on the other side of Cass. His voice was soft, almost tender when he spoke, "Now you see what it costs to defy me. But don't worry my lovely, I'll put another child inside you, then I'll torture you far beyond what you could ever conceive. But you'll be the mother of my next spawn, doesn't that please you?"

She spat in his face.

The Blacklord smiled at that and leaning over licked her face again, his desiccated tongue scraping along her cheek and over her lips.

He waved his hand and Davar withdrew Starsong from Cass' stomach, only to place it at her throat. "Now be a good girl and stay still while I defile you or I'll have my son kill you."

"I would rather die than let you have me!" Her hands were free, and she swatted at the Blacklord with a back-handed swing. It did little.

"As you wish." The Blacklord stood and waved his hand again. "Any last words to your whore, my son, before you kill her?"

Davar felt his head released from the Blacklord's hold. He could speak.

"I'm sorry, Cass, I love you." His eyes darted to the Black-lord. "And I'm going to kill you."

The Blacklord cackled a great long laugh. "You especially can't kill me! For if I die, you die!"

Deep down Davar had known this.

There had always been one ritual he'd been made to perform that had confused and baffled him. As a boy, he'd be forced to kill one of his surrogate mothers, a slave women who tended to him, and rip out her heart. Then the Blacklord had cast a spell on the still beating organ and made Davar eat it. There'd been more to the spell, but it had been only after that day that the tall and commanding man Davar knew as the Blacklord began to wither and grow, seemingly, frail. Yet that spell had also given the man immortality in his undeath.

Now he knew. The ritual had been more than just some lesson in evil. It had been a transference, the Blacklord giving over his mortal heart to his son so that he could be immortal.

And in that instant, everything fell into place.

Everything the Blacklord said was a lie, or some twisting of the truth, in this case, it was a literal reversal. It wasn't that if the Blacklord was slain Davar would die, it was the oppo-site. If Davar died, the Blacklord would be slain.

He knew what he must do.

Oh, Davar! I don't know if I can, Starsong said, fearful for the first time.

We all must do terrible things for those we love. We must all make sacrifices. Now he just needed to be able to move his body. He needed more power.

Then a plan began to form in his mind.

He contacted Cass. *I have an idea, but I'll need you to distract the Blacklord for a moment. I think I can kill him, but it may mean my death. I love you, Cass.*

I love you too, Davar. The tone of her mental voice was hard, resolved, sad. *I've something I can do to distract him and perhaps weaken him for a moment as well.* She was weak, the wound in her belly still bleeding. Her earth talent must be running low.

Then do that, but wait for just a moment, I need more power first.

The Blacklord waved his hand over Cass' belly and healed the wound in her stomach, the skin now smooth.

"I need you whole to carry my child," he said with a feral grin.

Davar had to act fast.

He knew he needed more earth talent to overpower the Blacklord's hold. He poured every ounce of his spirit talent into his body, draining it. He felt the hold weaken, but only just barely. He needed more. Where in the blazes of all the void could he get more?

The Blacklord was using a clawed finger to draw runes, across the pale skin of Cass' belly, each line blossoming blood. She didn't scream, her teeth were clenched, but Davar could see the terror on her face at what was to come.

He needed more power now!

He needed more spirit, but...

Wyllea, is Senia close? Can you grab her hand?

What why?

I need her spirit.

I don't know how to access it...

I can. Just touch her!

A moment, then through their mind-link Davar felt another mind join. He used his connection to Wyllea's mind to access Senia's spirit.

Spirit, like a vast well, opened before him and he drank it

in, pouring it into his earth talent and strengthening his magic over his body.

He broke free of the Blacklord's hold.

"Now!" he yelled to Cass as he stood, reversing his grip on Starsong.

She let out a feral scream and grabbed the Blacklord pulling him close. It was the last thing Davar had expected, but what happened next was even more of a surprise. She simply exploded in a great ball of spirit, body, and soul magic all directed at the Blacklord.

Davar stood stunned unable to act as he watched her flare out in one great blossom of pure energy. The Blacklord was launched across the dais, landing hard. Cass was gone, dead, vanished in one final fury of all of her powers.

Yet he regained himself quickly. He held Starsong before him, tip pressed against his chest, both hands on the guard. Cass had made her sacrifice. Now it was time for his.

"I love you, Cass," he whispered, then plunged the blade into his heart.

The Blacklord screamed a feral, horrible sound as a great gash appeared in his emaciated chest, pouring forth black blood. The wizard collapsed as more black ichor streamed from him, forming a pool.

Davar fell to his knees, then to his side.

He had killed the Blacklord but had paid the ultimate price.

CHAPTER 26

*C*assine was at peace.

She floated in a great, warm ocean of fog, which glistened with light in a myriad of colors. She'd been in pain moments before, physical and emotional, but now there was only comfort and calm.

Davar appeared next to her. He beamed, relief flooding over his features when he saw her. "I thought you were dead!"

She smiled sadly. "My love, I think we both are."

"Oh." He looked around the multi-hued clouds in which they floated. "I thought The Void would be darker, or more... on fire, like the legends say?"

"I don't think we're in The Void, Davar. This is The Heavens."

"That's not right. I don't deserve that after my life."

You sacrificed all you had to save the world. I think that will be enough to erase your other sins. This voice was so beautiful, so full of love and song and the vibrancy of life it nearly brought Cassine to tears.

A woman appeared in the nothingness with them. She

was as beautiful as her voice. Her hair flowed in weightless waves behind her, longer than she was tall. The locks shimmered in all hues at once, now gleaming white, then blond or even blue or silver, now fiery red, then darkening to brunette and black, only to cycle through once again. Her face was indescribable. Angelic, or Godly were the only words Cassine could think to use. Perhaps this was how Davar saw her, all those times he'd thought of her as an angel. The woman's eyes were all shades, like her hair, from darkest brown to palest blue, each blink a new revelation.

Her body was that of a matronly woman, full and round, covered by a gauzy robe.

I am Aehryn, Goddess of All Things.

Cassine had no words. This was impossible.

It was Davar who blurted out, "But you're dead."

Aehyrn smiled and Cassine's world lit up with it. *I was dead, yes. Only an act of truest love and sacrifice could return me to the Heavens. You have paid that price, and I have returned.*

Davar's mouth gaped.

In return for your selflessness and love, and also for ridding my world of a vast and potent evil, I am willing to grant you a great boon. I give you back your lives.

Cassine was crying, except she had no tears in this strange place. After everything they'd been through this last day, the trials and combat, the pain and suffering, her emotions overwhelmed her. For a long moment she couldn't speak. When she finally regained herself she could only manage a faint, "Thank you."

"What of our child?" Davar asked.

I feel it is time to return to the world. It will need me now more than ever to recover from the darkness spread by the Blacklord. Aehryn's hand touched Cassine's belly. *When you return I will be with you.* The Goddess looked from Cassine to Davar and back. *I have always been your child,* Aehryn said softly. *You, my son, were the only one who could see I had sent a greater spirit, an angel, to earth to host my return.*

"Oh!" Cass breathed. "But..."

And you, my child and my mother, Aehryn touched Cassine's face. *So pure of heart, so full of life. To you, I grant one final gift.* The Goddess's hand moved to Cassine's belly and there traced runes in light. *I will be but the first of many children, you will live a long, healthy life, surrounded by family, five generations you shall see before you return to my realm.*

This had been one of her most secret desires to have such a family. Now Cass did weep, but these were not tears, these were manifestations of joy, love, and hope in glistening drops.

Now go, return. Live well together. I will be with you always. She touched both of their foreheads at once. There was a great flash then...

~

reath!
    Life.

Noise... smells... the cold sensation of stone on her skin. A full inhalation of air, her chest rising, which meant she had a chest to rise and a mouth and nose and...

Cass sat up, eyes wide, as the pain of her death faded.

She was naked, her clothes had been torn apart by her dead-blast. She didn't think to cover herself, not yet. Instead, her first thought was for Davar.

She scrambled over to him. He lay on his side, Starsong plunged into his chest.

She pulled the blade out and his muscle and bone healed

even as it left. He drew in a desperate breath and then his eyes snapped open.

He saw her, reached for her, held her. He pressed her close in caring arms as they both wept.

There was a vague memory of a bright and loving place, but it was fading. There was only life now and a great well of joy at the miracle that had saved them.

She felt whole, so much more potent in her power than she ever had before. And in Davar's arms, she felt she could do anything.

This reminded her of the others in the room.

She rose and with a wave of her hand, not knowing the spell she summoned, a flowing white dress appeared over her.

"That's new," Davar said getting up next to her.

"I feel... completely different: reborn, renewed, stronger than before."

He shrugged. "I feel the same as always, but I do feel fully restored."

"Let's go help the others, shall we?"

Wyllea and Senia were freed from their cages. Ahrn was alive, but in great pain and unable to move. Cassine spent a long time healing him, making him whole once again. Davar took care of Tirol's wounds, which were mostly superficial save for a couple of broken bones.

"Is he truly dead?" Wyllea asked, nodding toward the shriveled form of the Blacklord. Davar went to investigate and when he returned he was nodding.

"He's nothing but dust now. His heart in my body was what sustained him. When that died, so did he."

"But if you're still living, won't he return?" Tirol asked, wary.

Cassine answered, "No. He's dead for good. Don't ask how I know, but I know. Davar's link to him was severed, his heart is his own now."

"Actually it's all yours," Davar said with a grin.

"Let's go home," Senia said.

"A fine idea, everyone take hands." Cass, still feeling strong in her abilities, teleported them back to St. Antin.

*E*mberthorn lit the room with a faint blue, flickering light.

Senia lay in Ahrn's arms, head on his chest, a glistening sheen on her skin from their exertions not so long ago.

It had been several months since the Blacklord's defeat and Cass had recently delivered her child. The baby was a girl. To thank the Gods for their miraculous survival and defeat of the Blacklord, the babe was named for the highest of the Gods, the Vanished God, Aehryn of all things.

Senia and Ahrn had been there for the naming ceremony earlier that week. Seeing the precious little girl had sparked new feelings within Senia.

"I stopped taking those herbs from the Daughters of Ehlani," she said softly into the quiet of the moment. Ahrn deserved to know, even if it was after the fact.

"What's that? Which herbs?" he asked, he might have been dozing slightly.

"The ones which kept me from conceiving children."

"Oh," he said evenly, then a moment later a more alert, more questioning, "Oh?"

Senia levered herself up, elbows on his chest, so she could look him in the eye. "I love you Ahrn, and the war is over. I think I want something more now."

"A family?" there was a faint smile on his lips as he spoke the word.

"Yes."

"I've seen this happen before you know." His tone was mock serious. "One woman has a child and all the other girls of the same age in the village want one too." He laughed a little and she joined him. After a moment, he spoke again. "But in all seriousness, are you sure this is what you want?"

She nodded. "Yes. Is it what you want?"

He smiled. "A family had never really been part of my plans. But then, neither were you, or a war, or most of this. I may need a little time, but... I love you and would love a family with you."

"Good." She leaned down to kiss him. Then speaking close, knowing her breath would be hot on his skin, she said, "Because I don't want to wait too long."

He grinned. "The child might take some getting used to, but the making of a child part, that I'm fully up for."

They shared a laugh before losing themselves in passion.

∾

"A child? Really? Me? Not right now. Why? Do you want one?" Wyllea paused in her dressing, wondering where Tirol's question had come from. Was this because of Cass and Davar's kid's naming ceremony not long ago?

Personally, she hadn't thought much about it.

Tirol shrugged, still lounging on the bed. "I might. I'm not as young as I used to be."

"We've still got lots of time, no need to rush things," she said. She finished putting on her clothes and returned to Tirol. "You've seemed a bit restless lately. Is everything well?" She tried as much as possible not to intrude on his thoughts unbidden, no matter how curious she was.

He sighed deeply, gaze going off to stare at the ceiling. "Wyllea, how long are we going to stay here?"

"At the Abbey?"

"Yes. The war is over, neither of us is really needed, and..."

"Are you getting restless?"

"Maybe a little."

"What did you have in mind?"

He shrugged. "I'm not quite sure. But there's a lot of world out there. Other people we could help. Other places we could see."

She considered this.

After a moment she laughed. "You know, this is the longest I've stayed in one place in all of my life. Perhaps it's time for a change." Another thought came to her. "Though I get the feeling the monks will want me to visit from time to time. I'm special. I don't think they're done studying me yet. But I think I could convince them to let me go on a few... excursions." She shrugged as she rose. "Besides, Cass can always find me and teleport me home if need be."

"Home?" he asked.

She looked at him questioningly for a moment.

"You said, 'teleport you home.' Do you think of this as home?"

She smiled slowly. "I think I do, sort of. But that doesn't mean I'm not willing to wander a bit."

He smiled. "Good."

⁓

*M*aster Elia once again waited in the High Abbot's chambers, not knowing why she'd been summoned.

The High Abbot believed Cass and Davar's child would be special, being the daughter of two multi-talents, and had asked to see the child. She'd asked Master Elia to be there when she did.

So here she was, sitting in one of the large chairs by the fire, waiting.

Davar and Cassine arrived, both glowing with joy at the bundle she carried. Though in the case of Cassine, the term *glowing* seemed literal. Master Elia could swear that Cassine's skin was actually slightly luminescent, radiant.

"May I see the child?" Ullanine said softly.

Cassine carefully handed the bundle over to the High Abbot who bounced and swayed the child for a moment.

"She's beautiful," Ullanine said, enraptured. Master Elia sighed, rose from her chair, and came to see what the fuss was about.

Elia wasn't one for children. She didn't like them much until they could speak full sentences and begin to train in fighting. That's when they became interesting.

Yet as soon as she laid eyes on the child, she knew this one was different. The baby's eyes were keen and intent, a pure and deep gold in coloring, much like her mother's. Her face was serene and she already had a silken patch of blond hair. She really was beautiful, not the usual grimy, grubby, drooling mess.

"Oh," was all Master Elia said. Perhaps the High Abbot was right in her belief that this child was special.

"Has she spoken yet," the High Abbot said casually, still looking at the child.

Cass laughed, "She's only a few days old. She can't speak yet."

"Oh, I doubt that," Ullanine said confidently. "Isn't that right, Aehryn?"

I should have known better than to try and hide among the keepers of all secrets. Embreth has told you of me. Hasn't she?

The voice, a woman's voice, was light and high yet still resonant and commanding. It spoke into their minds directly.

"Oh!" Cass started.

Davar looked stunned, blinking.

"Indeed she did, Great One. Rest assured, your secret is safe with us." The High Abbot smiled and handed the child back to Cass, who starred at it, an odd look on her face.

Keep only that I am among the mortals of this world a secret. Otherwise, spread the word that Aehryn has returned among the Gods to help heal the world.

"My daughter?" Cass said in awe.

Yes, my daughter and mother. But I am a child in all other respects and will need your love and care. Speaking of which, my body grows hungry.

"Of course," Cass said as calmly as if all children told their mothers their needs. She opened the top of the blouse she was wearing and lifted the child to her breast to feed.

"This is going to take some getting used to," Davar said with an odd grin.

"Less than you might think," the High Abbot said. "You're

lucky to have a child who can tell you what it needs. You may go now. I've confirmed what I was told. Thank you."

You're welcome, the Goddess replied.

"So," Davar said as he ushered Cassine from the room. "What's next?"

"More children, many, many more."

"We'll have to get started on that right away, then."

"I figured you'd like that part."

The door closed behind them and Elia heard no more. She turned to the High Abbot. "What are we to do? What does this mean?"

"It means our war against the darkness is finally at an end. We have won and the world is whole once more. As for what to do? You heard the Goddess. We spread the word of her return."

"Sounds like a big job," Elia said.

"Yes," the High Abbot said with a beatific grin. "I thought I'd put you in charge."

OTHER BOOKS BY R. MICHAEL CARD

TALES OF THE SEVEN KINGDOMS

The Goblin King

The Swordmaster's Apprentice

GUARDIANS OF LIGHT

Book 1: The Last Scion

Book 2: Scion Rising

Book 3: Scion's Sacrifice

ABOUT R. MICHAEL CARD

R. Michael Card has loved fantasy since he read his first Dragon Lance book so many years ago. He has been writing for twenty years but has only recently decided to start sharing his work with the world. He has always enjoyed the lighter side of epic fantasy, the grand adventure, and has infused that love into his works.

He lives near Toronto, Ontario with his beloved wife and their cat. He has had a plethora of careers, working in software, insurance, trades, and education, with jobs ranging from washing cars to career counseling.